New York Times & *USA Today* Bestselling Author

CYNTHIA EDEN

PROLOGUE

Or that time when opposites really, really attracted...

"You have bruises on your wrists." His voice was rough and deep, and it slid over her skin like the most sensual caress in the world. "I'm so fucking sorry. I wish that I'd gotten to you sooner." Cole's fingers slid along her inner wrist, carefully skimming over the faint marks that had been left by the ropes that her captors had used to bind her.

"You got to me, that's what matters." Her own voice was way huskier than normal, but Evangeline Lake—Evie to her friends and family—couldn't exactly do anything about the huskiness. Mostly because Cole was standing right in front of her. Cole was touching her. He was using his sexy rumble of a voice on her...

And her knees were getting all weak. A side effect of being so close to Cole.

Her gaze was locked on him, and she could not look away.

Cole was like a real-life action hero. She couldn't think of him any other way. *Her* hero.

When she'd been kidnapped while on a trip to LA, she'd been utterly terrified. Bound and gagged and thrown in a dark closet, she'd been so afraid that she would die.

Then Cole had come to the rescue. Literally breaking down the door. He'd carried her out of there. Rushed her to safety. And he'd been her bodyguard for the last week. Wherever she'd gone, he'd been there. He made her feel safe. He made her feel protected. He made her feel...

Super, super turned on.

Because Cole was the sexiest man she'd ever seen. Tall, with broad shoulders and muscles that wouldn't quit—like, *ever*—he had slipped his way into her dreams. His hair was thick and dark, his hard jaw always clean-shaven, and his eyes...God, his eyes...

Electric blue. Brilliant blue. Burn into your soul blue.

He'd been the perfect gentleman with her. So careful and courteous. He'd slept on the floor in their suite. He'd treated her with kid gloves, and he—

He let go of her wrist. Yet she could still feel the warmth of his touch.

"You should get some sleep," he told her, voice all gruff and rasping. "The plane leaves early tomorrow, and once you get back home, all of this..." He motioned vaguely with one hand. "It will be nothing more than a bad dream." He stepped away from her. Turned his back. Walked—

"It hasn't all been bad."

He looked over his shoulder at her. For a moment, she just had to admire him. The man's jaw—seriously, it was the most cut jaw ever. And his lips—*sensual* didn't even begin to describe them.

His dark eyebrows lifted. "You were drugged. Kidnapped. And trapped in a three by—"

"I didn't die. You and your team got me out. I met you." She licked her lips. She was so freaking nervous. When she was near him, yes, she felt safe, but her stomach also tended to feel as if a dozen butterflies were flying around inside. Giddy, nervous. "You weren't bad at all. I'm very glad that I got to meet you, Cole."

He gave her a slow smile. "Happy to be of service, Ms. Lake."

"Evie," she blurted. "You know that you're supposed to call me Evie."

His smile slipped. "You should get some sleep. It's almost time for you to go home. Your kidnappers haven't surfaced in the last week. If they're smart, they ran as fucking far as they could get."

But what if they come after me again?

No, no, she wasn't going to say those words—

"When you get back to New York, your step-brother will make sure you have the best security in place. You won't have to worry about anything."

"Too bad that security won't be you." She took a slow glide toward him. She hoped it looked all sexy and seductive, but it felt more like it was lurching and awkward. "Because I really like being with you, Cole." A pause. *Say it.* Evie gathered her courage and confessed, "I like you."

She was close enough that she saw his pupils widen. A very telling movement. Cole could control his expression perfectly—almost robotic control—but his pupils had just told her that her instincts weren't wrong.

Cole felt something for her, too.

Maybe...*maybe* he wanted her just as much as she wanted him.

There was only one way to find out.

Cole turned to fully face her. "Evie—"

Yes! He'd said her name, and it sounded like the sexiest thing ever coming out of his mouth. She rushed to him and locked her arms around him. "Will you kiss me?"

He sucked in a quick breath. "You don't want—"

"I want *you* to kiss *me*."

His gaze dropped to her mouth. That electric blue stare heated as he focused on her lips. His head began to lower.

She rose onto her toes. So very eager for him to—

"No." He shook his head, but his gaze didn't move from her lips. "You're confused."

Nope. "I feel crystal clear."

"It's adrenaline. It's mixed up emotions. You think you want me, but you're just riding the emotional roller coaster from everything that's happening."

"I hate roller coasters." Her gaze was on his mouth. "But I really want to know what you taste like."

A growl tore from him. "I have been keeping my control, every moment..."

parted. He kissed her back with an eagerness that matched hers, and, oh, but she loved the way he kissed. Such focus. Such skill. Such hungry need.

Ding.

The elevator doors opened behind her. Evie lifted her head. Smiled at him. "It's not like this will be our only elevator ride. I can reassure Harrison, and then we'll have all the time in the world."

Time to get to know each other better. Time to see what just might happen next.

Cole's eyelashes flickered.

She caught his hand in hers. Turned and led him out of the elevator. The rest of his team had remained downstairs. He was the one giving her personal guard service to Harrison's door. With every step that she took closer to Harrison's home—to the home she'd lived in since she was sixteen years old—nervous energy fueled her. Harrison had been twenty when her mother had married his father, Quint White. Harrison had been quiet, reserved. A bit arrogant.

And she'd been happy. So happy. Because she'd always wanted a brother. A big family. It had just been her and her mom for Evie's entire life, then with the new marriage, everything had been poised to change...

Until her mother and Harrison's father had died on their honeymoon. A traffic accident on a winding mountain road in France. Evie had been devastated. So sure that she was going to be on her own again.

But Harrison had stopped being quiet. Sure, he'd kept on being arrogant because that was just

Harrison, but he'd protected her. He'd loved her. He'd been her family.

She was going to tackle hug him as soon as she saw her brother.

"You'll like my brother," she said quickly as her steps rushed over the lush carpeting. "Some people think he can be intimidating, but I swear, he has a heart of gold." The heart was just hidden—very well—from most people. She paused and sent Cole a nervous glance. "But, wait, you've met him before, haven't you? I mean, if he hired you and all, you must have—"

"We've never met in person."

Oh. Okay. She tightened her hold on him. "You'll like him. He'll like you." She hurried forward.

"I highly doubt that," Cole muttered.

She was almost at the penthouse door.

Cole pulled his hand from hers. "You go in first and talk to him."

Unease slithered through her. "But...you can come in with me."

The door was just a few feet away.

Cole shook his head. "He wants to see you. I don't want to intrude on family time."

The unease got worse. "You wouldn't be intruding."

His hand rose, and his knuckles skimmed down her cheek. His lips parted, as if he'd say something.

The door opened. "Evie!"

Her head turned at the excited cry. Harrison stood in the doorway with a broad smile on his face. His green eyes gleamed, and the dimples on both sides of his mouth flashed. He grabbed for her and pulled her into his arms. She hugged him just as tightly as he held her. Harrison was home for her. Her safe place in a storm.

"God, I'm so sorry," he mumbled as he buried his face in her neck. "They took you because of me, and I swear, it won't ever happen again. You'll be safe. I promise it. Please, forgive me. I had no idea that you would—"

She eased back. As usual, his blond hair was tousled. He spent far too much time raking his hands through the thick mane. She smoothed back his hair. "I'm safe. I'm good." Evie nodded. "And it's all because of Cole."

Harrison blinked.

"Here, you two need to officially meet. In person, I mean." She exhaled and eased away from her brother. "Harrison, this is the man who rescued me—" Evie turned back toward Cole.

Except...

Cole wasn't there.

The hallway was empty.

"Cole?" A shiver raked over her. She took one step. Another. "Cole?" Her voice rose.

No answer.

He...he hadn't just vanished.

"Evie." A new note had entered Harrison's deep voice. A thread of worry. "Cole's job was to deliver you safely home. He's done now."

He's done now. Those words battered right at her heart. "He left...and didn't even say good-bye?" No, that couldn't happen. He wouldn't have just walked away while her back was turned. Not after last night. Not after they'd made love. Not after she'd confessed that she was falling in love with him.

He wouldn't...

But he was gone.

"Come inside, Evie," Harrison urged her softly. "This has all been a nightmare, and it's time for you to forget it."

No, it wasn't time to forget.

"You're home. You've come back to your life, and Cole has gone back to his life."

Her head swung toward Harrison. "Without saying good-bye?" There was too much revealed in her trembling voice. Too much pain.

"Oh, hell." Harrison's eyes widened. "Do I need to kick the ass of your bodyguard? Because, shit, he came with high recommendations from a friend. He was supposed to be able to get the job done, no matter what."

She flinched. *I guess he did get the job done.*

Then he'd left.

"Come inside, Evie," Harrison urged again.

Her steps wooden, she followed him in, but she couldn't help glancing back once more because she was still hoping that she was wrong. Hoping that Cole would appear.

He wasn't there.

She crossed the threshold.

Harrison closed the door.

And her heart broke.

CHAPTER ONE

Or...it's been two years, six months, and five days...not that Cole was counting...

The door swung open. "No." The beautiful woman was adamant. She shook her head, sending blond hair dancing over her shoulders. "I don't want any, but thank you and good day."

Cole Vincent lifted his brows. "Excuse me?"

"No soliciting is allowed in this building." Her voice was crisp. Her expression cold. Her dark eyes swept dismissively over him. "I'm not buying what you're selling, but thanks." She swung the door closed.

She tried to shut the door right in his face. Well, damn. Cole's hand flew up, and he caught the door before it could slam shut. "Okay, I probably deserve that."

"Probably?" Evangeline—Evie—Lake yanked the door back open. "You definitely deserved it. There is no question. Not even a single one. Not even half a question."

Was half a question even a thing?

"You left me without a word!"

If he'd been the blushing type, Cole knew that he'd probably be flushed crimson right then. "The job was over."

A determined nod of her head. "I am going to slam this door, and you are not ever going to bother me again."

"I, um, wasn't sure that you'd remember me—"

Her eyes—those gorgeous, dark chocolate eyes—widened, and then narrowed with rage.

Uh, oh. He'd obviously said the wrong thing.

"You think I forget the names and faces of the men I have sex with? Is that what you're saying to me right now?"

Oh, sweet hell. "That is not what I meant—"

"Then you think I forget the people who rescue me from asshole kidnappers?"

"No, that is, ahem..." Cole coughed. "Not what I meant, either—"

"Why don't you tell me what you *did* mean?"

God, she was feisty. And even more gorgeous. And he was suffering from the same problem he always had when he was with her. He said the wrong, stupid shit, and he also got instantly aroused. For a moment, he allowed himself to just look at her.

To see what I missed over the last two years.

Not like he'd forgotten her. Not like he could ever forget her.

Her blond hair was shorter now. When he'd met her before, her hair had trailed half-way down her back. Before, too, he'd never seen her with makeup. But now she had dark shadow around her eyes and her full lips were lined with a slick, sensual red. She was beautiful with or without makeup...

To him, Evie was just...*beautiful.* Always.

She wore jeans that showed off the pure, perfect temptation of her endless legs. High heels that made him swallow twice. Her tight-fitting black shirt hugged her breasts. She had a dancer's body, delicate in appearance but far stronger than most would ever realize. Strength hidden in delicacy. She was—

"You're staring at me like *you're* the one who's forgotten."

As if he could ever forget her. No way, not any damn day. "Your eyes seem even darker."

"Probably because I'm wearing eye shadow." Those eyes of hers were still narrowed. "Why are you at my door?"

"I..." *Tread carefully.*

"You'd better not be about to tell me that—after two years—you decided you couldn't live without me for even one more moment."

"What if I did say that?" Again, the wrong words burst from him. Cole had intended to say something else.

"I'd call you a liar."

He lifted his eyebrows. "Lots of people call me that."

She moved to slam the door again.

And, once more, he caught the door. "Your brother hired me."

Evie flinched. "I want you to leave. I want you away from my door. Out of my building. I don't know what Harrison told you, but I do not need you."

I do not need you. Those words hurt. Dammit. This scene was not going the way that he'd ever so optimistically hoped it would while he'd pictured the conversation on the plane ride from Atlanta to New York. In his fantasy, she'd opened the door. Seen him. Smiled. And thrown herself into his arms as Evie confessed that she'd desperately missed him.

Then they'd kissed and the fantasy had taken a far more adult turn but...

None of that shit is happening. Evie hates me.

"I'm not in danger, and I sure don't need you to swoop in and save the day. Things have changed since we knew each other before. I can take care of myself."

He'd read the updated file on her. Knew that after her abduction, she'd taken every self-defense class she could find. She was also an excellent shot now, and she was supposed to be wicked good with a blade. The lady had picked up all kinds of fun, new talents.

But...

Anyone could be a target.

And she *was* a target. "Harrison thinks the same kidnappers are going to come after you again."

She swallowed. "He's always been worried about that. They were never caught. They seemed to just vanish, and Harrison has been obsessed with the idea that they'd show up." Evie shook her head. "Not happening. I've told him that over and over again. He has to let the past go."

Sometimes, that was easier said than done. Cole was staring straight at his past, and the last thing he wanted to do was let go. Hold tight? Hell, yes. Walk away? Not ever again.

Walking away the first time had ripped his heart out.

He wasn't sure he'd have the strength to ever leave her again.

"This little meet and greet has been fun. Wait, no, it hasn't," Evie brutally corrected. "But I have things to do. Places to go. You know the drill."

She wasn't going anywhere without him. "I was hired to be your twenty-four, seven bodyguard."

At his words, Evie's cheeks turned a dark shade of crimson. "I didn't hire you for anything. How could I? You vanished while my back was turned."

He winced.

"You didn't exactly leave a forwarding address for me."

"You were better off without me." Oh, for the love of—why the hell could he not shut his mouth around her?

Her delicate jaw hardened. "I decide what's good or bad for me. My choice. No one else's." She straightened her shoulders. "My brother is worrying over nothing."

Cole would hardly call it nothing. "Harrison said you were nearly rundown in the middle of the street—"

"A careless driver. Not my previous kidnappers."

"The driver wasn't caught."

"He fled the scene." A firm nod. "But the police have a description of his vehicle. I have faith in the NYPD. I'm sure they will turn up something."

He stared at her.

"Thanks for stopping by."

Cole shook his head. He crossed his arms over his chest.

"I would love to say catching up with you was fun," Evie added.

He quirked one eyebrow.

"But I don't like to lie. In fact, I try to never lie. Mostly because I'm really bad at it." She sniffed. "It wasn't fun. It was as uncomfortable and awkward as I feared, and I hope our paths don't cross again."

Well, damn. She'd just cut him up as her voice stayed sugary sweet.

"Now, I'm going to shut the door. If you try to throw your hand up again, I'll just shove harder. Your hand may get broken." A shrug. "You've been warned."

She slammed the door.

He heard the lock click. "That's good," Cole praised, raising his voice so that she'd be sure to hear him through the thick wood. "Always lock the door. Set your alarm. Be alert and vigilant. Because if you are being hunted again, you need to be on guard every single moment."

Silence.

Was she staring at him through the peephole? Watching him?

His hands dropped back to his sides. He glanced to the left, to the right. No one else was there. They were on the top floor of the building, and she was the only tenant on that level. It wasn't an overly fancy place, not like the high-rise where her brother lived. No, Evie had made her home in a hip, casual apartment building.

Cole had never been hip a day in his life. He was battles and bloodshed. Tattoos and fist fights.

But Evie...Evie was sophistication. Class. She was Broadway and lights. She was the kind of woman who always seemed to fit in wherever she went.

She was the woman who'd fit *him*. Until, of course, he'd fucked everything to hell and back. Totally part of his charm.

"Evie..." His right hand lifted and pressed to the wood of the door. "I'm sorry."

Silence. The door didn't open. But then, he hadn't really expected it to open.

***

Her eye pressed to the peephole. Her left hand pressed to the door, uncomfortably close to the spot where Cole was pressing his own hand.

Damn him. He wasn't supposed to be sexier. Time wasn't supposed to have been kind to him. He should have gotten out of shape. Should have developed some thinning hair. Lots and lots of wrinkles.

He should *not* still have thick, luxurious, run-your-hands-through-it hair. He should not still have a hard, muscled body that made her quiver. He shouldn't have seriously sexy stubble on his jaw. And no way should his eyes be that electric shade of blue. She'd convinced herself that she'd imagined just how gorgeous his eyes were. A figment of her overstressed imagination. She'd learned that, in times of stress, people tended to overemphasize certain things. Reshape some memories.

She thought she'd imagined his incredible eyes.

She hadn't.

He was even better looking now than he had been before because, obviously, fate hated her.

She kept right on peering through the peephole. His tattoos were new. Cole wore a short sleeved, black T-shirt, and swirling, dark tattoos covered his arms. The tats looked seriously badass. Not that she was in to badass guys.

Not anymore.

Badass guys did nothing but bring trouble into her life. She was way over trouble. She wanted a nice, ordered routine. Was that so bad?

Did he have tattoos on his chest, too?

Why was she wondering about his chest?

"I'm sorry," he said again, and a fist seemed to squeeze her heart. How often had she dreamed of him apologizing? Of him saying that he was sorry for hurting her and leaving and that he would do anything to make it up to her for—

"I'm sorry, but I was hired to do a job, and I intend to do that job."

Her mouth dropped open. Cole wasn't apologizing for hurting her. He was apologizing because he wasn't leaving? What a jerk!

"I can't leave you unprotected. I told Harrison that he could count on me, and I'm here until I can figure out just who is after you."

He had just pushed all her buttons. Every single one with his half-ass non-apology. She nearly ripped the lock off her door as Evie flipped it and yanked that door open again—

Cole had the sheer, insane gall to toss his wide smile at her. "Figured you might open the door."

Her index finger stabbed into his chest. "You don't know a thing about me."

One powerful shoulder rolled in a shrug. "I knew you'd open the door."

She would not scream at him, but she wanted to—so badly. Did he think this meeting was a joke? Did he not get just how much he'd hurt her? She jabbed him again with her index finger. "You don't belong in my life."

His smile vanished. Something dark and dangerous flashed in his eyes.

She ignored the warning flash because Evie felt plenty dark and dangerous herself. "I don't want you in my life."

His hand rose. His fingers curled around hers. Warmth immediately shot through her hand. Up her arm. Right to her heart.

"Sorry, princess," he murmured, "but for the foreseeable future, you have me."

"Let go of me." She couldn't stand his touch. It stirred too many memories.

He immediately let her go. Took a step back.

"Do not call me princess." She wasn't some pampered princess. She worked hard for everything that she had. Twenty-hour days weren't uncommon for her when she was doing a show. She would come home, dripping sweat, and every muscle aching from choreography sessions. It was her job to make the routines. She came up with the steps, the sequences. She made them look beautiful and seamless when they were really grueling and gut-wrenching. Over the years, she'd had more broken toes than she could count. She'd had enough bruises to last a lifetime. Evie wasn't some spoiled princess. She was a flesh and blood woman, and she wasn't putting up with his bullshit.

"I don't want to fight with you," Cole said softly. He lifted both his hands toward her in that old, I-surrender gesture. "I'm here because I want to keep you safe."

"Why do you care?" He didn't. Obviously. She should not have asked the question. But then, he shouldn't have shown up at her door, either. Yes, she was bitter.

He'd vanished without even a backward glance. Just disappeared from her life. As if he'd never even been real.

A fantasy.

His lips thinned.

"You know what? Forget it. I don't want an answer." She tried to calm her racing heartbeat. "There was one near hit with a car. An accident. That stuff happens. I'll talk to Harrison and get him to seriously chill." Unfortunately, Harrison didn't know how to chill. "I'm good. Now, if you don't mind, I do have places to go."

"I'd like to come with you."

She squeezed her eyes shut. "This isn't happening."

"*Just* until Harrison ends my contract. I have a reputation to uphold, you see. I don't disappoint clients."

You just disappoint the women who fall in love with you? Nope. She was not going to say that. "If I leave, you're just going to follow me, aren't you?"

"Yes."

"You'll be a hulking shadow?"

"I don't think I'm particularly hulking. I like to think that I blend well."

Her eyes opened. Her gaze went to the top of his head then slowly trailed down his body. She stopped at his white tennis shoes. "You don't blend." Evie turned away from him.

"Is that a compliment?"

She headed into her place. Grabbed her purse. Slid the long strap diagonally across her body before she turned to face him. "Take it however you want." Evie exhaled. "I can't stop you from following me."

He started to smile—

"I could," Evie corrected quickly. "But it would involve calling the police and making a big scene, and I'm not one for scenes. I like things to stay quiet. Ordered."

"I remember that about you."

"Well, give yourself a cookie."

He blinked.

Shit. She thrust her shoulders back. "Try to do your *blending* bit. Stay out of my way, and after I take care of this one thing, I'll convince Harrison to cut you loose."

"I'll try to stay out of your way. Unless you need me. Then I'll step *up* and get in the way of the bad guys."

"Wonderful." A quick check in her bag confirmed that her keys were inside. Keys. Wallet. Mace. Good to go.

"I like your home."

Her head whipped up.

"The colors are great." He pointed to the wall. Stared at the series of lighthouse paintings that she'd carefully arranged. "You, um, do those paintings?"

"No." She cleared her throat. "My ex did them."

He'd been pointing, but now his fingers balled, and his hand became a fist. "You must have really cared about the guy if you keep his paintings on the wall."

"I like art." She didn't have to explain herself to him. "Doesn't matter about that guy."

"I see."

She didn't think he did. "Which brings me to my next point." She marched toward him.

He didn't back up. Typical Cole.

"This thing I have to do right now." Her gaze cut away from him. "It's a date."

A growl slipped from him.

The growl had her stare flying right back to him. "Is there a problem here?" She could actually think of at least a dozen problems but—

"He keeps his hands off you."

"What? What in the heck are you talking about?"

"I'm here to guard your body. If this date of yours touches your body, I'll see it as a threat." His expression had gone all cold and lethal. "So he keeps his hands off you."

"That makes zero sense!"

"Take it up with management."

Of all the— "You are management, aren't you?"

No reply.

"Then let's be clear." She stared hard into his eyes. She didn't even like blue. Especially not bright blue. Not like it was her favorite color or *anything*. "My body. I decide who touches it and who doesn't. Got it?"

A muscle flexed in his jaw, but he nodded.

"Excellent. Let's go." The sooner she put some distance between them, the better. She exited her place, locked the door, and headed for the elevator. She did not look back at Cole, but she could feel him shadowing her. She reached the elevator. Pressed the button to bring it up to her floor. The doors slid open a moment later and—

Oh, no. The last time that she'd been in an elevator with Cole...

I want to hit that emergency stop button. Press you up against the glass. And fuck you.

He started to walk past her and get in the elevator. She threw up her arm to block him. "Stairs! I'm taking the stairs because I need more cardio in my life."

He frowned at her. She ignored him and hurried for the stairwell. She yanked the door open.

"Your building needs to be far more secure. Anyone could get in here," Cole complained as he followed her down the stairs.

"Anyone *did* get in," she replied pointedly as she flew down those steps. He kept perfect pace with her. Probably because he worked out every available minute to keep that body of his in its rock-hard condition.

"Who's the lucky guy?"

There had been a definite edge in his voice as he asked the question.

"Who are you dating?" Cole pressed when she remained silent and worked on her cardio. "No boyfriend was mentioned in your file."

She jumped off the last step. Whirled to face him. "I don't like that you have a file on me."

His brows climbed. "You should take that up with—"

"Do *not* say management to me right now."

His lips pressed together.

"I don't like that someone thinks that my life can be crammed into a few nicely typed pages. I have secrets." Some. A few. Maybe one or two. Dammit. She needed to be more mysterious.

Cole nodded. "Duly noted." A pause. "Who's the guy?"

She spun away. Hauled open the stairwell door and rushed into the lobby. Evie tossed a quick wave to her neighbor who had just entered the building, then she made a beeline for the front door. Night had fallen outside, and soft streetlights fought the darkness. Cars rushed by on the street, and the warm air brushed against her skin as her stride quickened even more outside.

"You didn't tell me his name."

She stopped at the edge of the sidewalk as she waited for the light to change. "You don't get to act all jealous," she fumed. "Not like you and I are any sort of couple or anything."

"I didn't say I was jealous. I just asked for his name. Security protocol."

Security protocol, her ass. "Leopold Shepard."

"What in the hell kind of name is Leopold?"

She slanted a hard glance at him. "I don't know, *Cole*. A fun one?" It certainly belonged to an amazingly fun guy. Her friend Leopold could make her laugh even when she was at her worst.

And, okay, fine, she'd lied. She hadn't been able to look Cole in the eye when she'd bragged about having a date. It wasn't a date, exactly. At least, not a romantic one. It could count as a business date. Maybe. But, when your ex suddenly popped up out of the blue—the ex who'd shattered your heart and never looked back—a woman just might want to show him that she'd moved on. That she hadn't spent the last two years thinking about him.

Leopold would go along with her ruse. He'd probably find it freaking hilarious. Leopold—okay, Leo—loved to laugh. He was always telling her that if you didn't laugh, then you'd spend your days crying.

She didn't want to spend her days crying. She'd cried her last tears for Cole long ago.

"You're not taking this seriously," Cole snapped.

Her brows climbed. "That's what you think?" Her shoulders squared. "I will never forget what it was like to be held in that closet." Most people didn't know about that part of her abduction. Certain details had deliberately been kept from the media.

People didn't know that she'd been trapped in that old broom closet for so long that she'd gone hoarse from screaming. That her wrists had bled and bruised as she'd fought the ropes that had bound her. Cole had found her because she'd been weakly banging her bound hands against the locked door.

His lashes flickered. "Evie—"

"Evangeline. You can call me Evangeline." Hearing the shortened version of her name—the name that friends and family called her—hearing that name come from his lips hurt her. No, he was the one hurting her. Just seeing Cole had made an ache bloom in her heart. "I thought I would die. Every moment of my kidnapping is etched into my memory."

"And the moments after? The moments with me? What about them?"

A car horn honked. She jumped. "Do *not* try going there with me right now." She stormed away from him. The light had changed. Evie power-marched across the street, her legs kicking it hard. He kept perfect pace with her, of course, because...wasn't that what action heroes did?

Never faltered? Were always strong and seemingly perfect?

Not perfect. Not perfect at all.

When they reached the sidewalk on the other side of the road, she immediately turned left as she focused on her destination. "If you must know, then yes, I remember the moments with you perfectly. And I also remember exactly what it was like when I turned around and found you gone."

"The job was done."

She stopped. Caught her reflection in the glass of a nearby shop's illuminated window. Saw her own rage staring back. "If you say that to me again, I will not be responsible for my actions."

He cleared his throat.

She strode onward. A quick glance at her watch showed Evie that she was running late, because of Cole. His surprise visit. His reappearance that had just thrown everything in her life off balance. She hustled down the block, and told him, "I take my safety seriously, but I think Harrison is wrong about the current situation. I don't think I'm being targeted. After my abduction, he became hyper vigilant. He didn't even want me leaving the penthouse." She'd been suffocating. "I...couldn't live that way." He'd wanted to keep her sheltered all the time. "I moved out, and he hated it. But I can take care of myself."

"I have a team checking out the near hit from the mystery car."

"Of course, you have a team," she mumbled. "Don't you always?" His team was probably somewhere in the shadows, watching them at that very moment.

"If it turns out to be a case of some jackass who wasn't paying enough attention and almost hit you, I'll tell your brother that news immediately. I'll also make sure the jackass in question is never so careless again."

She could finally see the small Italian restaurant. Soft lighting drifted through the windows. Leopold was inside—he liked to sit right in front of the window near the door. He was a people watcher. He'd told her before that the table there gave him the best show.

"If you don't need me, I'll convince Harrison to terminate the contract."

She reached for the door. Pulled in a deep breath. Turned her head to stare at Cole. "Be very clear on this." She waited for his gaze to meet hers, and when it did, Evie crisply informed him, "I don't need you."

She hauled open the door, hurried past the hostess, and went straight to Leopold. He rose as she approached.

His blond hair was perfectly styled in his signature tousled look. His artfully ragged jeans fit his long legs. The designer shirt he wore showed off the muscles he carved on the Broadway stage. He opened his arms to her even as a broad grin split his handsome face. "I was starting to think you'd stood me up."

She sank into his embrace. Felt secure. "Never." Her racing heart slowed. She was with Leo. She was safe.

"Um...Eves..."

She didn't move.

"Eves, there is a very angry-looking man stomping this way." Leo's voice was a high stage whisper. "Should I be concerned? You know I'm a lover, not really a fighter. Got to keep the package safe from injury."

She sniffed. Let him go. Shot a glare at Cole.

Cole stopped in his tracks.

A flushed, young hostess was behind him.

"I'll sit here," Cole snarled as he took the table a few feet away from Evie and Leopold. He threw himself into the chair and snatched up a menu.

Evie nodded curtly toward him, then she sank into her own chair. She reached for her menu just to give her shaking hands something to do.

"Ahem."

Leopold. Crap.

He tugged at the top of her menu, pulling it down so that he could see her. Worry darkened his eyes. "Are you in trouble?"

"Nothing I can't handle." Wait, was she suddenly becoming good at lying? What? Since when?

A nod. He glanced toward Cole's table. Then back at her. "Who is he?"

"Someone I'd like to forget." She closed the menu. Put it down and leaned toward Leopold. To outsiders, it would probably look like she was leaning in for some romantic talk. "He's a bodyguard my brother hired, without my permission."

Leopold pursed his full lips. "He can guard my body anytime."

"*Leo,*" she warned.

"What? He's got that whole dangerous edge—"

"He is off limits."

"Dang, you just called dibs."

She had—oh, God, had she? No, no, that was *not* what she'd meant to do. "He's my ex. And it's complicated. And I need you to act as if you think I am the most amazing woman you've ever met." She bit her lip as she heard her own words playing back in her mind. "I am an asshole."

"No, you're not."

"I feel like one, and I can't believe I just said that stuff to you. I'm sorry. I don't know what I was ever thinking to—"

He reached for her hand. Squeezed. "He broke your heart."

She nodded.

"I can break him."

A laugh sputtered from her. "You just told me that you were a lover, not a fighter."

He smiled at her. His eyes twinkled. "I did, and I am, but for you, I can try to make an exception." He leaned ever closer. "But you need to tell me he's not nearly as tough as he looks. Like, the guy isn't some Navy SEAL who is gonna beat me into next week, is he?"

Um...maybe? She actually wasn't overly sure what Cole's background was. He hadn't shared a whole lot of specific details with her. But he definitely was as tough as he looked. The absolute last thing she wanted was for Leo to get hurt because of her. "How about no one gets anything broken? Let's just have our meal, and we'll pretend he isn't there."

Leo glanced over at Cole's table. "That will be so hard. Especially with the way he glares. Bodyguards aren't supposed to glare like that, are they? Must be the whole being-your-ex bit causing him to go all Hulk green with jealousy."

"It was a long time ago." She tried to focus on the menu even though she always ordered the same thing at that restaurant. God, she was predictable. *Maybe I'll have spaghetti instead of the cheese pizza.*

"It was a long time ago, and you don't care anymore?"

She looked around. "Where is the waitress? I could use a mega glass of wine."

"I see. You don't want to talk about what happened with him. Got it. Sharing about feelings isn't your specialty. I thought we were working on that."

Her gaze swung back to him. She lifted a brow. Like he was one to talk.

"Should we get down to business?" Leo rubbed his hands together. "Your last show on Broadway ended two weeks ago. Aren't you twitching to get started on another? Don't those feet of yours just long to dance and create new choreography routines? Because I have an offer for you, and I don't see how you can possibly tell me no..."

***

She'd moved the fuck on.

Cole got that. Could see it with his own eyes. Evie hadn't spent the last two years mooning over him. Of course, she hadn't. She was gorgeous, smart, and talented. She'd probably dated dozens of guys since they'd last been together—

"Oh, no, sir, are you okay?" The waitress frowned worriedly at him as she suddenly appeared—blocking his view of Evie and *Leopold*. "Did the glass cut you?"

He looked down at his hand. He'd squeezed the water glass too hard, and it had shattered. Great. Now he was dripping water and covered in glass. He pushed the glass shards onto his napkin. "I'm totally fine."

Just about to go completely insane.

He craned his head around the waitress. If that blond-haired jerk leaned toward Evie one more time...

They were on their feet. The blond-haired jerk was reaching out to hug her again.

Cole jumped up and tossed some cash onto the table. "I'm done, thanks." He hurried around the waitress. Dammit, why did the guy keep hugging Evie?

Cole imagined all of the ways he could incapacitate good old Leopold. He could have the other man on the ground within seconds and then he could—

"Your bodyguard is glaring at me again," Leopold said in the overly loud whisper that he had used when Cole first glimpsed the fellow. "Can you call him off? I'm afraid he's about to attack."

Evie gave a nervous laugh. "Don't be silly, Leo."

Leo?

"Why would he attack you?"

Why indeed? Maybe because her body was pressed to Leo's and Cole was—hell, yes—jealous. So jealous that the world was a haze of red. His own fault. He'd been the one to walk away from her before, and he'd known that when he saw Evie again, all of his emotions would get stirred up once more.

But he *could* stay in control. He would stay in control.

Evie eased back from Leo. "I'll think about the offer."

What offer?

Leopold beamed at her. Then he turned his head, and he kept right on beaming at Cole.

I do not like him.

"Eves is amazing," Leopold told him.

Eves? What the hell? Her name was Evie. E-V-I-E. And, as far as her being amazing...*Like I don't know that shit. I saw her strength firsthand after her abduction.*

But Leopold kept talking as he added, "She's strong and tough, and she's the most talented choreographer I've ever seen. Her body can move in ways that are truly stunning."

He had *not* just gone there. *Mention her body again, and I will kick your ass so hard.*

Leo nodded. "Oh, and, yeah, she's sexy."

Cole lunged forward. Caught himself.

"So sexy. And, sure, I don't know you, bodyguard man, but I think you're a dumbass. There." Leopold rolled one shoulder. "A hot dumbass, but still...dumbass. Such a waste."

What?

"Good night, Leo," Evie muttered.

His beam turned back to her.

But she was looking at Cole. Frowning at him. Nibbling on her delectable lower lip.

Since Leopold seemed done, Cole decided that maybe he should be able to say a few things, too. "I know she's strong."

Evie's eyes widened.

"And tough. And sexy. I also know she's smart. And funny. And she cares about people who don't deserve her." Hell, yes, he knew that. She'd cared about him—foolishly—because he would never deserve someone like her. "I know more about Evangeline than you ever could."

"Oh, yeah? Then you should know she hates to be called Evangeline," Leopold tossed right back. "Far too formal and stuffy for her."

Cole didn't look away from her. He couldn't. "I think the name is fucking beautiful." He thought everything about her was beautiful. "And she asked me to call her Evangeline," he said. "I want to do what she asks of me. I don't want to let her down this time." This time? Try ever again.

Because sometimes, you didn't realize you were holding a dream in your hand, not until you woke up and you were surrounded by nightmares.

"No." She shook her head. "No, Cole, you don't get to do this to me. *No.* I won't go down this path again." She spun and ran from the restaurant.

Dammit. "Evangeline!" He shot after her.

But Leopold had moved surprisingly fast, and he'd jumped into Cole's path. "You hurt her, and I will make you pay."

"Get the hell out of my way before I *move* you."

"I don't care how good of a jaw you have or what cool color your eyes are," Leopold continued doggedly. "If you hurt my Eves—"

That was it. Cole grabbed the guy. *Moved* him to the side. "She's not yours." He barreled toward the door. She'd already slipped outside.

"She's definitely not yours!" Leopold called after him. "That ship has sailed! It left the port! It's way out in the ocean now! Can't even see it with a spy glass!"

Cole shoved open the door. "Evangeline!"

She whirled toward him, putting her back to the street.

To the street...and to the black van that came to a screeching stop behind her.

"I can't do this," she cried. "I can't just see you again out of the blue and act like nothing is wrong. I can't do—"

The side door of the van jerked open. A man with a black ski mask jumped out and reached for her.

"*No!*" Cole roared. He grabbed for Evie even as that bastard tried to put his hands around her.

She realized what was happening. Her eyes turned into saucers, but she didn't panic. She drove her elbow back at the guy, a hard, fast hit, then she shot her balled fist toward his nose. He screamed out in pain.

Cole grabbed her wrist and wrenched her toward him. He pushed her behind him just as—

"Get the fuck out of here!" The masked man leapt into the back of the van. It raced away with a squeal of tires.

CHAPTER TWO

Or...the time when shit got real. Again.

"OhmyGod..." Leopold had burst out of the restaurant and caught part of the drama. "What just happened?"

Cole pulled Evangeline against him. "Are you hurt?"

A shiver shook her body. "No."

He looked back toward the street. The van was gone, and, like a freaking amateur, Cole hadn't gotten the vehicle's license plate number. "Do not move, understand?"

Other people were gawking. Voices were rising and falling.

He yanked out his phone. Dialed his partner. When James Smith answered, Cole snapped, "We had an abduction attempt."

"Already? Didn't you *just* get into town? Man, good thing you were there."

His gaze slid back to Evangeline. He hadn't done jack. "She fought him off herself."

She'd wrapped her arms around her body. Leopold was crowding in close to her. Cole pressed his lips together, tried to take a moment, but... "Shit," he snapped at Leopold. "Can you give her some air? Stop closing in on her!"

Leopold sniffed.

"Black van," Cole fired into his phone. "One guy in the back, wearing a ski mask. He's the one who tried to grab her. Driver never left the vehicle. Didn't get the tag number." He rattled off the restaurant's address. "See if our team can access street cams and figure out where the hell that van is going."

"On it," James assured him instantly. "And you'll be on her?" A deliberately mild question.

Cole's eyes narrowed. "Do not fuck with me right now."

"What are you talking about?" James was all innocence. "I simply meant you'd be staying with our target, that's all."

Bullshit. That was not all, not by a long shot. "I'll be staying with her." There was no way that he'd back off now. First order of business? Get her the hell off that street. He shoved the phone into his pocket and reached for her hand.

"Shouldn't we be calling the police?" Leopold asked. "That feels like the thing to do. That jerk was trying to grab Evie's purse!"

What? Cole squinted at Leopold. "That guy was trying to grab *Evie*. He didn't give a shit about her bag. He wanted to take her."

Leopold gulped. His face blanched. "That's why you have a bodyguard." His voice dropped. "Eves, you're in danger!"

"She is." Cole pulled her closer to him. "And that's why I'm getting her out of here." Too many people were around them. Too many unknowns. "We'll handle the police, don't worry."

"But—"

A white SUV braked near the corner. He recognized the ride and the driver who hopped out and hurried toward them. Chase Durant's weapon was in the holster under his arm. "James said you needed transport."

Cole nodded.

Chase opened the back door. "Your carriage awaits."

Cole urged Evangeline forward.

She dug in her heels. Her head turned, and she peered anxiously up at Cole. "Someone...that guy in the mask tried to abduct me?"

"Yes."

"Harrison was right." A tear leaked from the corner of her eye. "They're coming after me again."

That tear wrecked something inside of Cole. No, no, it made him want to wreck the bastards who'd hurt her.

I'm one of those bastards.

"They will not get you," he swore. "I will stay by your side. My team will catch them."

"But they didn't last time. The men who took me got away. They've been out there the whole time."

Chase coughed. "Uh, Cole, you coming?"

He didn't look at his buddy. "Things are different this time." He wanted her to fully understand this next part. "*I'm* different. I will not let you down. I just need you to trust me."

But...

She shook her head. "I can't."

A knife right to his heart. That was what her words felt like. Not unexpected, but it still hurt like a mother. "Then how about you at least just get in the SUV? Let me take you someplace safe."

She nodded. "Take me to Harrison."

Was Harrison her safe place? *I want to be her safe place.* He didn't say that, though, because he wasn't a complete idiot. "Fine."

She headed for the SUV. Stopped to look back at Leopold. "I'll call you."

"You'd better," he told her.

Cole slanted a glare his way. Leopold was gonna be a problem.

Evangeline jumped into the back of the SUV. Cole put his hands on the vehicle's door frame and ducked his head to follow her.

"You okay?" Chase asked softly. "I swear, man, you kinda look like you lost your best friend."

He immediately schooled his expression. "Not even close." He slid in beside her. His leg brushed against hers. She scooted over to the side, putting more distance between them even as Chase hurried back to the driver's side.

No, he hadn't lost his best friend. He'd lost something even more important.

Her.

I lost her two years ago. And I don't think I will ever get her back.

The SUV shot forward.

***

"He tried to kidnap me." Evie stared straight ahead as the SUV swept into the parking garage of her brother's building. She was far too conscious of Cole sitting beside her. The man seemed to take up way too much space. He was big and looming and, dammit, warm. Warmth seeped from him and surrounded her, heating her chilled skin. "Some jerk tried to grab me right off the street."

"We weren't followed to that restaurant."

Her stare whipped toward Cole. In the darkness of the parking garage, it was hard to make out his features. "How can you be so certain?"

"Because I was looking for tails. There weren't any."

"Like you couldn't have missed them," she muttered. Someone was awfully confident.

From the front seat, there was the sound of a throat clearing. "That's like Wilde 101, ma'am," the driver announced. "If you can't see a tail, you don't deserve to be lead on a case."

Her head was spinning. "What is Wilde?" Though the name was ringing a vague bell in her mind, she was just too dazed to fully piece things together. *Almost kidnapped. Right off the street.*

"It's our security agency." The driver was certainly being helpful. "Didn't Cole tell you about it?"

She strained to see Cole's features in the dark. "No, he didn't tell me about the agency." She licked her lips. Adrenaline coursed through her body. It was practically pulsing from her pores. "He did mention a team, though. I'm guessing you're on that team?"

"Chase Durant, at your service. I'm normally more of a shadow lurker on a case like this one, but when James called and said you needed fast transport, I got you out of there ASAP."

"James? He's another, uh, team member?"

"James Smith," Chase supplied. "Though I don't know how much you'll be seeing him, either. But he'll always be close."

"He a shadow, too?" Evie asked.

"More like a ghost." Humor trickled through Chase's words.

Humor that she didn't get. Evie frowned. "Did I miss a joke?"

Cole reached for her hand. His touch sent an electric surge right through her. She tried to pull her fingers back, but he held tight to her. "What are you doing?" Evie asked.

"Making sure you didn't break any bones when you slammed your fist into his face." Carefully, he stroked her fingers. "Great hit, by the way. I was impressed."

"Then my mission in life is complete. I impressed you. So happy."

His hold tightened a little more. "What can I do to make you not hate me?"

Her breath caught at his low question. "I...don't." Truth. "I don't hate you at all." Now sadness tugged at her. "In fact, I need to say thank you. You saved me back there."

"You saved yourself. Nice elbow attack, then perfect follow-up with the fist."

Silence.

The vehicle rounded a corner and stopped near a large column in the parking garage.

He let her hand go. "I don't think anything is broken."

She pressed her palms to the front of her jeans.

"If you weren't followed, then that means the would-be kidnappers knew where you were going." His voice was oddly careful, and she knew why, even before he asked, "Just how much do you trust Leopold?"

"He's a nice guy. One of the really good ones out there. He wouldn't do this." A slow exhale. "But we meet at that restaurant every Sunday night at the same time, so if anyone had been watching me for a while, they could have already known my routine."

A whistle from up front. Then Chase chided, "You should always vary routines. Where you walk, where you eat, where you shop. Don't ever let anyone know too much about you."

She knew that. And right after the abduction two years ago, she had varied everything but... "I thought I was safe. I thought that part of my life was all over." The bad part.

She'd been wrong.

"What happens now?" Evie could feel the tension gathering between her shoulder blades.

"We talk to your brother," Cole replied. "And I get the go-ahead from you both—you *both* agree to do exactly as I order on this case, no questions asked. Your safety will come first for me. I will do everything in my power to protect you, and Wilde will apprehend the people who want to abduct you."

"It's going to be hard," she warned him. "I like questions. I ask them all the time."

"I know."

She shoved open her door. The driver hurried out and came to her side. For the first time, she got a good look at him. Evie hadn't exactly been paying attention to him much earlier. Now she saw that he was built along the same similar, tall and muscular lines that Cole was. Only where Cole seemed all dangerous and he oozed that bad boy appeal, Chase had a more clean-cut veneer. He looked like a handsome, sexy version of the guy next door.

He offered his hand to her. "Like I said before, I'm Chase Durant, and I'm at your service."

She shook his hand. Felt the easy strength there and the calluses that told her his workouts were probably a whole lot like Cole's. "Evie."

A door slammed. Cole sauntered around the vehicle. "Oh, great. He gets to call you Evie, too, huh? Figures that you two would become fast friends."

They weren't friends, but if she was going to get through this mess, she couldn't treat the Wilde agents as enemies. She needed them. *All* of them.

She also needed to find out a whole lot more info about Wilde. Silently, she headed for the elevator. When the doors opened, the men followed in behind her, and she couldn't help cutting a side glance at Cole.

He was staring straight at her.

I want to hit that emergency stop button. Press you up against the glass. And fuck you.

She dug the elevator's security card out of her bag, used it, then hit the button for the top floor. Her eyes squeezed closed. "Just so you know, you totally ruined elevators for me."

"And every time I'm in one, I think about you."

Her eyes flew right back open.

"Um..." Chase shifted from foot to foot as the elevator headed high, high up. "Is there something I'm missing here?"

Lots. She wasn't going to enlighten him, either. They ascended in tense silence for a while before she said, "We need a truce."

His gaze never wavered. "The last thing I ever wanted was to be at war with you."

Then what did you want?

She'd shook hands with Chase, and now she offered her hand to Cole. "Let's start over."

His bright stare dipped to her hand.

"I'm Evie, and it looks like you're going to be my bodyguard."

He took her hand. His hand swallowed hers, but he was careful not to put too much pressure in his grip. "I'm Cole. I can be a bit of a dick some days, but when it comes to security and protection, you can be absolutely certain that I will not let you down. I will keep you safe. You don't need to worry."

The elevator dinged. The doors opened.

"He can be a dick," Chase cheerfully agreed as he exited the elevator. "But he does know protection. So do I. We've got you covered."

Cole still had her hand. She wiggled her fingers, and he let go. She hopped off the elevator and hurried toward her brother's penthouse. She could feel Cole stalking behind her. Heck, she could still feel his touch on her skin. Why did that always happen with him? Her hand fisted, and she didn't know if she was trying to hold on to the feeling or make it vanish.

Harrison's door opened before she reached it. He stood there in a rumpled suit, and he seemed to be paler than normal. "Heard what happened." His hands went to her shoulders. Tightened. "You aren't hurt?"

She shook her head.

His attention immediately cut to Cole. "I thought this kind of thing wouldn't happen when she had protection. How the hell did they get close to her?"

"It's not his fault," Evie quickly defended. "Cole warned me that I was in danger." Just like Harrison had been warning her. "I didn't want to believe it. I was the one who chose to be at that restaurant. I wasn't paying enough attention to my surroundings and I—"

"It sure as shit isn't her fault," Cole cut in to say. "But before we get into the blame game, how about we take this inside, hmm?"

Harrison's head moved in a jerky nod, and he retreated so that they could all head inside. The place was exactly as it had been when she moved out a year ago. Decorated by the best interior designer in New York to ooze money and taste. Nothing was out of place. Perfect artwork hung on the walls. The white furniture was both stylish and classic. The view over the city showed all the glimmering lights and—

The place felt cold.

Always had. She took a seat on the couch.

"Our team is searching for the van that was used in the near abduction," Cole said. He moved to stand behind her. Didn't sit, just stood back there, and for some reason, she found his choice of position oddly protective. "We'll access the traffic cams and see what we can find—"

"You can do that?" Harrison's eyebrows shot up. "The city just gives you access to their traffic cams?"

Chase coughed. "No." Another cough. "They don't." He smiled as he sat down beside Evie. "But we take it. Our techs can work all sorts of magic." He moved his hand around in a little swirl. "By the way, I'm Chase. We spoke a few times on the phone."

"Right. Chase." Harrison huffed out a rough breath. "Wait, back up, are you telling me that you're breaking the law?"

Chase nodded and, at the same time, he replied, "Absolutely not."

Harrison opened his mouth. Closed it. Then sat down—rather heavily—in a nearby chair. One that, of course, was a perfect mate to the couch.

For a moment, no one spoke.

"We need to get Evie to a secure location." Harrison peered at the floor as he seemed to consider options. "Maybe she should fly away." He looked up at her. "You know, I have that place down in Florida. You liked the beaches there, right, Evie?"

She had liked the beaches, but... "You want me to go and hide?"

His lips thinned. "Hiding seems far better than being taken by these bastards."

Giving up her life didn't seem like the best plan to her. "How do we know these kidnappers are the same ones who came after me before?"

Harrison tugged on his left earlobe.

She straightened. *Uh, oh.*

"I think we should just assume they are the same," he mumbled. "I mean, statistically, the odds of you attracting two different sets of kidnappers just aren't—"

"Stop."

He swallowed. Tugged on his ear again.

"First, I didn't attract the kidnappers. Not like I shined a bat symbol at them or something and invited them over to grab me."

Chase snorted.

"No, no, of course," Harrison rushed to say. "I didn't mean—"

"You're tugging on your left ear. That means you're holding back on me."

His shoulders slumped. "I got an email. That's why I went to Wilde in the first place. I turned it over to them, thinking they could track the sender. Hoping we could stop this mess before it went too far."

Goosebumps rose on her skin. "You didn't tell me anything about an email." Her head turned so she could look back at Cole. "Did you know about an email?"

"No. My boss didn't mention it to me." A pause. "Very *un*like Eric."

Her attention flew back to Harrison. "What did the email say?"

Harrison winced. "I mean, does it really matter? It was enough to put me on alert. Enough for me to think it was the same guys and to go and get the help that we needed to—"

"*Tell her what it said,*" Cole ordered.

Chase nodded. "Yeah, stop dicking around."

"It, um...said..." Harrison's gaze went back to the floor. "*This time, we'll send her back to you in pieces if you don't pay us what your father owed.*"

She almost jumped off the couch. "Your father? What does Quint have to do with any of this?"

"I don't know. I swear, I don't!" He *did* jump from his chair. "I'm not letting someone cut you into pieces. I'm not!"

"Damn straight, that's not happening," Cole added grimly.

Her breath sawed in and out. "No one could trace the email?" *Someone wants to cut me into pieces?*

"Eric Wilde's team tried, but they didn't turn up anything we could really use."

Eric Wilde. Yes, that name was definitely familiar. More familiar than she could show. Eric owned the huge security and protection firm. *Wilde.*

Harrison raked a hand through his hair. "That's when I knew you had to get protection. I told Eric that only Cole would do, and I got Cole to take the case so that—"

"Stop." Her heart slammed into her chest. Hard. "Go back."

His hand had frozen, mid-grab on his hair.

"Only Cole would do?" Evie repeated. She was trying not to think too much about the whole cut her into pieces part. If she thought about that, she'd freak the hell out. But now these other words from her step-brother made her think... "You forced Cole to take this job?"

How humiliating. Oh, God. Cole hadn't wanted to come back. He'd done it because Harrison had forced him to take the job. Her step-brother had *made* her ex come back to protect her. And here she'd thought that the day couldn't get any worse.

"Don't look at me like that, Evie. I needed someone you trusted," Harrison blurted. "You don't let people get close to you. I mean, you act like you do, but we both know you put up a wall." He pointed toward Cole. "Except you didn't do it with him. Your life is on the line. I couldn't leave your safety in just anyone's hands."

She could feel her face burning. He'd paid her ex to watch her. Wonderful.

"I want to talk to Evie," Cole announced. His voice was low and hard and menacing. "Alone."

Harrison's mouth opened.

"*Alone.* We need to clear the air about a few things before anything else happens. This is a non-negotiable point. That means, Harrison, I want you and Chase to get your asses out of this room. Now."

Chase rose. Headed toward Harrison and clapped him on the shoulder. "How about you take me on a quick tour of your place? Just so you know, I prefer tours that begin in areas that house alcohol. So if you've got some old whiskey, start me there."

Harrison frowned at him. "But...you're working."

Another clap on the shoulder. "Didn't say I was drinking. Said that was where I wanted to start the tour." He peered over at Cole. "Let me know when the private chat time is done."

Harrison and Chase filed out, but her step-brother didn't look happy.

Not like she was thrilled with the situation, either.

She could also not just keep sitting on the couch like everything was all casual and easy. Evie surged to her feet. "I'm sorry." She hurried toward the floor to ceiling windows. Stared out at the city but didn't see a thing. "If Harrison had told me that he was going to you, I would have stopped him. I would have told Harrison that he should never have forced you back to me." Jeez. That humiliation cut deep.

"That what you think happened? Your step-brother made me come back to you?"

There was something in his voice...A bitterness. No, more than that. Anger?

She turned toward him. "Isn't that what happened?"

CHAPTER THREE

Or...hell, no, I wasn't forced back. When you're in danger, nothing can keep me away from you. I'm kinda obsessed that way. Let's all deal with it.

"Didn't my brother make you come back?"

He knew that he had to tread very, very damn carefully. Because just from those few minutes of conversation that had involved jackass Harrison White, Cole had realized that the man had been keeping secrets from Evie. Cole wasn't just thinking about the fact that Harrison hadn't told Evie that he'd gone to Wilde in order to hire Cole.

No...he was thinking about...

About the time I came back to New York. Told Harrison I wanted his sister.

And he said that if I ever came near her again, he'd tell her all the dark and dirty details from my past. That he'd make it so that she'd never want me near her again.

But when Harrison could use those "dark and dirty" parts of Cole, he'd sure been quick enough to call.

Cole had never found Evie to be particularly standoffish with anyone. In fact, she'd been the opposite. *At least with me.* She'd been warm and open, and she'd drawn him to her before he'd ever thought of holding himself back.

So while Harrison had been bullshitting about that part, Cole knew he'd been serious when Harrison said that he couldn't leave Evie's safety in just anyone's hands.

He knows I will do anything to keep her safe.

Because Harrison knew exactly how Cole felt about Evie.

Or, the bastard *thought* he knew.

"Cole? You haven't answered me, and I'd appreciate your honesty." Her hands twisted in front of her body. "If he forced you to be here, I'm sorry."

She was apologizing to him? Hell, no. He stalked forward until he'd eliminated the distance between them. She tipped back her head and stared into his eyes.

"Never apologize to me." His words were rasped. "I'm a selfish, controlling bastard, and I'm the one who should apologize to you."

She shook her head—

"And something else you should know about me." His hand lifted. He just had to touch that silken skin of hers. His fingers trailed down her cheek before he brushed back a lock of hair that had fallen forward. "No one forces me to do anything."

"So he didn't go to...to Wilde, I think it was?"

"Wilde, my current employer. And, yeah, cards all on the table, he did. He contacted my boss, Eric Wilde, and demanded that I be put on the case. Said he'd pay any price."

Her thick lashes swept down to cover her eyes. "I see. It wasn't a matter of force. It was money. And I understand, I do. But if you didn't want to be here, the last thing I would ever try is to make you come back when you clearly want to be—"

"What I want right now is to have dirty, hot, mind-melting sex with you."

Her lashes shot up. Her stunned gaze held his. "You didn't just say that to me."

He stepped back from her. Put his hands at his sides. The better to not touch her, for the moment. "I did. I was on an honesty roll, and it kind of slipped out. But it's probably good that you understand where my head is at."

Her mouth was open. She had an adorable little gaping thing going on.

Why stop now? "Let me try being a bit more honest. I was jealous as all hell back at that restaurant. You nailed it. From the minute I found out that you had a date, I hated the SOB. To be clear, I'd probably hate *any* guy you ever dated. But that's my problem."

"Why...why would you be jealous?"

"Isn't it obvious?"

"I...no." She shook her head. "You left. You left me."

One of the worst mistakes of my life. "I'm here right now. I won't be going anywhere. You can count on me to keep you safe, I swear it. Don't think for a second that I'm here because I had to be forced to take this job. I could have told my boss no. There are plenty of other bodyguards out there."

She licked her lower lip. "Why didn't you say no?"

God, I freaking love her mouth. "Because it's you. Because I don't trust anyone else when it comes to you." Not even his own teammates because they didn't feel the same way that he did. They didn't know how scared Evie had been when he'd pulled her out of the closet in LA. How her body had been ice cold and racked with shudders but how she'd followed his every command perfectly and bravely in the dark. How she'd had him laughing the very next day, even though he should have been the one to help her. The one to chase the shadows from her eyes.

Others wouldn't get how sweet she was. How kind. They wouldn't understand how fragile her heart could be. He knew too well.

After all, he was the bastard who'd broken it.

"I'm not asking to go back," he told her quietly. The time for going back was long over for them. "I want to start again now, and I want to go forward."

***

"They have to be done." Harrison jerked his head all determined-like and turned on his heel, as if he'd return to the den. "I'm going in there."

Chase just side-stepped into the other man's path. "Nope, not done."

"Get out of my way."

No, thanks. "I have some questions for you. I can't help but feel like I've been dropped into the middle of a scene without getting all the right direction, know what I mean?"

Harrison shook his head.

"What? You didn't do drama as a kid? You weren't a theater brat? Huh, with your sister being a Broadway choreographer, I expected more from you. For the record, I was a theater brat." Because he'd always loved pretending to be someone else.

"She's my step-sister. Our parents didn't marry until I was twenty."

"Huh."

"What the hell does that mean?"

"How old was she?"

"Sixteen."

"Huh."

Harrison's expression darkened. "I don't get what the hell you're—"

"She's gorgeous now. I'm guessing at sixteen, she was probably just a younger version of—"

"*Watch what you fucking say about my sister!*"

Chase backed up a step. "Easy, bro. I was just testing the waters."

"Testing what damn waters?" It sounded as if Harrison had choked on something.

"Testing to see if you felt brother-like for her...or perhaps something more."

Harrison's eyes became slits.

Chase forged onward. "See, there's this whole weird, angry tension thing happening between you and Cole, and I'm trying to figure out exactly what is causing it. Like I said, I was dropped in the middle of a scene without any direction."

Harrison swung away and stalked toward the bar. He grabbed an empty glass, and his knuckles turned white around it. "Allow me to provide you with direction."

"Please do." He was waiting for it, ever so patiently.

"My sister was kidnapped two years ago. I hired Cole to get her back."

"Huh."

"I don't like when you say that." He whirled. "*What?*"

"Was a ransom demanded?"

"Yes," Harrison hissed.

"How much?"

"Five million dollars."

"Huh."

"You are a sonofabitch."

Sure, he was. "It's just that I'm doubting you paid Cole five million."

Harrison looked down at the glass. His hold eased on it. "You think I wasn't going to pay for my sister to be released?"

"I'm only figuring...it was certainly cheaper to use Cole."

"It was *safer*. I've heard about how badly these cases can go. I could've paid them the money, then never gotten my sister back. At least, not alive. Cole did the job he was hired to do. He got her back. But..."

Seriously? The guy was just going to stop his story there and let his voice trail away? Did it look like Chase wanted to be left in suspense?

Harrison carefully rearranged the glasses on his bar. "She wasn't the same."

Of course, she hadn't been. "She was kidnapped. I'd call that a life-changing situation." Anyone would.

"Evie wanted Cole."

Okay, now they were getting somewhere.

"When she had nightmares, she would call out for him."

Pay dirt.

"Cole saved her, and she fell in love with him." Harrison faced Chase once more. "The bastard walked away from her, and I had to see her pain every single day. So, yes, you're probably picking up on some tension between us. If this current situation hadn't happened, if Evie hadn't been in danger again, I never would've pulled that SOB back into our lives."

"Huh."

"God, I think I freaking hate you."

***

"Why did you say that part about having sex with me?" She probably shouldn't have asked the question, but Evie hadn't been able to hold back. "About, um, having 'dirty, hot, mind-melting sex' with me?"

Cole shrugged. "Because it's the truth?" He'd paced toward the other side of the room.

How was she supposed to respond to those words?

"But I get that you're with that asshole from the restaurant."

Her shoulders stiffened. "Leo isn't an asshole."

"Agree to disagree." He turned away.

"I'm not with him." *No, no, take those words back!*

Too late. Cole had whipped right back around toward her. "I thought you met him every Sunday at that Italian restaurant."

She licked her lips. "We do meet. We work together. But we're not romantically involved. I may have...embellished a little on that point."

"He wants to fuck you."

Now she smiled. "No, I don't think he does."

A rough laugh. "I saw the way he was touching you. Holding you. The man wants—"

"He was probably more interested in you."

Cole frowned.

Her smile had already vanished. "I lied, and I should never have used my friend that way. He deserved better. I just—I wasn't expecting you. I know I'm making excuses, but I—" *I wanted you to think I'd moved on.*

"I know you're not still interested in me, Evie," Cole growled. "I get that."

"Good." Wrong, but...

"Just because I've never been able to get you out of my head, it doesn't mean you feel the same way."

She'd misheard him. There was no way that he'd said what she thought. "You don't need to tell me these things."

He stalked toward her.

She resisted the urge to retreat. Instead, she straightened her spine. "You don't have to bullshit me and feed me lines about how you still want me."

He didn't stop that slow, deliberate advance of his, not until he was standing right in front of her. Why, *why* were his eyes so amazing?

"I'm not bullshitting you. I'm making sure you clearly understand the situation." His voice was rough. A little ragged. All sexy.

So much for her being immune to his charms. Maybe she just had a weakness when it came to Cole. Or bad boys in general. After him, she'd sworn off those guys. But here she was, only a short while after seeing him again... "Bad boys are such trouble."

"I'm not a boy."

No, he certainly wasn't.

"And I'm only trouble to the ones who want to hurt you. Because in order to get to you, the bastards will need to come through me. I'm going to be at your side until this is over. Until those jerks are rotting in a cell, I'll be with you."

Her heart raced even faster in her chest.

"I just want to cover the facts so you understand exactly what's happening before we move in together."

Hold on. "Before we do what?" Evie blinked.

"I'm moving into your place. If I'm providing twenty-four, seven protection, that means I'm with you when you sleep. I'm with you when you work. I'm there when any threat could come."

"I...don't have a guest room." Yes, she'd blurted that. Probably the least of her concerns but...

He smiled.

That smile of his sent heat churning straight through her. So much for being immune to his charm. Dammit. When it came to Cole, she still reacted the same way. Which was...*way too much.*

"Don't worry. I can sleep on the floor. I did that last time, remember?"

Until the last night, when he'd slept in the bed with her. Would things end the same way *this* time? "I have a couch," she told him crisply. "I'm sure you saw it when you came into my place. It lets out into a sleeper."

His eyes gleamed. "You told Leopold I was your bodyguard. You can tell everyone else that, too. Or, if you want to keep things on the down low, you can say I'm your lover. Not like that part is a lie, either."

"You're not my lover anymore."

"Who is?"

The jealousy was back. She could see it in his gaze.

Her stare shot to the door on the left. Where was her brother? Shouldn't he have been back by now?

"Still covering the facts," Cole added roughly. "And the fact is I am jealous as fuck when it comes to you. Two years didn't change that. I doubt twenty years will. When it comes to you, I tend to think one thing."

Evie was afraid to ask, but she could not keep the stupid question back as her attention slid to him once more. "What?"

"Mine. I tend to think you're mine."

Evie shook her head. "I only belong to myself."

"Once upon a time, I could have sworn you were mine."

"Cole—"

"And I was yours."

She'd wanted him to be.

"But you make the rules this time, Evie. You want my hands off you? Then they will be off."

Suddenly, all she could think about was the way it felt to have his hands on her. Dammit. Had that been a deliberate trick? A mind game he'd just played on her? Like when you do reverse psychology on someone so they'll do the opposite of—

"Protecting you is my priority. I wanted you to know how I still felt so there would be no confusion between us."

Confusion was making her head spin. "How you feel..." A breath. "You still want me."

"I never stopped wanting you."

But you left.

"Did you stop?" His voice had gone rougher. "Or do you still want me?"

The door to the left creaked open. "Evie!" Harrison's voice. Sharp. Worried.

Her head turned, and she saw his gaze jumping from her to Cole, then back again.

"There a problem?" Harrison demanded.

She hadn't answered Cole's last question. For once, her brother had exhibited absolutely perfect timing.

Chase sauntered out from behind Harrison. He slapped a hand on Harrison's back. "Of course, there's no problem. Wilde is on the case." But his focus shifted to Evie. "Aren't we? Do you want us to keep working your case?"

The pounding of her heartbeat sounded very, very loud. For a moment, she remembered being on the street near the restaurant. The sound of screeching tires.

The fear and fury she'd seen on Cole's face as he lunged for her.

Cole could be scary. He could be fierce. He could kick the ass of bad guys and get the job done. The problem? While he did all of that, he might just break her heart again. Because even though she hadn't answered him, the truth was that...yes, she still wanted him.

"I will protect you," Cole vowed roughly. "I will do everything in my power to keep you safe. But if we go down this path, you decide now. You follow my orders. You trust me."

That part was going to be tricky.

She licked her lower lip. There were other bodyguards out there. Plenty of them. But...

She'd never forget being in that closet back in LA. She'd never forget Cole's voice calling out to her and telling her that she was safe. That he was going to protect her. He'd broken down the door to get to her. Carried her out of her nightmare.

And...

"Do we have a deal, Evie?" Cole asked. He seemed to hold his breath.

She'd said they were going forward. When it came to kicking ass and taking names, Cole was a master. "We have a deal."

Some of the tension slid from his shoulders. He let out a quick breath.

"Good." His voice was still grim. Rough. "Now let's talk logistics."

***

Evie huddled close to her brother. Their heads pressed together as Harrison whispered something to her. From across the room, Cole's eyes narrowed.

"You could've mentioned to me that you were involved with our new client."

He didn't turn his head at Chase's low words. "Didn't see it as relevant."

"Huh."

"I hate it when you say that. You know that instead of saying 'huh' you're supposed to tell me what you really think. We've gone over this before."

"You slept with her."

"Don't see how you need to know that. FYI, Chase, I don't kiss and tell. That shit isn't cool. Should've learned that in high school."

"You still want her."

I will always want her. "What I want right now is for you to shut your—"

"I can see it when you look at her. If you don't want the world knowing, you might want to get better at hiding how you feel."

Finally, Cole glanced his way. "Just how do I look at her?"

Chase lifted his eyebrows. "Like you're starving, and she's the best feast you've ever seen."

"You're telling me that I look at her like I want to eat her?" His voice carried only to Chase.

"Eat her. Fuck her. Own her."

Cole locked his back teeth. "Watch it," he gritted out. His hands fisted.

"No, *you* need to watch it. I don't trust the brother, and I don't think you do, either." A pause. "I think he might hate you, by the way."

Cole looked back at Evie and Harrison. "The feeling could be mutual."

"Then explain to me why he called *you* in. I don't buy his BS about her not trusting anyone else—"

"It's simple," Cole responded quietly. "Harrison knows that when it comes to Evie, I would kill anyone who tried to hurt her." Because, once upon a time, he'd gone to Harrison and Cole had said...

I fucking love Evie. I want a second chance.

He hadn't gotten that chance, not back then.

I'm taking it now.

CHAPTER FOUR

*Or...second chance fun, anyone? AKA...the time
Cole tried ever so hard not to be an asshole.*

"I want a list of your enemies."

Evie stiffened at Cole's words. Harrison had
been whispering to her, making sure she was okay
and that she wasn't *super* pissed that he'd gone
behind her back to get Cole.

Super pissed? Really? *Ya think?*

But at Cole's curt order, she cleared her
throat. "I don't...I mean, there are some dancers
and actors who might say I'm a bitch because I
can be pretty demanding when I'm working a
choreography set, but I don't think I really have
any enemies. Certainly not someone who would
hate me enough to try and kidnap me." God, she
hoped no one hated her that much. If so, that was
a whole load of hate.

Cole shook his head. "I'm not just talking
about you, Evie. I'm also talking about your
brother."

Harrison had been touching her shoulder.
Now his hand tightened on her. "The email

referenced my father. My *dead* father. This is about him, not me or Evie."

"Could be." It was Chase who agreed. Chase stood next to Cole, with his arms crossed over his chest. His golden eyes gleamed. "But in cases like this one, it's standard procedure to investigate other avenues. The perps could be trying to throw us off by mentioning your dad. So we need to know who you've pissed off recently. Who you've *both* angered."

Evie took a steadying breath. "What are you asking for...exactly? Like the names of ex boyfriends?"

Cole nodded. "We already have a list going on them, but more information would help the investigation."

Helpful, huh? Why did it just feel like humiliation for her? "I haven't dated anyone in probably about six months. I was working on a production that just wrapped, and I didn't exactly have a lot of time for extra things."

His stare glittered at her. "I need the names of the guys you've rejected."

"Some men can't take that shit," Chase agreed flatly. "Dicks."

"I don't think this is about rejection." Evie shook her head. "This ties back to the first abduction. It's about money, not about someone's feelings for me."

"We can't overlook any avenue of investigation." Cole didn't look away from her. "We have to be thorough. Yes, it seems that it's the same. But we have to rule out that it's not some new bastard who knows about what happened to you before—"

"And sees an opportunity to imitate the crime," Chase finished grimly.

Great. So she could have *new* kidnappers?

"They're going down, Evie. New or old, doesn't matter. They'll be stopped," Cole promised. He seemed so very certain.

But they'd gotten away last time. Vanished into the air. Just as Cole had seemed to vanish.

Harrison cleared his throat. "I have enemies in my business. Real estate isn't exactly a friendly game." Harrison still had his hand curved over her shoulder. "My father made plenty of enemies, too. The way the asshole said in his email that we had to pay back what my father owed—sounded to me like it might be tied to some deal that went south."

Cole nodded. "Our agents are tearing into your father's financials even as we speak."

She felt Harrison stiffen.

"The first time you were taken," Cole told her softly, "I was a mercenary hired by your brother. I'd been part of Delta Force, but I was working freelance when Harrison reached out to me. I assembled my own team, and we got you out."

Wait, a mercenary? As in, like, a gun for hire? Was that a thing, outside of movies? She'd pretty much just thought of him as a hero, and she hadn't—

"This time, I'm working with Wilde. Eric Wilde has pretty much limitless resources. His tech team is the best. We're going to get the perps.

We're going to throw them in cages, and they will never get out."

At the lethal intensity in his words, a shiver slid over her skin.

***

"Cole!"

He hadn't been sleeping. Cole had been flopped on the lumpy, pullout couch in Evie's living room, staring up at the ceiling, and trying hard to *not* fantasize about her.

Then she screamed.

For an instant, his heart stopped.

In the next second, he was on his feet and racing to her bedroom. He shoved open the bedroom door—

"I'm all right!"

A lamp had been left on near her bed—it sent illumination pouring from the nightstand.

Evie sat up in bed. She clutched a white comforter to her chest. "I'm all right," she repeated quickly.

"You screamed." His heart slammed into his chest. His gaze cut around the room as Cole searched for threats.

"I'm all right," she said once more. "You can go back to sleep."

Seriously? Not happening. Cole strode forward. "What happened?"

Her cute little pink tongue licked over her upper lip. "Bad dream. We all have them."

His muscles tensed. "You screamed for me."

He saw her swallow. "Yes."

Okay, he did *not* like the growing suspicion he had. "Baby, do you always sleep with a light on?" He motioned toward the lamp.

Her stare darted to the lamp. "I...forgot to turn it off when I went to bed." She shook her head, hard, sending her hair swinging against her cheeks. "Wait, did you call me baby?"

He had. A slip. He wasn't about to be distracted. He strode toward the edge of the bed. Her scent—vanilla cream—filled his nostrils. "I thought you didn't like to lie."

She peered down at her comforter, not at him. "I don't like to lie," she mumbled. "Doesn't mean I don't try it every now and then."

Cole waited.

"You can go back to sleep," she told him again.

Obviously, it was a dismissal.

Obviously, he wasn't in the mood to be dismissed. At least, not until he got the answers that he needed. "Tell me what I want to know, then I'll head back to the couch from hell."

Her head whipped up. "Is it that lumpy?"

"I don't know that lumpy is quite the right word. Springs were shoving into my ass. I think they left impressions."

She winced.

"I've had worse." Plenty worse. A thousand times worse. "Answer my questions."

Her breath huffed out. She looked mutinous and way too cute as she snapped, "Fine. Ask them."

"Do you always sleep with a light on?"

Her lips pressed together. He didn't think she was going to reply even though she'd said—

"Yes, I do." Her chin notched up toward him. "After being trapped in a closet for over twenty-four hours, I developed a bit of a phobia. I don't like the dark, so I keep a lamp on when I sleep." Her nostrils flared. "Because when I wake up and it's pitch black, sometimes, I think I'm back there."

A fist grabbed his heart.

"Nyctophobia."

His brow scrunched.

"It's a fear or phobia of the dark. Lots of people have it. I'm not alone." She sounded defensive.

She didn't need to be.

I never want you to be alone, sweetheart. He pushed ahead with his questions. "Do you still have nightmares about the abduction?"

"My therapist said it would be normal to have nightmares."

"You're supposed to answer the question."

"What are you, a lawyer?" Now she let go of the comforter. It slid down to pool at her waist, and he saw that she was wearing a thin, white T-shirt. No bra. Her tight nipples pushed against the front of the fabric.

He swallowed. *She is probably cold. Not turned on. This is hardly the time for her to be turned on. Stop being an asshole.*

"Yes," she finally told him softly. "I do still have nightmares. Not often, though. Not like right after the abduction when I would—" Evie clamped her lips together.

"Don't stop now." He sat on the edge of the bed. Wanted to reach out and touch her. Cole held back that urge, barely.

"I would have them pretty frequently after the abduction, okay? But bad dreams can't hurt you. I learned that after a while."

Bad dreams could sure as hell screw with your mind. "The abduction attempt today probably stirred up memories for you."

Her lashes flickered. "Yes, I'm sure that's what it was."

"You screamed for me."

"Did I?" Her gaze darted away.

He almost smiled. Would have, if his heart hadn't felt so heavy. "You are a shit liar."

Her gaze flew to his face. She studied him a moment, then gritted out, "Fine. Yes, I might have called out for you. That's a habit that I thought I'd broken, too."

His own eyes narrowed.

"Though I don't think habit is the right word. I'm sure it should be called something else, but I don't know what that term is. It's late. I'm tired and I'm not thinking clearly, and we both should get back to sleep."

They should. Absolutely. But he wasn't moving, not yet. "You've woken up, screaming for me, before?" His heart seemed to stop beating.

She stared straight into his eyes. "Do you have any idea how humiliating this is for me?"

His breath expelled in a hard rush as his heart seemed to explode in a fast, frantic rhythm. "The last thing I would ever want to do is humiliate you." God, no. "I'm sorry. I was just—I'm trying to understand."

Because her brother had told him...

Evie wants nothing to do with you. She's put the pieces of her life back together, and those pieces don't include you. You were a mistake. She told me that herself.

Her brother's response when Cole had confessed how he felt for Evie—a response that had been burned into his brain.

"If you must know, my therapist said that I thought of you as my safe place. That in my mind, I saw you as an anchor in the storm. So, yes, when I had bad dreams for a while, I woke up calling your name."

An anchor in the storm.

And he hadn't been there. Fucking hell.

He hadn't known. "I'm sorry."

She blinked a few times. "For what?"

"I didn't know that you needed me."

Wrong thing to say. Her shoulders immediately stiffened. "I don't need you. I mean, yes, someone is after me now, so I guess I do need a bodyguard, and I appreciate the Wilde services, but...I don't *need* you."

"I understand." He did. He should move. Get his ass off the bed. Put some distance between them. "But I'm still sorry."

"Why?"

"I'm sorry I wasn't there when you called for me." His hand lifted, and he tucked a lock of her hair behind her ear. "I wish I had been there."

Her hand flew up. Her fingers circled around his wrist. "Don't say things that you don't mean."

"I didn't know. Your brother told me that you were adjusting just fine and—" Cole shut his mouth.

Too late.

Her lashes fluttered. "When did he tell you that?"

When I came back for you because I realized I'd made a colossal mistake. "I checked in with him."

A furrow was between her eyebrows. "He never mentioned that to me."

No, Harrison wouldn't have. *Because he didn't want me anywhere near you.*

"The only thing he ever told me was that you had other cases. That right after you left me, you'd taken another assignment somewhere in Europe, and there was no way to reach you."

There had been other assignments, but her brother... "I spoke with him." And it hadn't been just once. Hell, how did she think that Harrison had known he was now working with Wilde? Because when he'd signed on with Wilde, Cole had told Harrison exactly where he'd be.

The fact that the kidnappers were never caught kept me up at night. I worried about you. Told Harrison I would be there in an instant if you ever had trouble again.

"You talked to him—like, in person?"

In person. On the phone.

"When, Cole? When did you talk to him?"

"A little while...after." After...after he'd driven away and tried not to look back. After he'd given her his heart and tried to live like half a man. "When doesn't matter. I didn't—I didn't know, okay? I didn't know about your nightmares. I'm sorry that you were hurting, and I wasn't there." She was still holding his wrist. His head had bent toward hers, and he wanted to put his mouth on hers. Wanted to taste her. The night he'd had with her—she'd tasted so good. Perfect. "I won't let you down again. You call for me, and I will come running." Just like he had moments before.

Just like he would *always* do for her now.

Her hand slid away from his. "You—you're not wearing a shirt."

No, he wasn't. Actually, he was just wearing old jogging shorts. He'd just remembered that fact.

"You have tattoos on your chest."

He had a whole lot of tats. He didn't think the dim lighting from her lamp let her clearly see all the designs. "And some on my back." He wondered what she thought of tats. Some women loved tats. Thought they made a guy look badass. Other women couldn't stand them. Thought they made a man look too dangerous and wild.

He didn't particularly care about all those other women, though. He just wondered what Evie thought.

He'd gotten the tats for a very specific reason. One he wasn't going to tell her about. At least, not yet.

The way Cole figured it, there was no sense in telling her about what had happened to him. He'd survived. Time to move on.

His gaze lingered on her lips, though. What he wouldn't give to taste her....

"Good night, Cole."

A clear dismissal. He swallowed. If she glanced down, she'd realize that his eager dick was about to tear right out of his shorts. He stood and turned quickly for the door. Then he stopped. "I hope you don't have any other bad dreams." *If you do, baby, call for me. I'll be here.* He marched forward.

"Do you ever have bad dreams?"

Yeah, he fucking did. "Everyone does."

"What are yours about?"

His...

He looked back at her. "They're about getting to that closet in LA. Ripping open that door..." A hard exhale. "And not finding you."

My nightmares are about losing you.

He exited the bedroom. Closed the door. He stood there a moment, his heart racing, and rage churning in his gut. A quick glance at the nearby clock told him it was after midnight. Like he gave a damn. Cole snatched up his phone and dialed Harrison White's number.

It took four rings for a groggy Harrison to answer.

"Wh-what is it?" Harrison rasped. "Evie...okay?"

"You bastard, when this is over, I'm kicking your ass."

"What?" Now Harrison sounded more awake. More aware. And a little scared. "Why?"

"Evie has nightmares. She calls out *my* name."

Silence.

"And you didn't think it was important to tell me that shit?" If Harrison had been in front of him, Cole would have driven his fist into the other man's face.

"Evie was—was moving on with her life," Harrison sputtered. "Her therapist said a few nightmares were normal, and she—"

"Evie called for me." That gutted him. His hand almost smashed the phone because he held it so tightly. "And I wasn't there." A situation that would never occur again. "You kept me from her."

"You...you're not right for Evie, you're—"

"At this exact moment, considering the danger surrounding your sister, I'm more than *right* for her. I'm fucking perfect." He tried to choke down his rage. "You attempt to come between us again, and it will be the last mistake you ever make, got me?"

"You're threatening me? *Me?* I am paying for—"

"Screw your money. In case Eric didn't tell you, *I'm* footing the bill for any and all security measures that involve Evie."

"Why? Why would you do that?"

Because she's mine.

Her bedroom door creaked open.

He spun.

Evie stood in the doorway, wearing her white T-shirt, an oversize T-shirt that fell to mid-thigh. She wore the T-shirt and...

Holy hell, does she have on panties, or is she only wearing the shirt? He couldn't tell, and he really, really wanted to tell. With all of his soul.

"Cole? Are you listening to me?"

Hell, no. He was drooling over Evie. "Don't forget my promise." Cole's voice was a rough rumble. "I'll keep it when the case is over."

"But—"

Cole hung up on the dick. He tossed his phone aside and didn't even look to see where it landed, mostly because he couldn't look away from Evie. What sane man *would* want to look away from her?

She bit her lower lip. "Was that an important call?"

"Not really."

"But...it's after midnight." She took a tentative step forward. Her toenails were painted fire engine red, and her legs went on for fucking miles. "Was it about the case?"

"No." Hell. That had sounded like a growl. He tried again, saying, "It was about something I'll do when the bad guys are caught."

Her gaze darted to the couch—to the pulled-out sleeper. She winced. "I'm sorry that's so bad."

"It's fine. It's way better than the floor."

Her deep chocolate eyes came back to his. "You slept on the floor when you rescued me in LA. After that first night, when I woke you up—"

Her scream had woken him up then. Just like this time, he hadn't been able to get to her fast enough.

"Back then, you said you didn't want to leave the bedroom. And when you were there in the room with me, I felt safe."

"Evie..."

"That's the thing about you." She slowly crossed the room until she stood directly in front of him. "You always make me feel safe."

"I won't let anyone hurt you."

"I know." Her smile was wistful. "I used to think you were like some kind of superhero."

"I'm hardly hero material, and I'm certainly not super." His buddy James would say he could be a super asshole but...Cole was trying to be different, for her.

Trying to be better.

And that was why his hands were off her and currently clenched at his sides.

"I still want you," Evie confessed.

His jaw dropped.

"I'm not going to pretend that I don't. The attraction that I had for you before is still there. And, just, um, judging by your condition, I'm assuming you still want me, too."

His condition? Ah, yes, the giant hard-on that she probably hadn't been able to miss. He arched an eyebrow. "Yeah, Evie, I still want you." Still, always—whatever word she wanted to use.

"But you didn't do anything about wanting me. You just walked out of the room."

Bam. His heart thudded hard into his chest. "Do you *want* me to do something?"

"Back in LA, I had to come to you. I was the one who made the first move."

Yes, she had been. He'd been the one taking way too many cold showers.

Her head tilted. Her hair slid over her shoulder. "How long do you think you'll be guarding me this time?"

Her vanilla cream scent wrapped around him. Made him crazy. "I don't know."

"Last time, we only made it a week before we had sex."

Was it hot in there? It felt hot in there.

"I'm not seeing anyone. You already know I lied about Leo." Evie rocked forward. "Are you? I mean, are you seeing anyone?"

"No." An instant denial.

She nodded. "I just wanted to know."

"Now you do." He waited. Couldn't drag his gaze away from her mouth.

He heard her breathing hitch. "What do you want right now?" Evie whispered.

Since she'd asked... "I want to take your mouth. I want to see if you taste as sweet as I remember."

Her eyes flared. "This is a mistake. My brother would say it was a huge mistake."

"Yeah, well, your brother is a—" Cole caught himself, just in time. "It's a kiss, Evie. If you want to kiss me, if you want to see what happens when your mouth gets on mine, then let's do it. It's not about your brother." Hell, no, it wasn't. "It's not about what anyone else thinks. It's about me and it's about you."

"Right." She was staring at his mouth now, too. "Me and you."

He unclenched his right hand. Let it rise. Cupped her chin as he tipped back her head. "It's just a kiss. Not sex. You might kiss me and decide you don't want my mouth or my hands on you ever again." *Fucking perish that thought.*

"I might. Or you might decide that you don't want me."

Oh, that's a big hell, no. Won't be deciding that. Ever. "Maybe we should just kiss and find out what happens. That way, we get it over with."

She nodded. "Maybe."

But she didn't move. Neither did he. He didn't move because he did not want to screw anything up with her again. He was trying to hold onto his control. Trying to do things right this time, trying to show her—

"Fuck it," Evie breathed. She threw her body against his. Her mouth came toward his.

He took her lips. *Took* them. Her lips were soft and sensual. And they parted for him...

His tongue slid into her mouth. He tasted her, and dammit, she was even sweeter than he remembered. So sweet and good and he wanted to *devour* her. He could feel his control splintering. Could feel his need for her raging too hot and hard. His mouth was savage in his need as Cole took and took, and Evie kissed him back the same way.

There was no awkwardness. No hesitation because it had been so long since he'd had her in his arms. There was just an explosion of lust. A surge of white-hot desire.

She moaned.

He lifted her into his arms as he tried to drag her even closer to him. *Closer.* Her arms twined around his neck and her legs locked around his hips. His dick shoved toward her, pushing at the juncture of her thighs and the thin panties he could feel there.

He took a few steps forward and pinned her between his body and the wall. His heart pounded in his ears. The scent of vanilla cream flooded his nostrils. He kept kissing her. Tasting her. Wanting her.

It would be so easy to rip her panties out of the way. To sink balls deep into her and get lost in the madness of pleasure they would bring to each other. He could have her screaming. She'd have him roaring. Her nails could scratch down his body as he got her to come again and again.

Her hips arched against him. Her lips sucked around his tongue, and then she—

"No." Evie shoved her hand between their bodies. She'd torn her mouth away from his. "We...*no*."

He sucked in a breath. One. Two. Counted his pounding heartbeats. The beats were raging out of control.

"I'm sorry," she whispered.

"You don't have a fucking thing to be sorry for." His eyes squeezed shut. His hands were holding her hips—holding them way too tightly. "Just...give me a minute." To get his control back.

"I didn't think it would still be that intense." Her voice was soft. So husky. "It's...it's almost more than it was before."

With her, it was always more. She didn't get that. Didn't understand that she was different for him. Had been, from day one.

Slowly, he lowered her so that her bare feet touched the floor. He forced his hands to let go of her. His eyes opened as he stepped back.

"I don't know what I'm supposed to do with us." Her confession sounded lost. Uncertain.

"You do whatever feels right." His voice was freaking gravel.

She bit her lip.

He growled. *I want to bite. To lick. To suck. To take.*

"I...should go to bed," Evie mumbled.

And I would love to join you there. But he knew it was too soon. Too fast. He'd just come back into her life. After the day from hell that she'd had, Evie was riding one massive wave of adrenaline. Pair that with the fact that she'd woken up from a nightmare minutes before...

Yeah, he'd have to be one Grade A asshole to try and keep her with him that night.

Try not to be an asshole. This once. With her. Try. He locked down his body and told her, "If you have a bad dream, I'll be at your side in a flash."

Her gaze held his. "Thank you."

She slipped away. Headed back into her room. The door closed quietly behind her.

He looked down at his hands. They were shaking. Lust burned through every cell of his body. He wanted her more than he wanted breath. "Fuck me," he whispered.

This case was gonna be a real bitch.

***

So...she still wanted him. Maybe not still. More like, she wanted him *even more.*

Evie crawled into the bed, and she pulled the covers up to her chin. She stared up at the ceiling.

The lamp was on and spreading a faint glow around her bed—she couldn't remember the last time that she'd actually slept in the dark.

Before the abduction. You know exactly how long it's been. Stop lying to yourself.

She wasn't good at lying to others. Sometimes, though, she did try to lie to herself. She'd tried to lie to herself about Cole. Tried to say that she didn't still want him.

She did. When he touched her, electricity coursed through her blood. When he kissed her, her knees went weak and her whole body turned *on*. Desire pulsed through her. She wanted to haul him as close to her as she could and just let go of her control. To feel and enjoy.

But what happened...*after*? After the super awesome sex? Because sex with him was awesome. Amazing. Mind-blowing. Without a doubt, he was the best lover she'd ever had.

But...after?

When the bad guys were caught, she was certain that Cole would leave her life again. He'd disappear, just as he had before.

This time, though, she'd know that was going to happen. She'd know that what they had wasn't permanent. Know it couldn't last. Maybe...perhaps this time, she could just enjoy being with him.

She'd told Cole that she wanted to let go of their past.

So, what if there was no past? And no future for them?

What if they only had the present? The hot and sexy present.

Evie squeezed her eyes shut.
She could still taste him.

CHAPTER FIVE

Also known as that time Cole got stupid jealous and wanted to beat down a group of male dancers.

"Do they have to touch you so fucking much?" Cole growled when Evie finally took a break and headed toward him. She was wearing the tiniest, tightest pair of black shorts that he'd ever seen in his life. Shorts he would never forget anytime soon. Paired with those shorts, she wore some sort of camisole top that was form fitting and pushing up her breasts in the most awesome manner imaginable. The top was a thin bit of nothing, and it was driving him crazy. And seeing those assholes with their hands on her? Oh, that was just—

"Yes," Evie replied crisply as she grabbed her water bottle. "They do have to touch me. It's a choreography routine. I'm standing in for the female dancer because she's sick, and I told Leo that I would help out. We're working through the routine, and part of that work involves them lifting me up, spinning me around, and, yes, heaven forbid, *touching* me as they perform the dance sequence."

Behind him, he heard a snicker.

He shot a mean glare over his shoulder at Chase. "Don't you have something else to do?"

Chase shrugged.

Cole focused back on Evie.

"Neither one of you have anything to do." Her hand tightened around the bottle. "It's been five days since the incident with the van, and there has been no sign of the jerks who tried to grab me."

She was right. His gaze locked on a bead of sweat that was sliding down her collar bone and heading toward—

"We *did* find the van," Chase piped up to say. "But you already know it was wiped down. It had been reported as stolen by the owner, so, unfortunately, we're not getting a lot of leads from it at this time."

She sipped more water. Her throat moved as—

"Dude, you are drooling." Chase leaned closer. "Do you need a towel or something?"

Cole barely resisted the urge to elbow him.

Evie put down the water bottle. She bent, stretching, as she curved her body and touched her toes. Then she lifted one leg, straight up in the air, and curled her arms around it.

"Oh, damn." Chase sucked in a sharp breath. "You are *very* flexible," he praised. "I had no idea—"

This time, Cole elbowed him. Hard.

Chase choked.

Evie lowered her leg. Frowned. "He okay?"

She'd missed the elbowing because Cole was just that good and fast. "He's fine. Don't worry about Chase. He has allergy issues." *He's allergic to my freaking elbow.*

"Oh. Sorry." She looked back at the dancers. "Another half hour and we'll be done here."

Another half hour of watching those muscled assholes put their hands all over Evie? Another half hour of thinking about all of the ways he could so easily hurt them? Cole slapped a smile on his face even as jealousy tore into his heart. "Great. Wonderful. Another half hour."

Her gaze jumped back to him. A faint line appeared on her forehead. "You're bored."

Uh, nope, bored wasn't the right word. *How can I stay bored when I'm busy plotting all of the ways I want to kill a group of muscled dancers who are touching you all over that hot body of yours?* "Not at all," he assured her.

Her breath expelled in a low rush. "It's a waste of time." Her attention swung from him to Chase, then back to Cole. "For you both. For your whole team. It's been five days and nothing has happened. You can't keep up this protection detail indefinitely."

She thought he was just going to walk away? Not happening. "The perps are waiting for you to be vulnerable."

A shiver skated over her.

She needed to understand this part. "I'm not going to leave you unprotected."

He could see the worry in her eyes. "But how long can you keep this up? I can't let Harrison foot the bill for this time and all the manpower.

Actually, I already told him that I wanted to pay." Her chin notched up. "And I do fully intend to pay for the services you've given me this week."

Wait...Harrison was letting her think that *he* was paying? Hadn't Cole been clear on that point? He was covering Evie's protection.

"But I can't cover costs forever." Evie's voice was low. "I know Wilde is super expensive."

They were, only she didn't need to worry about that. "Who told you Wilde was expensive?"

She rolled back her shoulders and pointed toward Leo. He hadn't been one of the touching dancers. He'd been busy providing instruction and making lots of notes during the routines. "Leo told me he knew this Hollywood actress who used Wilde's services a while back. Gwenevere Solomon? And some rock star, too. According to Leo, Wilde caters to the rich and famous, so that means there has to be a heavy price tag."

"Your brother is rich," Chase reminded her.

"But I'm not. I make a good living, and I'm grateful for all that I have, but it's not like I can keep paying out for protection over weeks, months or—" She stopped. "You get the picture."

Cole did. "The bill is taken care of. You don't have to worry about it."

Her jaw tightened. "Because my brother—"

"Your brother is not fucking paying." Shit. Those words just burst out.

Her eyes widened. "Then who is?"

Do not speak. He was not going to dig his hole any deeper.

"Evie!" Leo called. "We need you to finish up this routine. The ending isn't working for me, and

I want to know how you think the final moments should go."

She didn't look away from Cole. Suspicion sharpened her gaze. "Who is paying for my protection?"

"We can talk about it when you're done."

One hand went to her hip. "We can talk about it right now."

Damn but she was even sexier when she was angry.

"Now, one more time, who is paying for my protection?"

"He is," Chase supplied, cutting in with his chipper tone. "Cole volunteered to foot the bill for your protection detail."

She stepped closer to Cole. "Why would you do that?"

Because it's you.

"Evie!" Leo hurried toward her. "We only have the studio for thirty more minutes. And don't forget, we've got the charity ball tonight. We need to finish up here and then go get gorgeous and extra glamorous before the big event." He stopped behind her. Smiled at Cole and Chase. "Oh, there are *two* of them now."

"You knew there were two," Evie replied without looking his way. "You never miss anyone in your studio."

"Well, of course, I don't miss anyone. Can't just have random people sneaking inside and trying to steal our choreography routines." He huffed. "And don't think that shit hasn't happened before." His voice rose. "Though, technically, it wasn't a random person so much as that wannabe Michael Simmons and—"

She put her hand on his chest. "Don't get worked up about him. You know you're way better than he is."

Leo exhaled. Seemed to calm. "You're right."

Evie's stare was still on Cole. "We are going to talk about this situation. It's not over."

He nodded. They could definitely talk, but he would still keep footing the bill. Because he had the feeling that Evie was trying to pull the plug on Wilde's services, and he wasn't about to leave her unprotected. He knew that was precisely what the perps wanted.

As soon as she's vulnerable, they'll strike.

That was the way the assholes always worked.

Without another word, she headed back to the team of *six* male dancers. Cole couldn't help it. He tried so very, very hard to keep his gaze up, but it fell because...

Evie's ass is a thing of beauty.

Then Leo stepped in his way and blocked his view. "For the record," Leo's voice was loud. "She is a million miles out of your league."

Of course, she was. "Tell me something I don't know."

Leo's gaze turned dagger-like in intensity. Leo didn't like Cole. Check. He'd gotten that message a few times.

They needed to work through this shit. "I'm keeping her safe," Cole growled. *So back the hell off.*

Leo moved closer, and voice low, said, "I don't want to see Evie get her heart broken just because some badass comes in and sweeps her off her feet. It would figure that Evie would have a weakness for badasses." Leo sniffed and pointed to Cole. Then Chase.

Wait, Chase? Why the hell was Leo pointing at Chase? Cole jerked his thumb toward the other Wilde agent. "She's not fucking interested in him."

"She's got a type. Obviously. Evie is the typical good girl who wants to walk on the bad side."

"There is *nothing* typical about her," Cole fired right back. "If you think that, you don't know her at all."

"Oh, I don't? And you're going to tell me that she's not typical because she's special and she's—"

"She damn well is special." Cole glared at him. "What the hell is your deal? I thought you were her friend. I thought—"

"He *is* her friend," Chase told him as he grabbed Cole's shoulder. "That's why he's pushing your buttons to see how you react. He wants to find out just how *in* to Evie you are."

He—aw, hell. Now Leo was smiling. More like beaming. "Looks like you are all *in*." Leo hummed. "Good to know. Maybe if you beg enough, she'll give you a second chance."

"I'm hardly the begging type."

Leo had already turned away. He waved his hand in the air. "Don't forget your tux for tonight! Maybe if you look good enough in it, you won't have to beg as long."

"I am *not* the begging type!"

A few feet away from Leo, one of the dancers was swinging Evie in front of him. He had one hand curled around her waist, and the other held her leg—the top of her leg, about three inches, maybe two inches away from her—

Chase's hold tightened on him when Cole surged forward. "You know you don't get to attack the dancers."

"Do you *see* where his hand is?"

"Yes, and I know you wish that was your hand, but it's not, and they're working, and this isn't about sex."

He still wanted that hand fucking *moved*.

"I don't think there is a threat to your Evie in this dance studio. I think the male dancers are in more danger than she is. And that danger is you."

Your Evie. His head swung toward Chase. "We're not sleeping together."

Chase's eyebrows climbed. "Did I ask? Did I ask you to tell me way too much information about your sex life? Because I don't think I did."

"You called her mine. She's...not."

"Yeah, but you'd like for her to be."

"I—" Shit. Yes. A thousand times yes.

"You're footing the bill for her security." Chase whistled. "You know I'm not cheap."

None of the Wilde agents were.

"That sure says a whole lot about how you feel regarding the woman."

"You're probing. Thought you didn't want too much info."

Chase let him go. "She's right, and so are you."

Right about what? Cole was lost. He was also trying not to glance back over his shoulder to see what the dancers were doing—

"Her protection detail can't go on indefinitely. I'm assuming you don't have limitless resources."

Chase could assume whatever—

"And the perps are trying to wait until she's vulnerable. If we backed off, if you made your presence a little *less* obvious in her life, then maybe they'd make a move. Have you considered that?"

"I'm not backing off," he snarled. What the hell? Chase wanted Cole to leave Evie vulnerable? Was he batshit insane?

"Okay, okay, easy there, killer." Chase shook his head. "Look, if they're watching her, then they've seen you around her. You're not exactly playing things low key. You're this big, tattooed guy who is watching her every move. That screams bodyguard, just so you know."

"I don't care what it—"

"If you want to catch the bad guys, you need to make your presence scream something else. Obviously, you don't want to leave Evie on her own. I don't want her on her own, either, just so you know. I'm not into the whole throwing lambs to wolves bit. Totally not what I was suggesting." He cleared his throat. "I thought that you might want to present a new image to anyone who might be watching from the shadows."

His gut clenched. "Just what image would that be?"

"So, the way I see it, there are two main reasons why a guy like you would be hanging out in a dance studio for hours, watching a woman like Evie."

He waited. "Enlighten me."

"One, obviously, is that you're her bodyguard. You're looking for threats."

Exactly, yes, he was.

"Two, you're an obsessed boyfriend who can't stand the thought of other men touching what belongs to him."

His shoulders stiffened even as he had the stupid, uncontrolled thought of—

Exactly, yes, he was.

"You're staying at her place. If the bad guys are watching—and we both know they are—then they know you've moved in with her. Again, two reasons why. Reason one, you're her bodyguard and you're giving her twenty-four, seven protection."

Sure, that was the case. It was what a good bodyguard would do. A thorough one. He believed in being thorough.

"Or, reason two, you're the lover from her past who came back, took one look at her, and realized you couldn't let her go again. You grabbed her, held on tight, and you moved in with her because you wanted to fuck her constantly."

Cole didn't speak.

Chase's gaze flickered over Cole's shoulder. "I, of course," his voice was smooth as silk, "know which option is correct, but we need to make sure the kidnappers see the narrative that works for us. We need them to change their thinking. Because an obsessed boyfriend is much easier to handle than a dedicated bodyguard. An obsessed boyfriend can be caught off-guard. An obsessed boyfriend can be taken down. He's not a threat."

Cole's breathing was nice and slow. But the muscles in his body were rock hard with tension. "You think I need to start acting like her boyfriend."

Chase smiled at him. "Give the man the biggest cookie in the world. Yeah, I do. I think you need to change the narrative here, ASAP. We need to pull the attackers in, and I know you aren't about to leave her undefended while that happens—"

"No, not even for a second."

"So we have to make sure that they stop seeing you as a threat. You look tough, but you need to look besotted."

Cole's eyebrows flew up. "What the fuck does that even mean?"

"Uh, it means infatuated, that you are basically emotionally drunk on the woman." Chase sighed. "Dude, try picking up a romance novel sometime. It will change your life *and* increase your vocabulary."

"You want me to act...besotted." Just so they were clear.

"We don't know exactly where our audience is, but yes, you need to act that way. All the time. Look at her like you can't wait to strip her naked. Look at her like you want to pull her into the nearest bedroom and never let go. Look at her like the sun rises and sets behind her. Look at her like she is the most important thing in your entire life."

Evie's laughter rang out behind him. It was light and sweet, and it had been so long since Cole heard that sound—

His head whipped toward her.

A faint smile pulled at his lips.

"Yeah," Chase coughed. "Basically, look at her that way. I think you've got it."

Cole's smile froze.

"Are you ready to change up the play? Because even our Wilde techs are hitting the wall on this case. We need to shake things up, and we need to do it now." A pause. "Are you ready to stop being the bodyguard and become the boyfriend?"

Like that was going to be some kind of hardship. Pretending to be wrapped up in Evie? Hell, yes, he could manage that one. In his sleep. "I'm ready."

"That's a wrap!" Leo called out excitedly. "We've got it! Time to clear this studio."

There were sighs of relief. Laughter. The dancers and Evie hugged each other. Her smile—though tired—still lit her face.

"No time like the present to start setting that scene," Chase advised.

Cole was already striding toward her. As he closed in, Evie's eyes widened.

He caught her hands. Pulled her against him.

"Cole?"

"I need to kiss you," he rasped.

"Um, okay. But I am really sweaty—"

"No, sweetheart, you are really fucking hot."

He took her mouth. Her lips were parted, and he thrust his tongue right into her mouth. He kissed her and he savored her, and he damn well worshipped her mouth. She tasted like his favorite treat. She smelled like vanilla cream.

He pulled her body closer to his. Kissed her harder. Hotter. Wilder.

Her hands dug into his arms as she held him just as tightly. Her body pressed to his, and he could feel the thrust of her nipples against his chest. He would love nothing more than to take those nipples into his mouth. To lick and suck them until she was moaning his name. Then he could strip off those teeny-tiny shorts of hers. Slide his fingers between her legs. See if she was wet for him. God, he wanted her wet. Then he could replace his fingers with his mouth. He could lick her until she came for him. The first time. The second time that she came, he wanted his dick buried so deep in her that—

Someone was clapping.

His head lifted. His heart thundered.

The clapping died away.

"That was so hot," Leo praised as he strode past them. The other dancers were smiling. "So much for being an ex, huh, Evie?"

She blinked. Her gaze had been unfocused, dazed, but at Leo's words, her stare sharpened. Her lips were red and swollen from Cole's mouth.

Cole really, really wanted to kiss her again.

"What was...?" Evie's voice trailed away. She shook her head. Stared at Cole. "Why?"

"I'll explain everything soon." He backed away, but reached down to thread his fingers with hers as he carefully held her hand. "For now, just follow my lead."

Her head moved in a jerky nod.

Play the lover? Play the "besotted" boyfriend? Sure, he could do that. He could play that role forever.

CHAPTER SIX

I knew what "besotted" meant. I was just messing with Chase. Man is an ass. And maybe...maybe I *am* besotted with Evie. So what?

"So it was an act." Evie sat in the back of the limo. Cole had just slid in right next to her, and the man was already taking up far too much room.

The driver slammed the door and headed to the front of the vehicle.

"I couldn't exactly explain when we had an audience."

There was no audience any longer. Just her. Him. Then again, there hadn't been an audience in her home, either, but he'd only had time to give her the briefest of explanations before they had to rush and get ready for the charity gala. She'd committed to the event months ago, mostly because her brother's business had organized it.

"Chase thinks we needed to mix things up. If you're being watched—and, honestly, I'm sure that you are—then we want those watching to think I'm your boyfriend, not just a bodyguard who is dodging your steps."

Her gaze slid over him. He was wearing a tux, and frankly, it should be illegal for a man to look as hot as he did. When she'd come out of her bedroom and seen him standing in her den, wearing the tux that fit him perfectly...

"You okay with this plan?"

She cleared her throat. "That's why you kissed me at the studio—because you wanted the dancers to think we were involved."

"I want everyone to think it. A possessive boyfriend who can't let his gorgeous girlfriend out of his sight—that kind of guy is much easier for the bad guys to take out."

"As...opposed to you. The kick ass bodyguard."

The driver had started the car. He pulled away and began heading toward the charity gala. The vehicle drove slowly down the busy New York streets.

The driver was another Wilde agent. Those guys seemed to be everywhere.

"I'm glad you think I'm kick ass," Cole murmured. "I do try."

She peered out of the window. "To make sure I'm clear on things, you're going to act all obsessed with me tonight?"

"The way you look in that dress, trust me, it won't be hard."

Her head whipped around toward him.

"You look beautiful." His voice was low. "The blue is perfect against your skin, and the silk hugs your body like..." He cleared his throat. "Well, it does a very good job."

"You look, um, good, too."

"I feel like an idiot."

His words surprised her.

"Tuxes aren't exactly my thing. I'm much more comfortable in the shadows."

"So am I," Evie confessed.

But he laughed. "You work on Broadway, Evie. You live in the city that never sleeps. You're surrounded by energy and light and—"

"I work as a choreographer. That means I'm not on stage. I'm not dancing for the crowds."

"You could be on stage. You're a phenomenal dancer."

Her chest warmed. "Thank you."

"You're such a great dancer." A pause. "Do you sing, too? Are you secretly a double threat?"

A little laugh escaped. "No, I'm not. Trust me, Broadway does not want to hear the madness that is my singing voice."

"You sure about that? I think your voice is sexy as hell."

He...oh. Her laughter died away. "My singing voice is different than my speaking voice." The limo was still driving slowly down the street. "And even if I could sing, I wouldn't want to be on the stage. I like being in the background. Too much attention has always made me nervous." That was why she was so comfortable doing the choreography work. She had the opportunity to orchestrate all of the wonderful dance sequences that she could imagine in her head, she got to bring those moments to life with the performers, but she didn't have to step into the spotlight.

The limo slowed down.

She nervously tapped her index finger against the seat. "What's the plan for when we go inside?"

"I don't take my eyes off you."

She shivered.

"Are you cold?"

"Yes," Evie replied quickly. "Super chilly. Brr."

"The dress doesn't have sleeves. Do you have a wrap or—"

"I'll be fine once we're inside. The crowd will keep the room warm."

Silence. Then... "You're nervous."

"Why would I be nervous? I mean, I'm just heading into a party with over five hundred people. A giant crush that you told me already was a security nightmare, and the bad guys could have slipped inside. No biggie."

A very biggie.

"I have something for you. As a precaution..."

He pulled something out of his pocket. A black jewelry box. Not a ring box, but a long and lean, velvet box, and when he opened it, she saw the glitter of diamonds on the bracelet that waited inside. It looked expensive as hell. "*That's* a precaution?"

"There's a tracker hidden in one of the diamonds. As long as you're wearing this bracelet, Wilde can find you." He circled the bracelet around her wrist. "*I* can find you. Anywhere you go."

The bracelet felt cold against her skin. "It's beautiful. Ah, for a tracker."

"The other diamonds are all real. Only one is fake."

She lifted her wrist. The diamonds sparkled. "This seems like very expensive tech."

"Does it matter?"

"Yes. It does." That brought her back to another point. "You aren't paying for my security."

He looked down at the glowing dial of his watch. "We don't have much time. There's something else I need to discuss with you."

"Uh, what you're trying to do is distract me, but I'm telling you—"

He tilted his head. Focused on her. "Several suspects will be at the event tonight. Wilde techs found some disturbing ties between a few of the guests and your family, and I need you to be on guard with these people."

A fist squeezed her heart. "What people?"

"Robert Demakis."

"Robert?" He was familiar to her. "He's a great director. I've worked with him before and he wants me to work with him again on his next—"

"Your step-father bankrupted Robert's parents."

"*What?*"

"Seems that, once upon a time, his parents and your step-father were good friends. Your step-father convinced them to invest in a real estate opportunity—promised them huge returns—but the property turned out to be worthless. A freaking swamp. They lost everything."

The thud of her heart seemed very heavy. "He never mentioned that to me."

"Gia Eastman."

"The artist? What has my family ever done to—"

"According to my sources, she and your brother had quite a volatile relationship."

That was news to her. "Harrison was involved with Gia? When?"

"At the time of your abduction, they were together. According to Gia's friends, she was even hinting they might become engaged. Then you vanished. When you returned, Harrison broke off the relationship with her."

She shook her head. "I-I didn't know." Harrison had never mentioned Gia to her.

"Two years ago, Harrison was supposed to invest in her new gallery, but he withdrew funds for it. The gallery didn't open, and she also lost several other investors."

The news was just sucking more and more. "Anyone else I need to know about?"

"One more person we know who will be at the party. He ever so helpfully RSVP'd."

She waited.

"Stephen Lowe."

Now she stiffened. That name *was* familiar. "He and Harrison were bidding on the same project about a month ago. But—"

"But your brother outbid him. Got the deal. Made millions. What *wasn't* common knowledge—and still isn't—is that Stephen's company is barely staying alive. He needs an infusion of cash, and he needs it now."

"An infusion..." She licked her lower lip. *The kind of infusion you could get from a kidnapping?* When she'd been taken in LA, the kidnappers had demanded five million dollars. "I really don't want to go to this party."

"Then let's turn the limo around and head the hell back home."

Her lips parted. "Just like that?"

"Just like that." He was already leaning toward the privacy window so he could talk to the driver. "You don't want to go, then we don't go."

She grabbed his arm. "But isn't this a chance for us to try and draw out the bad guys, especially since you already seem to have three suspects lined up for us tonight?"

"It is." His muscles felt so tight beneath her touch. "But if you aren't comfortable, we don't go in. Hell, I didn't want you in there anyway, so—"

"I'm going in." She was definite. Her hand slid away from him. "I want this over. If we can make progress on this case by going in there and parading in front of our suspects, then I'm doing it." She forced a laugh. "I'm scared, all right? But the fear won't stop me. I'll do it." She squared her shoulders. "Besides, I've got you, don't I?"

"Yes." Soft. "You have me."

"I also have my new bracelet." She looked down at it. Saw the diamonds sparkle once more. "You can find me anywhere."

He slid back toward her. His body pressed to hers. "Yes. I can find you anywhere."

The limo stopped.

She looked through the rear window. Saw the big crowd that had gathered near the red carpet. Her heart raced, but she schooled her expression. She had this.

"I need to get my life back." She didn't like being afraid. "So let's do this."

She started to ease past him.

He caught her. Pulled her onto his lap. Her dress slid over his thighs. "Cole?"

"Let's give them the right show when they open the door..."

His hand sank into her hair. Her head tipped back.

She knew what he meant. He was obviously planning some super sexy, hot kiss. Something for the crowd to see. An image for any cameras to catch.

The door began to open.

Maybe I want to be in charge of the show.

Evie licked his lower lip. Sucked that lip. Heard him growl. Then she kissed him. Deep and sweet, slow and savoring. She enjoyed his mouth, and she let the world see it.

***

"What in the hell are you doing with my sister?" Harrison grabbed Cole's arm and hauled him into the nearest corner. "You're supposed to be guarding her, not—not—"

"Putting my hands on her? My mouth?" Cole smiled at him, a tiger's grin. "If she wants them on her, if she wants me, then I will give her exactly what she wants."

Harrison's fist swung back as if he'd punch Cole right in the—

Cole caught his wrist, stopping the blow. "I think we need a come to Jesus meeting."

Harrison choked. "Excuse me?"

Cole glanced over Harrison's shoulder. As soon as they had entered the massive ballroom, Chase had appeared at Evie's side. He was currently sticking to Evie like glue while Cole took care of her jerk of a brother. "You won't keep me away this time."

"Uh, yeah, I *hired* you. That's hardly the definition of keeping—"

"She woke up screaming my name last night."

Harrison looked away. "She...stopped having those nightmares a while back. It must have been the stress that caused them to return. It must have—"

"*You* told me that she was better off without me."

"I stand by that."

"And I stand by the fact that you're a giant dick."

Harrison's angry stare snapped back to Cole.

Once more, Cole smiled. "An audience is watching us so how about you act like we're best friends? After all, I am the man who is currently dating your sister."

"You are *not*—"

"That's the cover we're using. The perps will think I'm easy to eliminate if they believe I'm her obsessed lover, the guy who follows her twenty-four, seven because he can't stand to be away from her, as opposed to the bodyguard trained to protect her."

"That's BS. If anyone looks into your background, they will find out the truth about you! You're former Delta Force. That shit isn't hard to figure out."

"You'd be surprised at how quickly records can change." He snapped his fingers together. "In fact, if you try to find my background, you'll see that it's quite different from what you might suspect." His brows climbed. "The folks at Wilde are great at creating false trails. Delta Force?" Cole paused, as if to consider that option. "No. Not me. I'm a real estate developer. Your father and mine were friends ages ago. I knew Evie in the past. In fact, we had a hot and heavy relationship about two years ago." It was always better to include bits of truth in a lie.

Harrison flushed a very unbecoming shade of red. "Stop talking about fucking my sister."

"We broke up," Cole carried on smoothly, quietly, "but we're back together. And we have your full blessing."

"The hell you—"

Cole lowered his voice a little bit more. "I can break you in about fifty different ways, and if it weren't for the fact that your sister is currently staring at us, I'd be doing just that."

"You're *threatening* me—"

"You came between me and something I want very badly. You misled me. I won't ever forget that." He grabbed Harrison's shoulder. To onlookers, it would look like a casual touch between friends. It wasn't casual. He was squeezing those nerves just right.

Harrison wasn't flushing any longer. He'd turned stark white.

"I need this cover story to be close to her. You're going to back me up, *Harry*. The attackers are waiting for a moment where she's vulnerable. If they think I'm the boyfriend, then I'm no threat."

Sweat dotted Harrison's upper lip. "You're...using my sister? R-risking her...?"

"Hell, no. I'm not. I'm not planning to let her out of my sight." He could see her right then, and he had Chase on her. Across the room, James Smith had also just made his appearance. The "contract" Wilde agent with the codename of Ghost—a guy who happened to be a former assassin—had slipped in and blended easily with the crowd. Ghost often worked as Cole's partner on high-level cases. To Cole, this case was of the highest possible level, so he'd gotten Ghost to come in and help. "Evie is not being put at risk, not for a moment. If you believe nothing else, know that I would *kill* before I let anyone hurt her."

Harrison jerked his head in a nod. "L-let...me go."

Cole let him go. Stepped back. Nodded. Projected his fake air of friendliness. "I love our talks, man."

"Me, too," Harrison mumbled.

"Ah, bring it in. We're practically family."

Alarm flared in Harrison's eyes right before Cole grabbed him in a hug and yanked him close.

"Three suspects are here tonight," Cole told him quickly. "Including your ex, Gia. Watch out for Robert Demakis and Stephen Lowe. You see anyone else suspicious, you alert me immediately."

Harrison had stiffened at the mention of Gia's name.

Cole let him go. "Got to head back to Evie. Promised her my first dance." He brushed past Harrison. As he closed in on Evie, Cole let his gaze casually sweep the crowd. Jeez, you could practically smell the money in the room. Jewels dripped from the women—from their necks, their fingers, their wrists, and their ears. Diamonds, pearls, rubies, emeralds. A jewel thief's frigging wet dream.

There was a lot of fake laughter floating around. The kind that said someone had just told a really shitty joke, but refusing to laugh just wasn't acceptable in those circles. Oh, how those circles got on his nerves. The people seemed too polished and perfect, and Cole knew that he didn't fit in with them. The tux was too tight and constraining and he would love to rip the damn thing off right then and there.

"You look like you want to kill someone, buddy," Chase drawled. He lifted the flute of champagne he held. "Why don't you have a drink and relax?"

Cole barely resisted the urge to tug at his collar. He felt completely out of place, while Chase seemed to have fit right in without any trouble. He was all relaxed and casual, and he didn't twitch in his perfectly fitting tux.

He stood next to Evie and, damn, but she looked sensational in the beautiful blue dress that she wore. The neckline plunged, revealing the top of her pert breasts. She'd carefully curled her hair in one of those magical ways that women did, she'd used shadow to make her eyes look darker and bigger, and the red lipstick had her full lips glistening. She and Chase stood together, and hell, they looked like a couple. Like they were two people completely at ease in this world of fake laughter and—

Evie slid to Cole's side. She put her hand on his arm. "Did I see you hug my brother?"

Her touch scorched straight through him. "Yes."

"Harrison isn't a hugger."

Chase choked out a laugh. "Neither is Cole."

At his laugh—a *real* laugh—several heads turned their way. One of those heads belonged to Gia Eastman. Dressed in a red evening gown and with rubies hanging around her neck, her gaze locked on Chase and seemed to heat.

"I think you should go make a new friend," Cole advised him.

"Already on it." Chase put his flute on a passing waiter's tray.

Then it was just Cole and Evie. The band began to play and slow, romantic music filled the air. An unusual tension trickled through Cole as he stood there. Other couples were already moving onto the dance floor. Their bodies glided together easily. Perfectly. He *knew* Evie was a phenomenal dancer, of course, but...

"Would you like to dance with me, Cole?"

He...um. His eyelids flickered.

He caught the flash of hurt on her face.

"You don't have to," Evie rushed to say. "I just thought it was part of our cover, you know, us being a couple and all, and I didn't—forget it. How about we grab some food?" She turned away.

He reached out and curled his fingers over her arm.

She trembled.

"Evie?"

She looked down at his hand on her. Then her eyes lifted and met his.

He pulled her closer. "I want to dance with you." Having her in his arms? Hell, yes. "But I'm probably not like the partners you're used to having."

"What do you mean?"

"I mean I can't dance for shit."

Laughter sputtered from her. *Real* laughter. Her laughter and Chase's both were filled with amusement, and that happy sound cut through the fakeness like a knife.

Evie eased even closer to him. "I can help you."

"Promise?"

"I happen to be very good at teaching people how to dance. You just have to trust me."

He couldn't look away from the darkness of her eyes. "I do." He'd trust Evie with his life.

She smiled at him.

She was the most beautiful thing in his world.

"Take my hand."

She held one hand up. He curled his fingers around hers.

"Good. Now put your other hand over my ass."

He put his hand on her ass.

"*Over*. As in, above. Like, near my lower back."

"My bad." He slowly moved up his fingers.

"You knew where you were supposed to put that hand."

"I'll put my hands anywhere you want them, sweetheart," he promised.

Her lips parted. Oh, how he wanted to lower his head and press his mouth to hers.

"Move with me," she whispered. "Focus on feeling the music. Nothing fancy, just a soft sway."

His hand tightened on her lower back as he pulled her forward a bit more. He wasn't feeling the music, he was feeling her, and, as always when Evie was near, his body had a most definite reaction.

A reaction she probably wasn't missing considering how close they were to each other.

"You're doing great," she praised him.

He smiled down at her. "You're being nice. We both know that I almost smashed your toes twice."

She winked at him. "Almost, but you didn't."

Warmth filled his chest. His body swayed with hers. Moved slowly. "I missed you."

She faltered, just for a moment, then kept dancing. "You don't have to lie and tell me those—"

"I missed you. It should have been easy to forget you. I mean, I was in your life for only a week."

Evie looked away. "Don't worry about pulling your punches. Please, tell me more about how easy I should be to forget—"

"You *weren't* easy to forget. That was the problem. You haunted me. And I wanted you back."

She didn't look at him.

"I still want you back. In case you wondered where my head was at. In case the freaking giant hard-on shoving at you wasn't a clue."

He saw her swallow. "I did notice that clue."

"But you're the one in charge. You want to slip out of your bedroom and kiss me at night? Then come do it. You want more? *Do it.*" He was so in for that. "Or if you don't want to do a damn thing—that's fine, too. I just wanted to tell you how I felt. I missed you. And I still want you."

Her slick red lips pressed together a moment. Then she put her head on his shoulder.

It was his turn to falter.

But he focused on *feeling* her, and he kept moving. Cole caught a glimpse of Leopold. The guy gave him a quick thumbs-up before vanishing into the crowd.

"I missed you, too," she confessed as he bent to pull in her sweet scent. "And I still want you. I'm just not sure what to do with that desire."

"When you figure it out, I'll be here. I'm not planning on going any damn place." Did she get what he was saying? He wasn't vanishing from her life. Not this time. This time, he had a second chance. He wouldn't screw it up.

They kept moving like that, slowly, carefully, until the music ended.

Evie's head lifted. She stared up at him. His head began to lower toward hers. He wanted nothing more than to get her mouth beneath his.

"*Evie!* I thought that was you."

And some jackass had just interrupted his moment. Some jackass with truly shit timing.

Locking his teeth, Cole wrapped his arm around Evie's waist and turned toward the jackass.

Robert Demakis.

He recognized the director because Wilde had sent a full dossier on the guy. Robert's hair was a deep black, his eyes a light brown. A Rolex glinted on his wrist, and a wide smile curved his lips. The smile was directed completely at Evie.

"Hi, Robert," Evie said, voice soft. "How are you?"

He glanced around the room. "Feeling a bit suffocated. Thought I'd step out on the balcony for some air." He offered his arm to her as he wiggled his brows. "Want to come with me? We can—"

"No, my girlfriend doesn't want to fucking come with you," Cole interrupted as he stepped forward. "And who the hell are you?"

Robert blinked.

Evie shoved a hand against his chest. "Cole, calm down. This is my friend, Robert Demakis."

He knew she was making the explanation just for the sake of appearance, but he still had the thought...

Not your friend, Evie. The guy is a suspect.

"And, Robert..." She offered a smile tinged with apology toward the other man. "This is, um, Cole."

Why was she being all apologetic to Robert? That shit needed to stop.

"Cole is my..."

"Boyfriend. Partner." Cole shrugged. "The guy who makes her scream at night."

"*Cole!*" Evie gasped, seemingly horrified. Hmm. Was that all an act? Or had he pushed too far?

"Whatever you want to call me." He shrugged again but kept his focus on Robert. "I'm also the guy saying, hell, no, you're not taking Evie away to have a private chat on the balcony." Like that didn't scream suspicious.

You're not taking her. Not on my watch.

CHAPTER SEVEN

I'm a jealous bastard. But I'm *her* bastard.

"You're embarrassing me," Evie muttered. "Cole, stop."

Robert swept his gaze over Cole. "Yes, Cole, stop. Before you piss Evie off and cause me to have to teach you manners."

"Are you serious right now?" Cole laughed. It wasn't a particularly pleasant sound. "I would love to see you try to teach me how to—"

They looked like they were about to fight. At a charity gala. Not happening. Evie shoved between them, putting a hand on each puffed-up chest. "This is ridiculous." She glared at Cole. "Robert is not interested in me that way."

She turned her head.

And caught Robert's smirk.

"*Why* do you want to talk to me alone?" Evie asked him. That smirk set off alarm bells.

The band was playing again. Couples were dancing. And she was trying to act like she was totally cool and composed. She wasn't. Not even close. She'd worked with Robert. Spent grueling hours in production sessions with him, and he'd never once mentioned that her step-father had basically wrecked his family.

Not like that was exactly something casual that you dropped into a conversation, but still...

"I have an opportunity that's opened up on my latest show," Robert inserted smoothly. "My lead choreographer had to step back, and now there's a spot that needs filling." A pause. "I thought that Leo might have mentioned this to you already. He was advocating quite strongly for you. Told me that you were the only one who could make my show perfect."

It was *Robert's* show? Leo hadn't mentioned that part to her. He had dropped some hints about a new project, but—

"If your boyfriend can bear to be separated from you, I'd love to give you more details." Robert waved one hand vaguely in the air as he took Cole's measure. "What do you think I'm going to do, exactly? Steal her away in a ballroom full of people?"

Her stomach sank. The wording was obviously intended to be a joke, but with the way her life was currently going—

So not funny.

Then she caught sight of Stephen Lowe. He was standing against the wall on the right, and he was watching her. His gaze was locked straight on her with a hard intensity.

Why was he staring at her so fiercely? Stephen had barely spoken to her in the past when they'd met at events like this one.

She looked over her shoulder, wondering if her brother might be close and perhaps Stephen's attention was actually on him—

But, no, there was no one behind her. Stephen was definitely staring straight at her.

Before she could speak, Cole leaned toward her. He put his lips to her ear. "Talk to Demakis. Push and see what you can learn. I'll keep you in sight," he barely breathed to her. "And, yeah, I see the asshat with his eyes locked on you. Got him."

Then he eased back. Cole lifted her hand to his lips and pressed a soft kiss to her knuckles. Oh, God, had his tongue licked over her skin? Sure felt like it.

"I'll be waiting for you, sweetheart," Cole murmured. "Don't go far."

She saw the hard intent in his eyes. He might as well have said—

Seriously, I fucking mean it. Do not go out of this ballroom.

Then he turned and strolled across the ballroom.

Her gaze followed him.

"Evie, seriously, since when did you start falling for the psychos?"

Her shoulders snapped together. "He's hardly psychotic, Robert."

"Uh, it looked like he wanted to rip me apart. Guy is obviously obsessed. That's never a good sign."

Her chin lifted. "I can handle Cole."

"Can you?" His tone said he doubted that she could.

The smile that curved her lips felt wooden. "Absolutely. I have him wrapped around my little finger."

His laughter boomed around her.

***

When he heard the bastard's laughter, Cole gave serious thought to turning around and marching right back up to the dumbass director. He hadn't liked the way the other man's gaze darted over Evie's body and lingered for far too long in the wrong places.

Evie might not have known it, but the director was lusting after her. That shit needed to stop.

"I'm on her," a voice said in his ear. When he'd turned away from Evie and started marching across the ballroom, Cole had casually slipped his comm link into position. Super tiny and quite awesome, the tech was top-of-the-line Wilde merchandise. It let him hear his other team members and transmit information quickly.

"Don't worry," the low voice continued. "She's covered."

He knew she was covered. Otherwise, he wouldn't be heading anywhere. But he'd wanted to see what Robert Demakis might reveal to Evie when Cole wasn't nearby.

Divide and conquer time.

Chase was currently chatting up Gia.

That voice in his ear—it belonged to James Smith—and there was no doubt that James would keep watching Evie.

As for Cole, time to see why Stephen Lowe had been staring so very intently at Evie.

There was a cash bar to the left of Stephen. Cole headed for it and slapped a twenty down after he got his drink. His fingers curled around the glass, he lifted it toward his mouth, and just like clockwork...

"You're with Evie Lake?"

Stephen closed in.

Cole lowered his glass. Studied the guy near him. Tall, lean, with slightly long hair and a hard gaze. "I am." He paused. "And you are?"

"Stephen Lowe."

"Cole Vincent." He inclined his head.

Stephen glanced across the ballroom. "I need to talk to Evie."

It seemed like the whole freaking world wanted to talk to Evie.

"But I saw how you reacted when Robert cut in, so I didn't think this would be the best time."

He put down his drink. "It's never a good time when some bastard thinks he's going to take my Evie away from me."

Stephen threw up his hands. "No! No, I'm not—I'm not interested in her that way. I just..." He huffed out a breath. "I need to talk to Evie about her brother."

"Harrison?" Cole acted dismissive. "He's here. You should talk to him yourself."

"No, you don't get it. Evie doesn't *know* the truth about him."

Color me curious. "And what's the truth?"

"He's a cold-blooded, back-stabbing bastard."

Keep talking. I hear motive.

"He put a spy in my company. A corporate spy! That's how he beat me on that last bid. Evie thinks he's some good guy—hell, half the city does. But Harrison is only out for himself."

Cole nodded. "So you hate him because he beat you on a deal."

"Corporate. Spy." Each word vibrated with fury. "He's going down. I am going to make it my mission to take him out."

Oh, yes, not suspicious. At all.

"But I don't want Evie getting caught in the fall-out. So I just...I wanted to tell her to watch herself."

Was that a threat? "Evie isn't getting caught in anything." He advanced on Stephen.

The guy backed up a quick step.

"If you've got some revenge plan in place, know that it had better not so much as touch her. Because as long as I am around, anyone who hurts Evie? Anyone who *tries* to hurt her?" *Get this message. Burn it into your mind.* "I will hurt them. I will destroy them."

"You sound just like Harrison."

Hell. Not exactly thrilling news but...

Stephen shoved a hand through his hair. "Bastard was always way too obsessed with Evie. She's his weakness, but I'm not like the others."

"What others?"

"I won't use her against him." He pointed across the room. Right at Robert Demakis as he leaned in close to talk with Evie. "He will, though. He'd use her in a heartbeat to get what he wants." With that dramatic announcement, Stephen spun on his heel and stormed through the crowd.

"That seemed like an enlightening conversation." James's voice drifted into Cole's ear. *"Do you mind if I ask—oh, hell, I don't care if you mind, I'm asking anyway—just why is the brother so obsessed with his sister?"*

Cole lifted his hand as if he was rubbing his jaw. Really, he was covering his mouth as he replied, *"Step-sister."*

"Oh." There was way too much meaning in that response.

"Not fucking like that," Cole growled with his hand still rubbing along his jaw.

"You sure about that? Because I heard you haven't seen the lovely Evie in two years. Maybe you're missing out on a few important details about what has been happening in her life."

Harrison was making his way through the crowd. Going for Evie. He closed in on her as she spoke with Robert. He reached out for her. Curled his hand around her hip and brought her in for a hug.

"Huh," Cole said.

"Now you sound like Chase."

Harrison glanced across the room. Made eye contact with Cole. He was still touching Evie.

Cole had tried to set the man straight when he'd first entered the ballroom. Seemed like someone hadn't gotten the hint.

It was also time to figure just what the relationship was between Harrison and Evie. Step-siblings. Or something more?

It had better not be fucking more.

***

"You okay?"

Cole was in front of her again. Glowering. He seemed to be doing that a whole lot.

Her brother had slipped away right before Cole approached, and Robert had also vanished somewhere in the crowd.

Okay? She thought of Cole's question, and decided that no, she really wasn't okay. Far from it. "Can we leave soon?" They'd done their job. Gone in, acted like a couple, even talked to his suspects. The knot in her stomach was getting worse with every moment that passed. These events weren't really her scene, she'd just gone because Harrison had helped to organize things—his company, but all the funds raised were going to her charity pick. Because of that, not attending hadn't been an option for her.

"We can leave whenever you want."

Her shoulders sagged. "Let me hit the restroom, and we're out of here." Out of the tight dress and the shoes that made her feet ache. Back to her place where she intended to put on yoga pants and a loose top at the first available opportunity.

She turned through the crowd and made a beeline for the bathroom.

It took her a moment to realize that Cole was tailing her. She stopped a few feet away from the bathroom door and raked her gaze over him. "I'm okay on my own in there."

He blinked.

"You...weren't planning on following me in, were you?"

Did he flush? A little? "No."

"You were."

He winked. "I was just going to watch the door, promise."

Jeez, his wink was sexy. "I'll be right back." Shaking her head, Evie hurried inside. She passed one lady as she made her way to the sink and—

"Hi, Evie."

Gia Eastman stood there. Almost as if she'd been waiting for Evie.

"Hi, Gia."

As usual, Gia was drop dead gorgeous. Her long, dark hair slid over her shoulders and her pale eyes gleamed. The dress she wore hugged and accentuated every curve of her body.

Gia had plenty of curves, too. Curves Evie couldn't help but envy. Evie knew she was on the smaller side when it came to her breasts, she had a light, delicate build—a ballerina dancer's body, she'd once been told. Men didn't tend to drool over her.

They drooled over Gia.

And Harrison was thinking about marrying her? He'd never said a word to Evie.

"Noticed you were with someone new tonight." Gia smiled at her. The smile didn't warm her eyes. "Surprised Harrison let the guy within five feet of you."

Evie hurried toward the sink. Washed her hands. Robert had accidentally spilled a little of his champagne on her, and she'd wanted to get the stickiness off her hands—that had caused her beeline for the bathroom. "Harrison likes Cole."

A throaty laugh. "He finally found someone good enough for his sister? I'm impressed."

Evie looked up and caught Gia's reflection in the mirror. "He didn't find Cole."

Gia's head tilted. "Your brother has been avoiding me."

Evie turned off the water. Dried her hands.

"Do you have any idea why?"

"No." Evie spun around to face her. "Do you?"

"It was a mistake," Gia suddenly snapped. "We all make them. Even precious Harrison. Remind him of that fact, will you?"

Then she stormed away.

Evie blinked. Well, okay. She glanced around the bathroom. No one else was there. Hell, she might as well use a stall while she was inside.

She made her way to the left—

And all of the lights plunged off in the bathroom.

***

"Hi, there." Gia Eastman strolled from the ladies' room and put her hand on Cole's chest. "I don't think we've met."

He lifted one eyebrow. "No, I don't think we have."

She gave him a slow, flirtatious smile. "I'm Gia, and I'm bored."

"I'm Cole, and I'm waiting for someone."

She laughed. "A man like you shouldn't have to wait."

"And just what kind of man am I?"

She leaned onto her toes. Her lips were painted a dark, dark red. A red to match her dress.

"The kind of man who wants more than the lukewarm fun that Evie Lake will give him."

His jaw hardened. *You did not just talk about Evie that way.*

She pushed her lips out into what she probably thought was a sexy pout. "You don't have to wait. I'm right here. How about you and I slip away? I promise, I may be many things, but I'm definitely not lukewarm."

"Neither is Evie."

Some of the sensual confidence faded from her expression.

"I'd describe her as freaking red-hot, an inferno that burns me alive. Or maybe I'd say she's the best fuck I've ever had." He shrugged. "But I'm sure you get the idea. Oh, yes, she's a dancer, too, but I'm figuring you're aware of that." He whistled. "Woman is flexible as all hell. The things she can do with her body...*damn.*"

Gia eyes turned to slits.

"Sorry about your boredom, ah, Gia, I think it was? Hope you find a cure for that shit soon."

"Your loss." She spun on her heel and stormed away.

"You know the comm link is still on, right?" James asked in his ear.

Cole tossed a quick glance across the ballroom. Saw James standing against the far wall, with a champagne flute near his mouth. Cole gave a slight nod.

"I mean, glad you're happy with your girlfriend and all, but seriously, man, TMI."

"She's not my girlfriend," he growled. It was just a cover, though he wanted so fucking much more.

He wantcd her.

Cole glanced down at his watch. How long was she going to be in there?

"Do not think of going into that bathroom after her. Seriously, we need to have a talk about the concept of space."

But Cole was thinking about going into that bathroom. He turned away so no one in the crowd would see him talking. "Pull up her GPS. I want to make sure she's still inside." Sure, he could be worrying for nothing but...

This is Evie.

James wasn't the only one on the comm link. Chase was tied in, too, and so was a Wilde tech agent who was working remotely. The tech agent should be able to tell him—

"Evie's device shows that she is two floors down," the female tech agent told him, her voice strained with worry.

What the fuck?

He lunged for the bathroom door. Tried to shove it open. But the door was locked or jammed or—

He kicked it in. Wood splintered. "Evie!" Cole roared her name. The lights were off in the bathroom. He hit the switch, but they didn't turn back on.

"She's moving. Two floors door, heading toward the parking garage."

He whirled and rushed back to the ballroom. From the corner of his eye, he saw Chase bounding forward, too.

"What's happening?" Harrison stepped into Cole's path. *Slowing me down.* "Why are you rushing away? Where is Evie?"

Cole shoved him out of the way. He and Chase hit the stairwell at the same time. He flew down those stairs, jumping over several steps. The tech's voice was in his ear, telling him status updates and all he could think was—

They're taking her to the parking garage. They're trying to put her in a vehicle. Trying to take her away.

He shoved open the door to the parking garage. "Evie!" Cole bellowed her name.

He didn't see her, but...were those her shoes? Her heels, just dropped on the pavement?

A sedan rushed toward him, the bright lights blinding him. He could smell burning rubber and could hear the screech of the tires as that vehicle hurtled right at him.

"Get out of the way, Cole!" Chase yelled.

Cole dove to the side with Chase just as the sedan shot past them.

"She's moving fast," the tech operator said in his ear. *"On the road, going down to turn left—"*

"She's in the fucking car!" Cole snarled. She'd been taken—taken on *his* watch. Fear poured through every cell in his body as he leapt back to his feet.

I'm going to get her back.

CHAPTER EIGHT

I will never let her out of my sight again. I'm going to chain her to my side.

It was happening again. Evie cracked open her eyes but saw only darkness around her. It had been dark in the ladies' room. The lights had gone off, and she'd stumbled and she'd slammed into—

Someone. Someone else had been in the bathroom with her. Someone had shoved a smelly cloth over her mouth, and she'd felt dizzy and sluggish and the next thing she knew—

I'm here. Only she wasn't sure where here was, exactly.

Too dark.

She hated the dark. Her body was all twisted up, so she tried to straighten and—

Evie rammed her head into metal. Her hands flew up. Touched the metal. She grabbed to the left and the right, and just a few inches away from her—

Wait, am I moving?

There was a steady hum of sound, and then...a jerk.

Her body rolled with that jerk.

Oh, God. I'm in a car. I'm in a trunk! Someone had stuffed her into the trunk of a car. Even as Evie had that realization, the car was accelerating forward again.

Fear twisted inside of her. No, this could *not* be happening.

She shoved her hand up, hitting the top of the trunk. *"Help me!"* Evie screamed. She felt her bracelet slide down her wrist. *Her bracelet.* She grabbed it with her right hand. As long as she had the bracelet, Cole could find her.

The darkness closed in around her.

Hurry up, Cole. Please hurry.

***

"Keep giving me directions," Cole ordered. "Do not lose her, do you understand me?"

"I've got her signal. She's about two miles ahead of you." The response carried easily to the comm unit he still wore.

"The bastard should have figured for New York traffic," Chase said from beside him. "Not like it's easy to slip away in this snarl. It'll slow him down."

But *they* were slowed down, too. They hadn't taken the limo in pursuit. They'd taken the SUV that Chase had used for his arrival at the ball. As for the other Wilde agent who'd been at the gala, James—hell, the last time Cole had seen him, the guy had been hot-wiring some motorcycle that was in the parking garage.

Cole's heart was racing in his chest, and his grip on the steering wheel was brutally tight. "I promised to keep her safe," he muttered. But she'd been taken again. On his watch. He'd screwed up.

"Take a breath, man," Chase urged him. "We'll get her back. It's going to be okay."

"Uh, the vehicle just turned. There is...there's a problem."

"Do not tell me that!" Cole snarled. The traffic eased a bit, and he shoved the gas pedal to the floorboard as he lurched to the right.

"I'm checking traffic cams, and if you don't stop the perps in the next five minutes, their path will open up and they will be free and—"

"Oh, shit!" Chase grabbed for the side of his door. "Are you driving on the sidewalk? That is illegal. You know that, don't you?"

"So is fucking kidnapping."

***

Her body rolled again. The car had stopped once more.

New York traffic. Most days, she hated it, but tonight, God, she loved it tonight. Her hands fumbled as she reached toward the back of the trunk. After the abduction two years ago, her brother had brought in several of what he called "safety experts" to train her. One of the lessons?

How to escape from the trunk of a car. As long as this vehicle had been made after 2002, there should be a trunk release lever back there with her. She just had to find it. The thing *should* have been glowing in the dark. That was what her safety expert had told her. Only nothing was glowing. It was supposed to be near the trunk latch, and it should have been some kind of button or handle or—

Her fingers closed around it. Or at least, Evie hoped what she was grabbing was the right handle. She jerked on it, hard, and...

The trunk popped open, just a few inches. That was all she needed. Light spilled inside, and Evie shoved the trunk open all the way. The car was still stopped. This was her chance. She jumped out of the vehicle.

And straight into traffic.

Cars were buzzing by her—to the left and the right, and horns were honking and she was barefoot in an evening dress and stumbling because her legs didn't seem to be working quite right. Nausea rolled in her stomach as she staggered forward. "Help!" She had to flag someone down. A taxi was close by, and the driver was frowning at her. She lunged for his vehicle. "I need—"

"You are not fucking going anywhere, bitch," a voice grated in her ear as she was grabbed from behind. "You're coming with me, *now*!"

The hell she was.

He'd locked her arms against her sides and he was lifting her up, holding her tight against his body.

"*Evie!*"

She knew that roar. It was Cole's roar. Her frantic gaze flew to him. He'd just jumped out of an SUV that was parked halfway on the sidewalk, and he was rushing toward her.

Cole gripped a gun in his right hand.

The man holding her yelled, "I will slice her open!" He put a knife to her throat, but kept one arm locked around her body.

Cole didn't stop. He ran forward. "And I will put a bullet in your brain. Let her go!"

Cars were still passing by. As if this was a normal occurrence. *Nothing to see here. Just keep going.* The taxi driver was gone. She was in the middle of the street. Tears were on her cheeks. A knife was at her throat. She wanted to punch back at her attacker, but that knife was already pressing into her skin. Could he slice her neck open before she escaped him?

"Evie." Cole's voice. Flat. Calm.

How could he be calm?

Chase stood just a foot or so behind him. Like Cole, Chase's expression was completely controlled.

"Evie, you're going to be okay," Cole told her in that steady, calm voice of his.

"*Get the fuck back!*" Her attacker yanked her against him. The blade slipped over her skin. "Get back or I will let her bleed out right here!"

Cole's gaze didn't leave Evie's face, but he said, "You won't get paid if she's dead. I'm sure that's part of the deal."

"You don't know a damn thing! *Get back!*"

A woman saw Cole's gun and screamed.

Oh, sure, scream at that. What about the creep with the knife at my throat?

Evie's attacker tried to drag her back toward his car.

"I want you to duck and run to me, Evie," Cole ordered.

What? He wanted her to run—like, right then? There was a knife at her throat, and she couldn't get her elbow free to drive at her attacker in order to loosen his hold.

"Duck and run," Cole told her again, his voice harder.

"No!" Her kidnapper's voice blasted in her ears. "We are getting in the car and getting—"

A motorcycle was hurtling toward them. She saw it from the corner of her eye, and Evie screamed. So did her attacker. He let her go.

Duck and run. Run to Cole.

She ducked, and she ran.

"No!" Her attacker's bellow followed her as he grabbed for her arm. *"You aren't going to get—"*

Bam.

One blast of a gunshot.

She kept running. Cole grabbed her and hauled her against him, twisting his body at the same time so that he was shielding her. He shuddered against her and held Evie in a death grip.

She held him just as tightly.

"Check the bastard!" Cole roared.

She could hear sirens. Their screams were growing closer and closer. Someone had called the cops. Maybe it had been that nervous-looking taxi driver. Whoever it had been...*thank you!*

"Baby, are you hurt?"

She lifted her head. Blinked. "Little...dizzy. They...*he* put something over m-my mouth and nose. Knocked me out."

"It's clear," she heard Chase shout out. "Car is empty. Attacker is down."

The motorcycle's engine growled.

Her head whipped toward it. That fast movement made her dizziness worse. The man on the cycle swept his gaze over her.

"That's James," Cole told her quickly. "It's okay. He's with us."

Her attention darted back to her attacker. He was still on the ground. He was...

Oh, God.

"Who shot him?" she whispered. Everything had happened so fast.

"I did."

Her gaze jumped back to Cole.

"He was going to stab you, Evie. You didn't see it, but he was swinging the knife down at your back. I had to stop him."

He'd...She stumbled away from Cole. Her horrified attention went back to the man sprawled on the street. The man who wasn't moving at all.

When Chase had said her attacker was down...

Had he meant that the man was dead?

Her knees buckled. Maybe from whatever drug her attacker had used to knock her out. Maybe because she might be staring at a dead man. Maybe because she'd just been freaking abducted. Whatever the reason, they buckled. Before she could hit the pavement, Cole grabbed her and scooped Evie into his arms.

"It's all right," he reassured her quickly.

It was *not* all right. It was a million ways from all right.

"I've got you."

He'd just shot a man because of her. Killed a man...*because of me.*

Feeling numb, no, icy, her attention drifted around the crowd. People were gaping at her. Some were lifting their phones and filming the scene. Filming this nightmare?

A police cruiser raced toward them and braked with a jolting stop. The officers jumped out with their guns drawn. "Freeze!"

Cole's hold tightened on her. "Everything is going to be okay," he promised her. "Just trust me."

Another tear leaked down her cheek.

"God, baby, you're bleeding."

She was?

His head whipped toward the cops. "He cut her throat! We need an ambulance, *now!*"

***

"You...good?"

Good? Cole turned away from the window in Evie's place and put his hands on his hips as he faced Chase. "I don't think good covers it."

Chase winced. "You want me to stay with her tonight?"

"I've got her." A growled, guttural response. Leave Evie? Hell, no. His gaze slid to her bedroom door. Shut. They'd had to answer dozens of questions from the cops, had to stay in the police station for far too long, before Evie had finally been allowed to leave.

Before we were all allowed to go.

He'd pulled the trigger, so there had been lots of grilling from the detectives in charge for him. Did he regret what he'd done? No, not even for a second.

The bastard had been swinging his knife at Evie. He'd been intending to stab her in the back.

There were plenty of witnesses to back up Cole's story. Hell, there were videos. Tons of them currently were flying around social media. The beautiful woman in her long evening dress, being carried from the scene by the guy in the tux. The fact that the guy in the tux had *killed* a man...well, that just made the story even juicier.

"You get that the media will be camped out on her doorstep."

"They're already downstairs." Chomping at the bit for a story.

"We'll make sure Wilde runs them off. Don't worry. We can keep her insulated from them."

That was only partially the truth, and they both knew it. Her story would circulate for a while, bringing attention that Cole knew Evie would not want.

"Where is she?" Chase asked, frowning. "Sleeping?"

"She's in the bathroom." EMTs had taken care of her throat. Luckily, the wound hadn't been deep enough for stitches.

If that bastard had sliced her throat open and let her bleed out in front of me...

No, Cole shut down the thought.

"Huh." Chase shoved his hands into the pockets of his jeans.

Cole's eyes narrowed. "What in the hell does that mean?"

"Oh, you know, just...with what happened, I thought you'd never let her go to a bathroom by herself again."

Cole bounded toward him, so not in the mood for the guy's shit—

The bedroom door opened. Evie stood there. She wore jogging shorts and a black cami top. She was pale. Far too pale. A white bandage covered the small wound on her throat.

Every muscle in his body hardened. He wanted to run to her. To haul her in his arms and never let her go.

Instead, he stood frozen to the spot. In his mind, he saw her lunging toward him as that bastard raised his knife behind her.

Yes, I killed him. I would kill anyone who threatened her. With Evie, he'd never pretended to be anything more than what he was.

The first time they'd met, he'd been a mercenary.

The second time, he'd shown her that he was a killer.

He would never, ever be good enough for her, and it was a truth that he well knew. Wasn't it the very reason he'd walked away from her before?

"How are you feeling, Evie?" Chase cleared his throat. "Any more dizziness?"

She shook her head. "No." Her shoulders hunched a little bit.

They hadn't discovered what the perp had used to knock her out. Detectives and the EMTs had thought it might be something like chloroform. They had sent a team to search the restroom she'd been taken from—and the parking garage at the charity gala. A doc had checked her out and run several tests to make sure that Evie was clear, and he'd ordered someone to stay with her during the night, just in case.

As if I would leave her.

"I-I didn't know him." Her hands twisted in front of her. "I saw his face. When the cops arrived, I-I looked, and I didn't know him."

"Probably because he was a hired thug," Chase supplied. "Someone to do the grunt work so his boss wouldn't get his hands dirty."

She flinched.

Cole shot a glare at Chase.

What? Chase mouthed.

"So you're saying...it's not over? Even though he's dead, it's not over?"

Cole's head swung back toward Evie. "No." She needed to be prepared for this. "It's not over."

She inched forward. "Then you're staying with me?"

I'd like to see someone force me to leave. "Yes, baby, I'm staying."

Shit. He'd called her baby again. The endearment kept slipping out. He'd have to be more careful.

"I'm glad," she said as she lifted her chin. "I didn't want to be alone tonight."

They were separated by about five feet, but when her eyes met his, Cole swore that he could *feel* her. The darkness of her eyes seemed to burn with a thousand emotions, and he stepped toward her before he could stop himself.

"I'll be staying, too," Chase piped in. "But, ahem, I'll be stationed outside the building to keep an eye on the perimeter. You know, in case you should need me."

She swallowed. "And the man on the motorcycle?"

"Ghost?" A low laugh spilled from Chase. "Don't worry. He's around, even when you don't see him."

"Ghost? But Cole said his name was James."

"James is his name. Ghost is just a codename we use for him sometimes." That wasn't the moment to tell her exactly how the former assassin had earned the nickname of Ghost.

Evie's arms hugged her body. Her focus was on him. "I thought I was safe. You were right outside the bathroom door. I was only a few feet away from you."

She was a few feet away from him now. Too far. He wanted her in his arms.

"I didn't even have a chance to call out for you."

He took another lurching step toward her. He should stay away, he knew he should stay away, but he felt pulled toward her. And if he got his hands on her, if he touched her...

My emotions are out of control. I can't hold back. I want to grab her and never let go.

If he touched her, he wouldn't be able to stop.

"When Cole realized you were missing, he kicked in the door to that bathroom. All bad-ass-like." Chase was still talking. Why was Chase still there? "And he burned rubber to save you, but you got yourself out of that trunk. Well done, Evie."

Cole choked down the lump in his throat. "Damn well done."

Her gaze fell. "No one would help me."

Rage twisted in his gut.

"I was begging for help, but the cars kept passing me by."

He wanted to *destroy* something.

"Then...after...after the man was shot...those people—they were all just watching. Filming me on their phones. Like it was some kind of show for them." Her breath shuddered out. "Why is this happening? Why do they keep coming for me?"

He saw a tear slide down her cheek.

That's fucking it.

"Chase," he barked.

"Yeah, man?"

"Get your ass out." He didn't look away from Evie. Her head bowed forward. Her shoulders hunched more. She was crying, and it was ripping him apart.

Chase coughed. "Getting my ass out." His steps thudded for the door. A moment later, the door shut. Cole heard the flip of the lock.

He should go set the security system. He'd gotten an upgraded system for her when she'd been working at the studio with Leopold.

Go set the system. Then...

Get her.

His steps were wooden as he moved away from her. His back turned to Evie as he armed the security system, then he flipped a few more of her dead-bolts. She'd had the dead-bolts *before* the Wilde crew came to work their magic. He knew she'd had them because she'd been afraid that someone would come for her again.

And someone did.

His hand rose and flattened against the wood of her door. "Do you want a drink?" Or maybe several? He'd seen wine in her kitchen.

But, hell, she'd been knocked out, so wine probably wasn't—

"That's not what I want."

He didn't turn toward her. "Are you still crying?"

Silence.

His eyes squeezed shut. "That's a damn yes, isn't it?"

"It's been a really bad night. So, yes, I'm crying a little bit and—"

His control shattered. He spun toward her.

Evie's eyes widened as she stared at his face. He could only imagine how savage he looked, but there wasn't much he could do about it.

There were tear tracks on her cheeks. Freaking tear tracks. On her beautiful face. There was a bandage on the delicate column of her throat...*because that bastard put his blade to her neck.*

"I wish I could kill him again." His voice was barely human.

She shook her head in a frantic *no* movement.

He stalked to her. His hands fisted at his sides. "But I do, Evie. He hurt you, and that drives me insane."

"You killed to protect me."

"I could have fucking shot him in the shoulder." His words were guttural. His steps slow but certain. She stiffened as he approached. "I'm a very good shot, and I hit what I want." He'd wanted the guy's heart.

Because he tried to take mine.

She backed up until her shoulders hit the wall. Fear flashed in her gaze, blocking out all the other emotions.

"You should be afraid," he warned. "You should have been afraid of me from the very beginning. I am not the kind of man who should ever be touching you."

He hated the sight of the tears on her cheeks.

His hand rose and gently wiped away the tears. The moisture seemed to burn his skin.

"You're touching me right now." Her scent teased him.

"I want to touch you every moment." He leaned in closer to her. "That's part of the problem. Someone like me should never be this close to someone like you."

Her breath hitched. "But you are this close."

"I want to be closer." He wasn't holding back. Couldn't. The wall he surrounded himself with had been shattered.

Knife at her throat.

"I want to be so close that you can't tell where I end and you begin."

Bastard was going to stab her in the back.

"I want to be in you, Evie. Buried so deep that I'm fucking marking your very soul."

He was trying to take her from me.

"Because you marked mine. And now, I think you belong to me. Just like I belong to you."

The darkness swirled in her eyes.

"When someone tries to take what belongs to me..." His voice was too rough. His whole body seemed too rough compared to hers. *She's fragile. Delicate. I need to stay away.* Yet all he wanted was to be closer. "I lose my damn mind."

She licked her lower lip.

A savage growl tore from him. "He was dead the minute he took you."

"You don't mean what you're saying."

He leaned even closer. Wanted her mouth. Was barely an inch away from it. "I have never meant anything more." He could all but taste her. Just that one inch. One...

She surged up. Grabbed his head and hauled him toward her.

Their lips crushed together in an explosion of need and desire. Unchecked. Wild. His mouth was open, so was hers, and their tongues met in greedy lust. No care. No tenderness.

He was too far gone for that.

And she didn't seem to want it.

Her mouth fed on his. His devoured hers. He was kissing her frantically, desperately, over and over, locking his mouth to hers. He'd been without her for too long. Had missed her for too long.

And then tonight, the bastard had tried to permanently take Evie from Cole.

Never.

He would kill anyone who tried to hurt her.

He was a monster, had always been. But, he was *her* monster.

His hands curled around her hips. He lifted her up, pinning her back against the wall, and her long legs wrapped around his hips. Her hands had flattened against his cheeks as she cupped his face, and she was still kissing him fiercely.

As fiercely as he was kissing her.

His dick shoved against the front of his jeans. He'd changed when they got back to her place, ditching the tux for jeans and a T-shirt. He wanted the jeans gone. He wanted her shorts gone. He wanted his dick in her as deep as it would go. He wanted her screaming his name.

He tore his mouth from hers and began to kiss a path down her neck.

Her neck.

He froze. Ice seemed to pour down his back.

"Too rough," he gritted out. He could see the white bandage against her skin. "I'm...sorry."

Her breath heaved in and out. Her hands slid down to curve around his shoulders. "Cole..."

He squeezed his eyes shut. He needed to let her go. Right—

"If you don't finish what you just started, I will *make* you sorry."

His eyes flew open.

"Finish," she ordered, voice husky and sensual and designed to drive him insane. "Fuck me."

CHAPTER NINE

I would kill to have her. That's not an exaggeration. It's the truth. What? Did you think I was the nice guy? Wrong.

He carried her into her bedroom. Evie couldn't pull in a deep breath. She was panting, and her heart was racing and her panties were wet, and she just wanted him.

She didn't want to think about the attack.

Or the dead man.

Or the gunshot.

Or—

No.

She wanted Cole. Wanted the wildness that came from him. Only him. Because he'd been the only one to ever make her feel this way. There was no fumbling with him. No uncertainty. There was just this earth-shattering need that blew everything else away.

He lowered her onto the bed. Put her down in the middle of the mattress. He stood to the side and stared at her as the overhead light illuminated the room.

He was big and muscled and looming. His expression was cut into hard, savage lines of desire. His eyes seemed even bluer—something that should be impossible, but they blazed with his need.

He looked...

He looked as if he could eat her alive.

He yanked his shirt over his head. Tossed it to the floor. Her gaze slid over the tattoos on his chest. They moved and seemed to undulate as she watched. So many. Twisting lines. Curves. And...

Wait...what was that? Right on his chest, over his heart...

Those curves. Were those letters? They...

OhmyGod.

He leaned over the bed, caught her shorts, and hauled them down her legs.

Need tore through her. Everything else was forgotten. "I want you. Right now."

"Do you know what I missed?"

He was still wearing his jeans. Leaning over her like some kind of hungry jungle cat, but hello—still wearing jeans.

His long, tanned fingers slid under her panties. "I missed your taste."

"Cole—"

He pulled the panties down her legs. Pushed her legs apart. Then put his mouth on her.

She nearly lunged right off the bed. Would have, if one of his hands hadn't held her hips locked to the mattress. She buckled against him as his tongue slid between her folds. He licked and sucked her, his tongue greedy on her clit. Over and over, hungrily, desperately. She grabbed for the sheets and fisted them in her hands. His tongue drove into her, then pulled back. He blew over her clit. He licked her—

She cried out his name and came.

"I missed that," Cole rumbled. "Missed hearing you call *my* name. Nearly went insane imagining you calling for some other bastard."

Her heart thundered in her chest. Her sex quivered with little aftershocks of pleasure.

Two fingers slid inside of her, and she hissed out a breath.

"Missed the way you feel, squeezing me so tight. Like you don't ever want to let me go."

She licked her lips. "Come...inside." How many times did she have to tell the man?

He rose over her. Grabbed her camisole.

She lifted up so that he could toss it aside. She hadn't bothered with a bra, and her breasts—with tight nipples—thrust toward him.

"Missed how beautiful you are." His head lowered. He took one nipple into his mouth and lashed it with his tongue.

She was always extra sensitive after she came, and the feel of his mouth on her, of his tongue moving against her...Evie arched up against him even as her legs curled demandingly around his hips. "I want you inside. Finish what you started."

"I will finish, baby. I will finish and you will rake your nails down my back and you will scream for me again. Because I missed that." He turned his attention to her other breast. Licked and sucked and she couldn't stop her moans. "I missed everything about you."

Her hand shoved between their bodies. She caught the top of his jeans and yanked them open. The zipper flew down, and his cock shoved into her hands.

"God, yes, squeeze me."

She squeezed and pumped and stroked him. The head of his cock was wet. He was ready, so was she. *More than ready.* Why was he waiting?

"Missed your touch."

His words were getting harder to understand.

"Condom...in wallet." He moved away and ditched his jeans. She heard a packet tear, and then he was rolling on the condom.

She couldn't take her eyes off him.

I missed you, Cole. I missed you too much.

He came back to her. His cock shoved at the entrance to her body, but he didn't thrust inside. Not yet. "I won't give you up again."

Had she heard him right? Her heart pounded too loudly. Her breath heaved. She was arching toward him and trying to pull him inside.

"Never again," Cole vowed. "Never...give you...up again."

He sank deep.

He stretched her. Filled her completely. Pleasure, but almost pain. So good. So complete.

"Evie?"

Two years was a long time. Too long to wait and want.

"Baby?"

"Finish," she whispered. She squeezed her inner muscles around him. "Make me come again."

He withdrew. Thrust deep. Harder. Her nails flew over his back and scraped over his skin. He knew just what she liked. Knew how to drive her crazy.

"I missed the way you fuck me, Evie."

He slammed into her.

She screamed his name. The pleasure was even stronger this time, the kind of pleasure that burned away every thought and had your whole body shuddering.

She was panting and moaning as wave after wave hit her.

He kept thrusting, and every move had pleasure lashing at her. It was too much. She couldn't—

He stiffened against her. *"I missed...you."* She saw the pleasure wash over his face. He held her even tighter, and when he kissed her, she swore she could taste the pleasure on his tongue.

He held her, didn't let go, and she knew she was in trouble, but Evie didn't care. Because...

I missed you, too, Cole. So much.

***

Cole grabbed the sink top in Evie's bathroom. His knuckles whitened as he held on, too tightly.

Just as I held her too tightly.

His control had been gone. He should have been careful. Instead...

He'd fucked her without care. Fucked hard and deep. Fucked her wildly.

Had he hurt her? When he'd first thrust into her tight, hot core, she'd stiffened. She'd tensed, and he'd been afraid.

Can't hurt Evie. Not ever.

But...had he?

His head lifted. He forced himself to peer at his reflection in the mirror. Why the hell hadn't Evie run from him at her first opportunity?

He didn't look like a prize, surely not like those other fancy jerks in the ballroom. His gaze seemed feral with sexual hunger—*because I want to fuck her again already. Already? Try endlessly.*

His hair was tousled, and his face almost savage with need.

Tattoos covered his body. His chest. His arms.

He swallowed. Had she seen? The overhead light in her bedroom had been bright. He'd been able to see her perfectly.

Did she see all of me?

Had Evie seen?

Had she noticed that, right over his heart, her name marked him?

The tattoos. She'd ask about them, sooner or later. Ask why he had so many. Then he'd have to tell her the truth, and he didn't want to see pity in Evie's eyes.

Not that. Not ever.

He shoved back his hair. Sawed a hand over his jaw and the stubble there.

I killed a man tonight.

Not the first time. Evie didn't know that, though. Evie didn't know about his life. She didn't know what the tattoos hid. She didn't know who he was, deep inside.

He'd tried to warn her.

But the warnings were all too late now.

She'd let him have her again. Taste her. Touch her. Fuck her.

There was no way that he'd give her up again. No way that he could ever let her slip through his fingers a second time.

So...

He would have to convince her to stay. Have to get Evie...

To fall in love with a monster.

He ran some water over a wash cloth. Got it nice and warm, then went back to Evie. She was in the middle of the bed, and she'd hauled the covers up to her chin. Her eyes darted toward him.

He stopped. Smiled. "My, what big eyes you have."

She eased her grip on the covers. "Am I the big, bad wolf?"

Slowly, he made his way to the bed. "I think that's me." He lifted the cloth. "In case you're sore, I warmed this up for you."

"Oh, yes." Soft color bloomed on her cheeks. "That would be helpful." She held out her hand.

He lifted the covers up and slid the cloth between her legs.

"*Cole.*"

"I made you sore, so it's my job to make you better." Carefully, tenderly, he caressed her. "Been a while?" Cole asked the question ever so casually when *casual* was the last thing he felt.

She stiffened.

He looked up at her.

"Do you really want to go there?" Evie responded with a low question of her own.

"No. I would prefer not to ever think about any lucky bastard who had the extreme good fortune of touching your body." He kept up his gentle ministrations. "Because when I think of the bastard, I want to rip his head off." He moved the cloth. Pulled the covers back over her. "Better?"

"Uh, yes."

He nodded, curtly, and strode back to the bathroom to get rid of the cloth.

Shouldn't have asked. Shouldn't have brought up that shit. Now jealousy gnawed at him. He'd been the one to walk away, so he knew that he didn't have any right to feel the way he did. He didn't have the right to want to drive his fist into the faces of all the men who'd been with Evie.

He sucked in a deep breath, and, once more, returned to the bedroom. He turned off the bright, overhead light, then immediately turned on the lamp near her bed. The soft glow made a faint circle near the bed.

"I'll tell you about my lovers, but only if you tell me about yours."

She wanted to know about who he'd been with since her? "That's easy."

She'd grabbed a T-shirt while he'd been in the bathroom. It covered her chest, unfortunately. He had to admire the fact that she'd moved so quickly, though.

Even as he hated the shirt. *It can go.*

"It's easy." Her head cocked as she considered his reply. "Because you count all of your lovers? Because you have an instant tabulation in your head?"

He slid into bed beside her. Plumped up the pillow. "Oh, I should have asked...do you want me to sleep here tonight?"

She blinked at him.

"Because I was afraid you might have a nightmare," he continued carefully, "and if you did, if you woke up and you called out for me, I wanted to be close."

Her throat moved as she swallowed. "I'd like for you to sleep here."

Tension eased from him. "Good." Because beside her—in her bed—was exactly where he wanted to be. "And it's easy because the answer is zero."

"What?" Her voice shot up.

"You wanted to know how many lovers I've had since us? Since I made love to you in LA? Zero."

Silence.

He waited. Attempted to be patient.

She eased back down on the mattress. Put her head on her pillow. Turned her face toward him.

He turned his toward her. "It's your turn," he finally prompted.

"Are you lying to me?"

"I don't like lying to you, so I try not to do it."

More silence.

"And, no," he added when that stretching silence got to him. "I'm not lying. There haven't been others since you."

"Why not?" Soft.

"Because the others wouldn't have been you."
Hell, even flirting with any other woman had felt
wrong. Some of the Wilde agents had tried to push
him and had tried to get him to pick up women in
bars because they hadn't known about his past.

He hadn't been interested in other women.
They just weren't Evie.

"Does that shit sound stalker-like?" Cole
wondered.

"I..." Her voice trailed away.

"Evie, you haven't told me your number." Yes,
it was the stupid freaking jealousy pushing at him,
and he needed to get that shit under control. The
woman had been through more than enough that
night. The last thing she needed to do was deal
with his possessiveness. "Forget it. Doesn't
matter. The only thing that matters when we're
together—it's us. Me, you. No one else. Shouldn't
have asked."

"You really shouldn't have," she told him,
voice husky.

Sleepy?

"I don't want to know." He didn't. Ignorance
could be his bliss. Besides, what if he found out
that she'd slept with say, one of those muscled
dancers that she spent so much time with? The
next time he saw them together, Cole would have
the uncontrollable urge to drive his fist into said
dancer's face, and that shit wouldn't be cool with
Evie. Better to not know. Better to not—

"Zero."

The word was so low he thought he'd imagined it. Mostly because he wanted that number to be zero so very, very badly. "Evie?"

"Didn't feel right. Didn't...meet the right guy."

I can be the right guy.

Actually, hell, he was wrong for her in so many ways. A million ways, but for him, no one had ever felt more *right* than Evie. She soothed something in him. Gave him peace and happiness when he wasn't used to feeling either.

A man would do a whole lot to keep someone who made him feel that way.

He'd lie.

Trick.

Kill.

When it came to Evie, he'd already done all three.

He tucked the covers around her. Her eyes had closed. "I'm sorry...that you saw me kill him."

Not sorry the SOB was dead. The guy had deserved that. *He tried to hurt you.* But Cole hated that Evie had seen how cold-blooded and brutal he could be.

Her eyes opened. "I'm sorry that you had to kill for me."

He didn't look away from her dark gaze. "Baby, I'm not. For you, I'd do anything." Those words were probably the wrong ones to say. They might terrify her.

Her hand slid toward him. Her palm stretched over his heart.

And Evie fell asleep, touching him.

Cole didn't sleep, at least, not right away. He stared at Evie. Why look anywhere else?

He had her back in his life. Finally. He'd had a plan in place, one churning in his head, long before he'd gotten the orders from his boss that Evie needed protecting.

He'd been plotting. Making arrangements. Trying to figure out exactly how he could slip into Evie's life once more. He'd reached the decision— two months back—that he couldn't keep going as he'd been. He'd wanted another chance with her.

He'd been willing to do whatever it took to get that chance.

Her breathing was slow and steady. His hand rose. Hovered over her cheek. He wanted to brush back her hair, just wanted to touch her, but he didn't risk waking her.

He had Evie back.

Now, he just had to keep her.

CHAPTER TEN

Commence operation "Convince Evie That I'm Not a Monster"—step one will involve, hell, I don't know what yet. I'll figure it out as I go.

"This is cozy." Chase followed Cole into Evie's kitchen and waved his hand toward the spread that covered the large bar in the kitchen. "Did you make all of that? Like, seriously, I didn't think you could even boil water, man."

Cole grabbed the powdered sugar and carefully sprinkled it over the pancakes. "That shit is insulting."

"You're cooking. And it looks good. And it's the most surreal thing I've seen in a while." Chase's eyes narrowed. "Do you have an apron? *Were* you wearing an apron right before I came inside? Please tell me it has flowers on it. Or one of those awesome sayings like, 'Kiss me, I'm the cook.'"

"None of the breakfast is for you. You get to stare at it and not eat a single bite."

Chase sucked in a deep breath. "That is not cool. Friends don't do that to friends."

He lifted his eyebrows. "Why are you here this early?"

Chase sobered. "Because I just got some intel that I wanted to pass along to you." He rubbed a hand over his jaw. "The next shift of agents arrived, so there are still eyes outside. I'm going to the hotel and crash for a while, but I'll be back as soon as I recharge."

"What's the intel?"

Chase glanced over his shoulder. "She still sleeping?"

"She is." Evie had looked like an angel in bed. He'd woken up hard and aching for her, and he'd wanted nothing more than to make love to her. Over and over.

But, ah, considering how rough he'd been the night before, he'd decided to try a different tactic with her.

Breakfast. She'd see it and think...*Maybe he's not such a prick. He cooked for me.*

Or...not. Cole was still working out the logistics on all that.

"We don't have concrete evidence just yet, but Eric has his suspicions, and he's got his contacts digging as much as he can. It's hard, though, because the incident occurred so many years ago *and* it happened in another country, so it's not like we can easily get our hands on the vehicle and have our own team go over the evidence—"

"Wait. Back up." Cole's voice was low. Chase had been rambling and had lost him. "Another country?" He straightened. "Are you talking about Evie's mom and step-dad?" Because he knew their fatal car accident had occurred while they were honeymooning in France.

A grim nod from Chase. "Eric thinks they might not have died in an accident."

That was definitely new intel.

"Some forensic accounting work turned up the tidbit that her step-father's company was on the brink of bankruptcy. Oh, sure, it *looked* healthy enough at first glance, but when our techs dug, they could see through the numbers." A sigh. "Quint White owed a lot of money to a lot of people, and they were not going to get paid."

Cole stepped back. "The perp told Harrison that he would have to pay what Quint owed him."

Another nod from Chase. "That's what prompted Eric to dig deeper into the step-father's finances." He moved closer to Cole—and swiped a piece of bacon. "The family was going to lose everything. Even the penthouse that Harrison still resides in. But then Quint White and Evie's mother died. Everything changed."

His stomach knotted. "That's her bacon. Eat another piece and you'll lose a finger."

Chase's gaze lingered longingly on the bacon. "How did things change?"

Chase's gaze rose. "Insurance policy. They both had *huge* insurance policies. Evie wasn't legal at the time, and Harrison was the beneficiary. He got everything. And, since then, he's used that influx of cash to turn around the family fortune."

Cole heard the bedroom door open. His attention immediately shifted to Evie as she advanced toward them. Her face looked fresh and clean. Her hair swayed loosely around her shoulders. She wore jeans that were old and faded and fit her like a second skin. Her blouse was flowing and a deep emerald. Cute little ballerina flats were on her feet.

She looked good enough to friggin' eat.

He was suddenly famished.

"I cooked for you," Cole blurted.

"And he won't share," Chase muttered. "What a greedy punk."

Evie hurried into the kitchen area. Her eyes widened when she saw what waited. "You cooked *all* of this for me?"

What? Were twelve pancakes—chocolate chip with powdered sugar on top—eight eggs, ten pieces of bacon, and four cinnamon rolls too much? It looked right. "Yes."

Her face softened. "That's really sweet of you."

Chase choked.

Cole cut him a glare. If that bastard was choking on a piece of stolen bacon...

Chase waved his hand in the air and coughed. "She thinks you're sweet!"

"I am sweet. Now move your hand *away* from the bacon."

Evie reached for a plate. "I don't mind sharing."

Chase gave him a Cheshire cat grin.

"I do," Cole rasped.

Evie offered Chase a plate.

"Thank you very much," he told her. "It's so nice to find someone who is a good hostess." He helped himself. To a lot.

Cole crossed his arms over his chest.

"I-I heard a bit of what you two were saying." She bit her lower lip. She hadn't reached for the food yet. "You don't think my mother died in an accident?" Worry made her eyes even darker.

Tread carefully. "We don't know with certainty yet. Wilde is just following the clues to see what we can turn up." But he had to push and ask her, "Did you know that your brother was the beneficiary on their insurance policies?"

"Yes. He even used part of the money to set up a trust for me."

Cole and Chase exchanged a glance that clearly said, *Mental note. Check out that trust. Make sure the cash is still there.*

Because, while Evie might not realize it, Cole completely understood what Chase had been hinting at before.

A fatal crash in the mountains. One that possibly *hadn't* been an accident. And suddenly a ton of money for good old Harrison?

Hello, new suspect. It's nice to see what you look like.

She reached for one of the cinnamon rolls. Brought it toward her mouth.

Voice as mild as a spring breeze, Chase asked, "Did you know that Gia Eastman thinks you and your step-brother are sleeping together?"

She froze. "What?" Evie dropped the cinnamon roll onto her plate. "That's not funny."

Chase munched on bacon. "I didn't intend for it to be," he replied around a bite. "It was a question. You didn't answer it."

Evie shook her head. "No, no, of course, I didn't know that."

"Huh."

Cole narrowed his eyes on his buddy.

Evie's fingers fluttered around the cinnamon roll. "Why would she think that?"

Chase glanced at Cole. Lifted one eyebrow.

"It was a question," Evie gritted out as she tossed Chase's own words back at him. "You didn't answer it."

A bark of laughter came from Chase. "God, man, I can see why you love her. She's got fire."

Silence. The deafening kind.

I am going to hurt him.

Evie pushed away from the bar. "Cole doesn't love me. That's not a funny thing to say."

Chase choked down the bacon. "I was...kidding." His gaze jerked to Cole. "Sorry."

"You will be," Cole promised him. He could taste rage. He swallowed it. Motioned toward Evie. "You should eat."

"I'm not hungry."

He growled. She wasn't hungry now *because of Chase.* That sonofabitch had upset her. Cole was going to—

"No, I'm sorry." Evie sat down on the barstool. "You went to all of this trouble for me, and I really appreciate it. Thank you, Cole. It was kind."

He waited for a sarcastic comment from Chase.

None came.

"Thank you," Evie said once more. She picked up a cinnamon roll. Took a bite.

He hurried to her side. "Don't make yourself eat it." Okay, looking at things from this angle, it *did* look like he'd made some sort of hotel-size buffet. "The food doesn't matter. If you're not hungry, just forget it."

Her eyes grew wider. "This is delicious."

It was? She thought it was?

She took another bite. Moaned.

His body tensed.

There was a little bit of icing on her upper lip. He should help her by licking it away. He leaned toward her.

"I asked the question because Gia flat out told me last night that Harrison had broken up with her because of you," Chase said with his usual bad timing. "She said that there wasn't room for any other women in his life. Only you."

Well, he'd certainly gotten the woman to be chatty.

Cole had a quick flash of Gia coming out of the bathroom. Trying to pull *him* away from Evie. The fact that she'd been the last one in the ladies' room with Evie, right before the abduction?

Suspect.

"You'll be interviewing her again, ASAP," Cole ordered.

"You know it's already on my To-Do list." Chase saluted him and grabbed a pancake. "Chocolate chips are my favorite. Did you make these for me?"

"You know I didn't."

Evie had finished the cinnamon roll. As he watched, she licked away the icing.

Sweet mother of...

"So, are you going to tell us?" Chase pushed.
Cole blinked.

"Tell you—what?" Evie's eyebrows shot up.

"You and your step-brother. Just how close
are you?"

And Cole realized just what Chase was doing.
An old technique. Distract and question. Keep
pushing until you got what you wanted. Chase was
throwing out bits of info, Evie was off balance, and
Chase obviously thought she might slip up and
reveal something useful.

Only Evie *wasn't* a suspect. She was the
victim. Chase shouldn't be using any
interrogation techniques on her.

Cole stalked around the bar. Snatched the
pancake from Chase.

"Hey!"

"You don't interrogate her." He glowered at
his friend. "You don't play mind games with her.
You don't do *anything* to upset her. Not now. Not
ever. Are you hearing me? You getting this
message?"

Chase searched his eyes. "Don't you want to
know?"

"I already do." *So take that shit.* Evie had told
him last night that there hadn't been anyone else
since they'd been together. He believed her. He
trusted her.

End of story.

"Ahem."

Cole glanced over his shoulder.

Evie had scooped up some bacon. And
gobbled down a pancake.

He smiled at her.

"You're a really good cook," she told him. "I had no idea that you possessed these, ah, skills."

Oh, baby, I can show you some skills.

"And the answer is no. For the record. To be as clear as possible." She lifted a glass of orange juice. Took a long gulp. When she put the glass back down, her hand lingered—and tightened—around it. "I'm not involved with my step-brother. Never have been. Know why? Because that's gross. *He's my brother.* Consider Gia Eastman misinformed." Her chin notched up.

She was so beautiful. "I will consider her both misinformed," Cole assured her, "and a chief suspect."

"*Gia?*" Evie let go of the glass.

Definitely Gia. "She was the one closest to the bathroom. The last one to see you in there. *And* she tried to get me to leave. Wanted to pull me away with her."

Evie's gaze hardened as her head tilted. "Exactly how did she try to get you to leave?"

Ah...

"Did she flirt with you? Is that it? While I was being shoved in a trunk, she was flirting with you?"

Gia had actually been telling him that Evie was a boring lover, but there was no way he'd mention that detail. *And, sweetheart, you are never, ever boring.*

"All three of our main suspects were there when the abduction went down." Cole had spoken to the cops about them all during his very lengthy interrogation. "The NYPD will have their chance to run at them, but Wilde will be up next. We'll be investigating them all." A pause. "Those three, and our other chief suspect."

He saw Evie's shoulders stiffen. "Just who is your chief suspect?"

In light of the news about her mother and step-father... "We need to pay a visit to Harrison."

Evie reached for her napkin. Cole saw that her fingers trembled slightly. She quickly patted her lips. "I-I will get my bag and be ready in a moment."

"Evie—"

But she'd hurried away.

He watched her go.

"So...out of curiosity, I just have to ask..."

Chase was still there. Chase was still talking. Cole swung toward him with a growl.

"Did you think cooking breakfast would make her forget that you killed a man last night?"

Cole's shoulders squared.

"Because that's not going to happen." Chase rose. His face appeared oddly solemn. "You can't wave a wand and act like someone else just because you're trying to charm the woman you want."

"You don't know anything about me and Evie."

"I think I do. I'm not blind." His lips twisted as sympathy flashed on his face. "She has to accept you for who you really are. Not who you pretend to be."

"I don't remember asking for advice."

"At Wilde, we're often undercover. Often pretending to be someone else entirely. It's easy for us to lose sight of who we truly are."

"I know exactly who I am."

"But does she?"

***

Evie shut the bedroom door, muting their voices, and she realized that her hands were still shaking. She lifted them up and balled them into fists.

She'd tried to act in control out there. Tried to act as if each new detail didn't batter away at her.

My mother didn't die in an accident? If that was true, if her mother had been murdered...

Evie had to blink away tears. Her temples throbbed as pain cut through her.

And Harrison...they actually thought Harrison could be behind all of this? Impossible. Harrison had been the only one there for her after Quint and Evie's mother died. He'd taken care of her. Had given her everything that she could possibly need. There was no way—*no way*—he would ever do anything to hurt her.

Right?

I have to be right.

Her eyes squeezed closed.

***

"Something is wrong," Cole said. His gaze had moved to the closed bedroom door. Unease slithered through him. When she'd walked away, Evie's shoulders had been so straight. So stiff.

"There are lots of things wrong. Like the fact that your girlfriend was thrown into the trunk of a car last night. I'd call that super wrong."

"She's not my—" He stopped. He wanted Evie to be his girlfriend, lover, partner—whatever the word. *I want her.* "Evie was too stiff when she walked away. Normally, she walks like she's flowing. Freaking grace in motion. A sexy dancer thing."

"Sounds like you spend a whole lot of time watching her walk."

Cole was already bounding for the bedroom. "Something is wrong," Cole said again.

"Well, we did just tell her that her mother might have been murdered, then we dropped the bombshell that her step-brother—her only family—could have been behind things. But, hey, you made her one big-ass breakfast, so I'm sure everything is cool."

Cole flipped him off, then pounded his fist into Evie's bedroom door. "Evie!"

Footsteps rushed up behind him. "Dude, you need to use some tact." Chase's voice was low. "Don't pound. Knock. Try some care."

Cole spun toward him. "Did you or did you not just tell me that she had to see the *real* person that I am?"

"I...guilty."

Cole jerked his head in a curt nod. "Lock the front door on your way out. I've got Evie."

"I'm sure you do," Chase murmured.

Cole whirled back around. The *real* him...he pounded again. "Evie, I know something is wrong." He'd knocked, so now he could open the door, right? He grabbed the handle.

Locked.

He sucked in a breath. "Please don't be crying in there."

The front door shut behind Chase.

"Evie?" Cole's back teeth were clenched. "It's just us. You don't need to put on an act any longer." And he realized that was exactly what she'd done.

Private, quiet Evie. She didn't like to reveal too much about her feelings to others.

He'd been such a damn ass. Standing in that kitchen. Dropping bombshells on her and wrecking her world.

The door cracked open.

Her eyes gleamed with tears. Her lashes were spiky with them. "My mother was murdered?"

Oh, hell. His heart twisted.

"Someone might have killed my mother?"

He hauled her into his arms.

CHAPTER ELEVEN

Try to keep me from Evie again. Go on, try. I dare you, dumbass.

"You're fired." Harrison made the announcement as soon as Evie and Cole entered his penthouse. He also grabbed Evie's wrist and pulled her toward him. "You're moving in here, and I'm going to keep you safe."

He was going to what? Evie tugged on her hand. Harrison didn't let go. What was his deal?

Cole glanced to the left where a hulking—and obvious—bodyguard stood. "By any chance," he asked the fellow, "you have orders to throw me out?"

"I do," the man agreed with an eager smile.

Evie's heart seemed to jump right to her throat. "No!"

"Yes," Harrison assured her. "I tried to call you last night. Multiple times, did you know that?"

No, because she'd been sleeping like the dead...in bed with Cole.

"I attempted to gain access to your building. I wanted to see for myself that you were safe." He waved his left hand toward Cole. "But this bastard and his friends wouldn't let me up to see you."

"Cole was asleep last night," she mumbled. He had been...hadn't he? In bed with her?

Cole nodded. "I didn't leave last night, sweetheart. I stayed exactly where you needed me to be."

Her shoulders relaxed.

"*Sweetheart?*" Harrison snarled. "Evie, tell me that you did *not* sleep with him!"

Her chin lifted. "Actually, that's the best way I do sleep." In Cole's arms.

Harrison stabbed his finger toward Cole and the hulking bodyguard. "Get him out of here, Tommy! Toss his ass out—the same way that jerk Chase tossed me out of Evie's building last night!"

Chase had done that? He'd certainly been busy.

And Chase thinks Harrison could be involved in all of this mess.

The bodyguard in the straining white T-shirt reached for Cole.

"Don't." Cole shook his own finger at the guard. "It will just be embarrassing for you. I mean, you've got considerable bulk, and when I lay your ass out, it will look bad. Word will spread—because I am the type who will spread that word—and you won't be able to get other jobs. Won't even be able to be a bouncer at your favorite club and—"

Tommy lurched forward and grabbed for Cole.

Evie screamed and tore away from Harrison.

But Harrison yanked her back.

Cole's head swung toward Evie. "*Let her go. Now. You're too fucking grabby with her.*"

The bodyguard's hand plowed into Cole's side.

He grunted, and fury flashed on Cole's face. "I warned you." He fired off with his own punch. A left, then a right hook. The bodyguard staggered back, and Cole grabbed his arm. He did a twist that Evie could only admire, and in the next moment, using perfect pressure and pain, Cole had the guard on his knees. Cole had angled the guy's arm up high behind him, and the bodyguard's face turned white.

"This is what I warned you about." Cole shook his head in admonishment. "Now you look like a dick."

The guard wasn't moving. Probably because if he moved, Cole would break his arm. She'd been taught that same technique but never used it.

"Harrison, your hands are still on Evie. Get them off."

"You can't tell me what to—"

Evie pushed away from him. "Call off your guard."

Cole laughed. "Doesn't really need to call him off. He's not exactly on. But we do want to send the bozo outside."

She glared at Harrison.

"Fine," he muttered. "Go outside, Tommy."

Cole finally let him go. "Outside, Tommy, you heard the boss. I saw your buddy waiting by the door. Go join him."

Tommy practically ran outside. And, yes, Evie had seen the other guy waiting out there, too. Another new guard.

At this point, neither of Harrison's two guards were inspiring a whole lot of confidence in Evie. Because they weren't Wilde?

"Please tell me that you don't think you're going to fire me, then replace me with that dude?" Cole jerked his thumb over his shoulder. "Because that's bad planning."

Evie put her hands on her hips. "You're not firing Cole."

Harrison's eyes were hot with fury. "You were *taken* under his watch! He's not competent!"

"I was recovered under his watch, too. He *killed* the man who took me. What more do you want?"

Harrison's gaze snapped to Cole. "A lot more."

If possible, the tension in the air grew even thicker.

"It was a mistake to bring him back." Harrison nodded. "I can see that now. I thought he'd do anything to keep you safe, but the problem is that he can't see past you. He's too involved where you're concerned. He cares too much."

Her gaze slid to Cole. But there was no reading his expression.

"Thought he'd be over it by now. Or at least, have that shit controlled, but it's working against you. He's putting you at risk, and I can't have that." Harrison's voice thickened as he added, "You are my only family, Evie. I can't lose you."

Hadn't she had the same thought about him? That he was her only family?

"About that..." Cole cleared his throat. "I think we need to talk."

Harrison frowned at him. "You're fired. I have been over this several—"

"You can't fire me because I don't work for you."

Harrison opened his mouth. Closed it.

"I *have* been over that with you, too. You're not paying for Evie's protection. I'm watching out for her. Case closed."

She could easily read the fury on her step-brother's face. But then...that fury...it turned sly.

"I'm going to tell her," Harrison threatened. "Is that truly what you want?"

"And is the ass kicking I promised you truly what *you* want?" Cole tossed back, almost casually. "Because I already warned you it was coming. If you want it now, I am happy to oblige."

Her temples throbbed.

"But, keep in mind how easily I took out your guard. So just know going into this that you will have zero chance against me." Cole rolled one shoulder. "The ass kicking will be fast."

Harrison glared at him. Then looked at Evie. "He's a killer."

Her spine snapped straight. "He was protecting me. Cole did not have a choice last night—"

"Not talking about last night. I'm talking about before you met him. *Since* you met him."

"Harrison," Cole growled. "Shut your damn mouth."

But Harrison's mouth kept going. "When I hired him, he was a mercenary. He would do anything for money, Evie. Anything. You get what I'm saying? He was hired, knowing that he might need to kill the abductors who held you in LA, and he didn't hesitate. Told me it wouldn't even be his first time."

She sucked in a sharp breath.

Cole lunged forward.

She put her hand on his chest, right over his heart, stopping him before he could get too close to Harrison. Tension poured from Cole's body, but at her touch, he stilled.

Harrison's voice sped up as he quickly added, "After he left you, he worked for criminals. The mob. Do you hear what I'm saying? He's not some good guy knight—"

"They lied to me." A muscle jerked along Cole's jaw. "As soon as I found out the truth, I did what was right. I didn't hurt any innocents. I have never hurt—"

"Do you think that makes it okay?" Harrison shook his head. "You're a gun for hire. You don't have a soul. You do the dirty work for the highest bidder."

"No, no, I work for Wilde now. We protect people. We help—"

"You're trying to clean up, but it's too late. You can't wash the sins away."

The pounding in her temples got worse.

"Neither can you," Cole snarled back.

"What is that supposed to mean?" Harrison demanded.

Cole's heart raced beneath her touch as he snapped, "It means, jackass, that we know about the insurance policies on your father and Evie's mom. And Wilde knows their death wasn't an accident."

She was watching Harrison so closely—so very closely—and Evie saw the flicker of his lashes. Right before his hand reached up and tugged on his left ear.

"OhmyGod." Her stomach dropped straight to the floor. "What did you do?"

His eyes widened in horror. "I didn't *do* anything! Jesus, Evie, you think I would kill my own father? You know me better than that!"

"I do know you well." She nodded. "So I know when you're holding back. I know your tells. *You are holding back on me right now.* You can't do that. You have to tell us everything." How could he do this? "I was shoved into a trunk last night. That bastard had a knife. If Cole hadn't shot him, I would be dead right now."

Harrison flinched.

Cole moved around Evie and closed in on her step-brother. "Tell us everything."

Harrison's Adam's apple bobbed as he swallowed. "I didn't have proof."

Evie waited.

"I suspected their deaths weren't an accident, but...I didn't have proof."

"What made you suspect?" Cole's rough voice pushed for more information.

"My father had mentioned that he'd been...harassed, right before the wedding. Told me it was an angry competitor. He'd stepped up security, just as a precaution. But when he went on his honeymoon, I think he believed he was safe in France, so he didn't bother with the guards there." A painful laugh. "Of course, he didn't want guards with him there. He'd just married. For the first time in years, he was in love again. Happy."

Her mother had been happy, too. The last time Evie had seen her, her mother had been beaming. Her wide smile had stretched from ear to ear. Evie treasured that memory of her mom. Evie wanted to always remember her being so happy.

"My dad was a great driver. Hell, back in his youth, he even had a race car. He took safety seriously. And he knew those roads. He had a second home there. Him losing control? In the middle of the day? I didn't buy it. But when I tried to investigate, I turned up nothing."

Cole crossed his arms over his chest. "You didn't investigate that hard, did you? Because you didn't want to alert the insurance agents who might halt that heavy payout you were getting."

"The agents would still have honored the policies—"

"Not if you were the one who killed the newlyweds. You wouldn't have received a dime then."

Harrison staggered back a step. "You seriously think I killed my father?"

A shiver slid over Evie.

Cole's expression didn't alter. "Did you?"

Harrison whipped his head toward Evie. "Do you think I killed them?"

"No." The answer was pulled right from her soul. "I saw your grief." They'd huddled together at the cemetery. She'd cried with him. "No, I don't think you did."

Harrison licked his lower lip.

"See, there's the problem." Cole's voice was flat. "Evie loves you. You're her only family, so she views you through blinders. I don't. I see you for exactly what you are."

Now Harrison's shoulders stiffened. "And what's that?"

"A greedy, driven, ambitious prick who will stop at nothing to get what he wants."

Well, that had been blunt. And she actually did know all of that about Harrison, but she also knew that he had good parts, too. He'd helped her. Taken her in. Always made sure she had everything that she needed and—

"You're possessive," Cole continued darkly. "And controlling. You've been controlling Evie's life for years, and that shit is over."

No, Cole was wrong. "He...hasn't been doing that."

Cole glanced at her. "You sure about that?"

She nodded.

"Then you know that one month after I left you, I came back."

Her heart stopped. She'd misheard. Must have misheard. There was no way that he'd said—

"Harrison wouldn't see me the first time I came back. He had guards meet me at the door. I never got close to him—or you."

That wasn't true. That wasn't possible. Cole hadn't come back for her.

"I took another mission. Missed you like hell. Realized it wasn't really possible to keep walking around without my heart, so I came back, again. This time, Harrison met with me."

Her breath was coming out in hard heaves. She'd been heartbroken when Cole left her. Harrison knew how hurt she'd been. And Cole had come back? *Twice?*

"Evie..." Harrison's voice seemed very, very careful now. "He's trying to turn you against me. I don't know why. I don't know what game he's playing, but don't let it work."

Cole lunged forward. Stood toe-to-toe with Harrison. "You think this is a game?"

Harrison's chin jutted into the air. "Do you?"

"I don't think a damn thing about Evie is a game."

Evie hurried toward them. She curled her fingers around Cole's arm.

Instantly, he turned toward her.

"You came back?" Her whisper was so unsteady. Hoarse.

He nodded.

Her heart stuttered in her chest. The ache grew and grew. Her hold tightened on him even as she swung her gaze to Harrison. "He came back?"

Harrison's lips thinned.

He came back.

"Why didn't you tell me?" Pain throbbed in her words.

"Because you didn't need someone like him in your life, Evie! You don't know the stuff he's done. He's dangerous. I dug into his background. Hell, why do you think I hired him in the first place? I wanted a man who wasn't afraid to get his hands dirty. Someone who wouldn't look too hard at the law because I needed you back. I didn't care what had to be done to save you, and I needed a person without—without morals to do it. Someone who didn't mind hurting or even killing to get the job done."

She flinched, but didn't let go of Cole.

"That's who he is. He will do whatever is necessary. Even kill, for the highest bidder." Harrison's voice pounded at her. "He's worked for the mob, Evie. I wasn't lying about that. He's not choosy on his employers. He only cares about money. That's all he's ever cared about. Why do you think he came back? Do you truly think it was because he loved you? I know you're not that naive."

She couldn't speak. There wasn't an ache in her heart. There was fire. Fury.

"He knew how much money we had, Evie. That's why he came back. He got hurt on one of the missions he took after yours, and he decided he didn't want to be in the business anymore. Your money looked damn good, so he came back for that. Not you."

"That's not fucking true." Cole's voice wasn't a roar. Wasn't some bellow. It was low and lethal.

"He was caught on an assignment overseas," Harrison thundered on. *His* voice was high and wild. "Sliced over and over because the people who had him wanted Cole to turn on his team. But he didn't. He killed the men who held him. Slit their throats and left them dying in pools of their own blood."

She was going to be sick. Evie yanked her hand away from Cole and stepped back.

"Evie," Cole breathed. Pain flashed on his face.

"When I learned all that, I wasn't going to let him near you. I was going to protect you. I'm your family. It's my job." Harrison straightened. "So, yes, he came back. And I told him you wanted nothing to do with him. Because I knew the truth. I know *you*, Evie. You fell for him because he saved you, but when you got to know the real man, you wouldn't love him. You'd fear him."

Her hand rose to her mouth.

Cole was staring at her, his expression tense, his eyes blazing.

But he wasn't saying anything. Nothing else.

"Yet y-you brought him back into my life," Evie stammered. That meant—

"Because when you're dealing with criminals, you use whatever tools work the best. Cole is a tool that needed to be used. I knew he'd protect you. He killed the man last night, didn't he? So, yes, I guess he did his job, but things are getting too messy. He's trying to push his way back into your heart, and I can't have that. That's why it's better if we just fire him now and—"

"I need—I need a minute, I'm sorry." She whirled and pretty much ran from the room.

"*Evie!*" Cole called after her, but she didn't look back.

Right then, she couldn't.

Pain and fury twisted inside of her. She just had to get away. Had to get a moment to herself. She rushed to her old room. Threw open the door.

Everything was the same. All of the furniture was still in the same place. As if the room had been waiting for her.

As if Harrison had been sure that, eventually, she'd come back.

Her chest burned.

Her brother's words rang in her ears over and over again. *He was caught on an assignment overseas. Sliced over and over because the people who had him wanted Cole to turn on his team. But he didn't. He killed the men who held him. Slit their throats and left them dying in pools of their own blood.*

"Oh, my God."

CHAPTER TWELVE

Her name is tattooed over my heart. Like,
fucking literally. Because she owns it. Does she
get that she owns my soul, too?

"I'm sure you can see yourself out now."
Harrison smiled at Cole. His Delta Force buddies
would have called it a shit eating grin. "Don't let
the door hit you in the ass."

Cole laughed. The sound was low and hard.
Mean.

Harrison's smile faltered.

Just so they were on the exact same page, in
the exact same book, Cole told him, "I'm not going
any damn place."

"But—but Evie doesn't want you—"

"Oh, trust me," Cole said with far more
confidence than he felt, "Evie wants me." She'd
had *tears* in her eyes when she ran from the room,
and those tears gutted him. He prayed she wasn't
crying because she thought he was some kind of a
monster. Shit, but...

I am.

He'd tried to be better. To change. To do
more. For her. But she wouldn't know. He hadn't

told her. He'd tried to hide his past. Tried to pretend it hadn't happened. Then her dick of a brother had decided to air all the dirty laundry in the world. *Thanks, asshole. Another thing I owe you for.*

"Evie doesn't want—"

"Ask her downstairs neighbors. I'm sure they heard her screaming my name last night. She wants me plenty."

Harrison took a swing at him. Cole let the blow land, for shits and giggles. No surprise, Harrison couldn't punch worth a damn. Cole barely felt the blow on his jaw.

And Harrison stood there, all chest heaving and cheeks flushed, like he'd done something. Absolutely adorable. Not. *More like a pain in my ass.* Cole quirked a brow. "That the best you got?"

"I—" He backed up a step.

"Because since you had your shot, I think it's only fair I have mine." He drew back his fist and let it fly toward Harrison's face.

Harrison squeezed his eyes shut and turned his head away.

Cole stopped the blow, just centimeters away from Harrison's face.

It took Harrison far too long to realize that he hadn't been hit. His eyes cracked open, and he gaped at Cole.

"If you weren't her brother, you'd be on the floor, groaning in pain right now and probably spitting out teeth." Just so he understood the situation. "But then, if I were the uncontrolled, mercenary bastard killer that you want Evie to believe I am...I guess I wouldn't let the fact that you're her brother stop me. I'd beat the ever-loving-hell out of you just because I wanted to do it."

Harrison wet his lips.

"I do want to do it," Cole assured him. "But you're wrong about who I am. You've always been wrong. Now Evie knows it. She knows that you've lied to her. That you've hidden the truth, and that you aren't the hero she thought."

"What?" Harrison's eyes flared wide. "No, Evie didn't think—"

"You were the brother who swooped in to save her when she was sixteen. Instead of casting her out, you gave her a safe life. That made you a hero in her eyes. Freaking Superman."

Unease flickered on Harrison's face.

"I didn't want to be Lex Luther to your hero. That's not how I wanted Evie to see me, even if it's how *you* wanted her to view me."

"You *are* what you are—"

"And so are you. Right now, you're the dick who betrayed Evie."

Harrison's jaw dropped. His gaze darted toward the hallway. "No, she's mad at you, not me."

Cole laughed. "You are a clueless SOB, aren't you? Evie didn't leave crying because of me. She left because of you. Because her hero just fell from grace." His laughter vanished as he fought *not* to take that swing at Harrison. "Another sin at your feet. I don't like it when anyone makes Evie cry. Do it again, and I won't be holding back."

Harrison raked a shaking hand over his face. "Evie, no, she's not angry with me."

Cole didn't speak. He did turn on his heel and head toward the hallway.

"She's not going to want to see you!" Harrison blasted after him. "You read the scene wrong. Evie wants you gone. She was crying because she can't stand what you are."

Now Cole had to spin around and stare at the guy in confusion. "Are you truly that clueless when it comes to her? Don't you know her at all?"

"I know her better than anyone else—"

"Then you have no excuse for hurting her this way. Never do it again." His stare raked over Harrison. "There is one question I have to ask. This shit keeps coming up, and you know, I get where Evie stands on it, but I need to make sure I understand *you*."

Harrison peered at him in confusion.

"The wrong answer is going to lead to serious trouble for you. The kind of trouble that's life-changing."

"What the hell are you talking about?"

"Are you in love with Evie?"

Shock flashed on Harrison's face.

Cole's hands clenched.

Then disgust coated Harrison's features. "Are you crazy? She's my *sister*!"

Good answer. You get to keep breathing. "Gia Eastman thinks that you broke up with her because of Evie."

Harrison glanced away.

"Shit. You *did*."

Harrison paced toward the window. "I was supposed to be in LA. When she was taken, I was scheduled to be there. It was originally my hotel room, not hers. The trip was PR for the company."

"But Evie's not involved in the company."

"Sometimes, she helps out with PR work. Putting a family face on things, you know? Like she did at the charity gala last night." He blew out a breath. "Two years ago, I was supposed to go to LA. It was a photo op thing. But Gia wanted me to spend the weekend with her. So I asked Evie to go in my place."

"And she was taken."

Harrison's head sagged forward. "Yes, she was. I got the call about her while I was with Gia. Gia didn't exactly like it that I left her bed in order to run to Evie's rescue." He whirled around. "What kind of BS was that? My sister was abducted, but Gia acted like it was some kind of inconvenience. That I should just call the cops and let them handle things. I got the feeling she didn't care if Evie came back home or not."

Well, well...another reason for Cole to dislike Gia Eastman.

"Then when she found out that Evie was slated to inherit everything I had, hell, she started demanding I change my will. That I make new arrangements immediately. Gia told me that as soon as we were married, she expected to come first with me."

Cole lifted his hand. "Back up. What do you mean, Evie gets everything?"

"She's my sister," Harrison said simply. "I know that you think I'm an asshole. Join the club. Most people think that. But I truly only want what's best for Evie. In the event anything should happen to me, I've made arrangements for Evie to inherit everything that I possess." A rough exhale. "I didn't plan to marry Gia. She was making assumptions. And I," Harrison coughed, "may have told her—after Evie was safely back home— that I was stepping back from our relationship because I wanted to be there for my sister."

Hell. Harrison had used Evie as his excuse. "Now Gia has it out for Evie."

"Well, she probably doesn't like her much but—"

"Do you know that Gia was the last person in the restroom with Evie last night? Right before someone drugged her and threw Evie in the back of a sedan?"

"I...heard that."

"Well, hear *this*. Your ex might be a kidnapper, and if she is, I'm personally gonna throw her ass in jail." He squared his shoulders. "Now excuse me, but Evie needs me." He marched for the hallway.

"She might not want you anywhere near her—"

"Dumbass," Cole threw over his shoulder without looking back, "I'm the one she *does* want close." Confident. Cocky.

But that confident facade faded the minute he rounded the corner in the hallway and came face to face with a closed door. He stood there a moment and pulled in some fast breaths.

Jesus. Don't let that prick be right. Don't let him be right. Evie knew the truth about him, and maybe she *had* run away because she was scared. Or disgusted. Or a thousand other things. Cole hoped not. He prayed not. He'd been bluffing his butt off with Harrison. *Never let the enemy see weakness.* But the truth was...

Cole was afraid.

Afraid that when he opened that door, Evie would tell him to get the hell out of her life. She'd have tears on her cheeks, she'd absolutely break him with her pain, and she'd tell him that she never wanted to see him again.

If she did that, then what in the hell would he do?

He swallowed. Squared his shoulders. Lifted his hand. Knocked on the door. "Evie?" He held his breath while he waited.

"Come in." Her voice. Hushed and husky.

He reached for the knob. Turned it ever so slowly. Or maybe he wasn't turning it slowly. Maybe everything just felt slow because it sure seemed as if the door was opening in slow motion, too. The seconds took forever to tick on by.

His breath labored as he waited for the door to open. He could feel sweat on his brow.

Then he saw her. Standing at the foot of the four-poster bed, with her back to him.

Can she not even stand to look at me?

"I'm sorry," Evie said.

No, don't do it. Do not say that you're sorry, but we're done. Do not fucking do it. "I'm not leaving you while you're in danger." The words were growled. The only response he could think to say. "So you might hate being nearing me right now, but it's necessary."

She whirled toward him. Gaped.

Dammit, there *were* tears in her eyes. Tear tracks on her cheeks.

Give me a chance, please. I can show you that I am so much more than what the world thinks. He didn't say that, though. Instead, he growled— yes, another stupid growl—at her, "I will keep you safe. I won't mess up like I did last night."

She shook her head.

"I won't let you out of my sight. I'll stick closely to you. I-I..." Fuck, now he was stammering. "I will keep my hands off you, but I can't let you be alone."

She shook her head. She kept doing that.

Kept right on breaking his heart. The heart he'd decided—more than two years and six months ago—would always belong to her. "Evie?" He took a step inside the room, barely noticing the surroundings. "Why...no?" *Why are you telling me no? Why are you turning me away when all I want is to hold you close?*

But he knew the reason why. Because he'd lost her. Because she saw him for what he was. Because her dick of a brother was right.

He stared down at the floor. Not due to the fact that it was particularly fascinating—it wasn't. It was just a hardwood floor. No, he stared at it because he couldn't look at her right then. It hurt to see her. He wanted her so much that seeing her and knowing that he'd lost her gutted him. "I understand that you don't trust me to keep you safe. I messed up last night."

"You saved my life last night."

His head snapped up.

Her eyes—those beautiful but, dammit, still tear-filled eyes of hers—were on him. "The first time I shook my head, it was because you were wrong. You didn't mess up. You saved me."

He lurched toward her. Freaking moved like some mindless zombie.

"The second time I shook my head because I don't want you to keep your hands off me."

Another lurch. The woman probably *should* be running from him.

Instead, she reached up. Caught his right hand in hers. Held tight. "I want you to touch me as often as you can."

Hope burned, hot and bright, igniting within him. "Evie?"

"I'm sorry for what Harrison said to you. I'm sorry that I didn't ever know what really happened. Because if I had known that you'd come back...I would have run to you."

He was rooted to the spot. "What...about the other things he said?"

Her lower lip trembled. "You were hurt and I didn't know? Someone hurt you?"

His chest ached. "Do you think I'm evil, Evie?"

"No."

"He wasn't wrong about the things I've done. Harrison wasn't lying." Cole had heard the truth in Harrison's voice when he'd told Cole, only moments before, *I want what is best for Evie.* "I don't think I'm best for you. Hell, I'm probably one of the worst bastards in the world."

"I don't believe that."

She should. "I took jobs that I thought were legit, but later…" Shame coiled inside of him, but Cole wanted no secrets between them. He wanted Evie to know all that he was. "Later I found out that one of my employers had sent me after an innocent victim. I didn't hurt her, I swear it. And in fact, that's how I joined Wilde. I found out who the real good guys were, and I helped them to protect her. We brought down the bad guys. We stopped them. I knew that I never wanted to be wrong, never wanted to risk hurting an innocent, ever again."

Her gaze searched his. "That's why you started working for Wilde."

"I started working for Wilde because I wanted to be someone you could be proud of." He turned his hand so that he was holding hers. "Because one day, I was determined to have another shot with you, and when that chance came around, I wasn't going to screw it up."

I want that chance. Don't take it from me now.

"Did someone hurt you?" Evie whispered.

"You don't want to know about that."

"I do. I want to know everything." A pause. "After you left me, what happened to you?"

His lips parted.

And his phone rang.

What the hell?

He knew the ring tone. Chase. The guy had only left a little while before to go back to his hotel. Shit. A call from him so soon had to be about the case. Cole yanked up the phone. Shoved it to his ear. "Your timing could have been about a million times better—"

"Gia Eastman has vanished."

"What?"

"Our agents went to interview her. Only she's not at home. Not at work."

"Maybe she's with some friends who—"

"You think I haven't checked that angle? I have. I got Wilde to pull some strings—and by strings, I mean I got the tech people to tap into some street cams. You're not going to like what I found out."

He waited.

Chase didn't say anything else.

"Spit it out!" Cole snapped.

Evie winced.

"I'm so sorry, sweetheart," he immediately said.

"Oh, that's okay," Chase told him warmly. "We all get stressed. I know you didn't mean to snap at me."

I wasn't talking to you! "What. Did. You. Find. Out."

"Around dawn this morning, Gia headed out for a jog. She didn't make it back to her building. A black SUV swooped in behind her near Central Park. Guy grabbed her, and they shot out of there in a flash."

"You're telling me she was abducted?"

"It sure looks that way. I've notified the cops, sent them an anonymous tip to check for her and to take a look at street cams from this morning." Chase's voice roughened as he added, "We saw her as a potential suspect, but she could be the next victim."

Because after Evie, she was the closest person to Harrison White. Maybe the kidnappers thought that since they couldn't get Evie, they could use Gia against Harrison.

"Stay on this," Cole ordered. "See if you can get Wilde to track her phone. I'll talk to Harrison."

"You think he's going to get some kind of ransom demand?"

"If she's been abducted, is there anyone else in Gia's life who could pay?"

"No." Grim. "No family. No close romantic ties, not that I've found."

"My gut says this will go back to Harrison."

"And if your gut is wrong?"

Then he didn't know what the hell would happen to Gia.

He spoke to Chase a bit more, then shoved the phone back into his pocket. His gaze had been on Evie the whole time. "How much of that did you hear?"

"Too much," she said, voice shaky. "Someone kidnapped Gia?"

"Maybe." *Looks that way.* "We don't know exactly what's happening yet. But we're going to find out." He caught her hand in his. Threaded his fingers with hers and turned for the door. He kept his hold on her as they hurried down the hallway, then toward Harrison's office.

When they entered, Harrison spun around. He seemed pale. Nervous.

His attention immediately focused on Evie. His gaze swept over her, then...stopped at Evie and Cole's joined hands.

"Yes, deal with that shit," Cole told him flatly. "We've got other issues right now—"

Harrison's phone rang.

He ignored it. "What issues?"

"Who is on the phone?"

"What?"

The phone was still ringing. Harrison was still not answering it.

"Who is on the phone?" Cole asked again. "Look at it. Now."

Harrison scooped it off his desk. "Unknown number. Probably some damn telemarketer."

"Answer it."

Harrison's expression clearly said he thought Cole had lost his mind, but he answered the phone. His finger swiped across the screen, and he lifted the device to his ear. "Yes, hello—"

He stopped. His eyes widened.

Aw, hell.

"Who is this?" Harrison demanded.

Cole surged toward him. "Put it on speaker."

Harrison nodded quickly and put the call on speaker.

"We have Gia Eastman."

"Why?" Harrison asked. His face showed his confusion and shock. "Why the hell would you take her?"

"Because we could. Want her back? Then you'll have to pay."

Cole heard Evie suck in a sharp breath.

Shit. It was looking like his suspicions from a few moments before might have been right. *The kidnappers hadn't been able to get Evie, so they'd taken the next person who was closest to Harrison. The woman who'd once told her friends she was going to marry him.*

"What do you want?" Harrison's voice was low.

"*You.*"

"What?"

"*Want her to live? Then you'll pay us what we want. And we want you. Trade yourself for her or Gia Eastman dies.*"

CHAPTER THIRTEEN

Or...desperate times mean I kick some ass.

"Are they going to kill Gia?" Evie turned as soon as the door closed behind Cole. They'd gone back to her place, and she hadn't been particularly surprised to see the two Wilde agents at her building. One stationed outside, and one on her floor.

The Wilde team seemed to be everywhere.

"She's not going to die." Cole reset her security system. "We're going to get her back."

Because even though her brother had tried to *fire* Cole that morning, he'd also turned around and begged him to help before they'd left his penthouse.

Harrison had staggered after he'd gotten that phone call.

Trade yourself for her or Gia Eastman dies.

After dropping that chilling demand, the caller had then said he'd be contacting Harrison that night. Told Harrison to be ready.

The call had disconnected.

Harrison had asked Cole to get her back. He'd pleaded with Cole to use his connections and return Gia safely.

So now Wilde was on that case, too. Except it wasn't really a different case, was it? More like the same one. Only the kidnappers had turned their attention away from Evie and focused on Gia.

"Will you be able to get her back?" Evie asked softly.

"Wilde will get her back. I've got my buddy James running point. He has connections in this city you wouldn't believe. We will find her."

Evie nodded. Then headed into her bedroom. Dropped her bag. Put her phone on the nightstand. She took a moment to suck in a few deep breaths as she tried to steady herself. The attempt wasn't exactly successful. Evie hurried back into the den, and Cole glanced up at her approach.

Her arms wrapped around her stomach. "I feel helpless."

"Baby..."

"I want to do something. What can I do?"

He strode toward her. Looked as if he wanted to touch her, but he didn't. "You can stay safe, that's what you can do. We're going to find her, and when we do, we'll catch the bastards who took her, too."

"We thought she was a suspect." Shame burned inside of her.

"*I* thought that, you didn't."

Evie looked away. "No, I thought it, too. When I saw her last night in the bathroom, she was just so angry with me. I suspected her, too."

"Wait, she talked to you last night?"

"Well, yes, we were in the ladies' room together." She shrugged. "Women talk in there. It's a thing."

"Evie, what did she say?"

"Just, um, she was surprised that Harrison had let you within five feet of me."

"What?"

"That's what she said. That she was surprised Harrison had let you near me."

His eyes widened. "She knew I was a bodyguard. She knew exactly who I was."

"I don't think so." Evie shook her head. "It was more like she was saying she was surprised Harrison was letting any guy get close to me." But maybe Evie was wrong. Maybe Gia had known who Cole really was.

Cole didn't speak.

"She also told me to give Harrison a message." Which she hadn't done because considering the current situation, the timing had just been way, way not right. "She said he'd been avoiding her. Asked me if I knew why. When I told her no, Gia said there had been a mistake. That everyone made mistakes. Even Harrison."

"Yeah, your brother makes plenty of those. So the fuck do I."

Evie wet her lips. "She told me to remind him that everyone makes mistakes. I didn't tell him, though, because he was hurting enough as it was. I saw the pain in his eyes. He was wrecked because she'd been taken." No matter what was happening between them, Evie hated his pain. "I think he might still love her."

"Guess this is the test for that, isn't it? The ultimate test. If he loves Gia, he trades his life for hers. If he doesn't, then the kidnappers get nothing."

Evie felt an ache in her heart. "That's not the way it should work. In order to prove that you care about someone, you shouldn't have to risk your life." She paced a few feet and turned away as she swallowed down the lump in her throat. "That's not a price anyone should ever have to pay."

"No, it's not." His voice was low and rough. "But it's a price I'd pay for you in an instant."

She whirled back toward him. "*Don't say that.*" Anger churned through her, sharp and hot. "Don't put something like that out there in the universe! Do not ever say—"

"What, Evie?" Cole cut through her words as he walked toward her.

She instinctively backed up, but, dammit, there was a wall behind her. Nowhere for her to go. *Not* that she was running. She wasn't running.

"What don't you want me to say? Is it that you don't want me to say that I'd trade my life for yours, if you were the one who had been taken?"

"*Cole.*"

His hands closed around her shoulders. "Because I would. In an instant. No hesitation. Not ever."

She shook her head. "Don't say..."

Understanding flashed on his face. "Are you afraid to hear the truth?"

No, she wasn't afraid. She was—

"Because I want you to know it. I love you, Evie. I loved you two years ago, and I love you now, and to be quite honest with you, I'm sure I'll love you until the day I die."

Her body jerked in his hold.

"Is that what you didn't want me to say? You didn't want to hear that I love you because you don't love me?" He let her go. Didn't step back. Just stood there, all strong and resolute. "I know you saw the tattoo."

Her heart pounded too fast. Too hard. Too loud. "You...have a lot of tattoos."

"Because I have a lot of fucking scars."

Shock stole her breath. Even though she'd feared...

"Your brother was telling the truth. I did have a mission that went to fucking hell." His jaw clenched. Then, he gritted out, "*Hell.* I lived through it, though. Lived through that sonofabitch slicing me with his knife over and over because he thought he could make me talk. He thought he could break me. He couldn't. Because every single time that blade cut me, I just thought of something else."

She still couldn't draw in a deep breath.

"I thought of you, Evie. I thought of coming back to you. I knew I had to come back. I wanted a second chance. I wanted to tell you I was sorry, and I wanted a shot with you."

But you came back, and Harrison never told me, and I spent too much time being angry and hurt.

"The SOB wanted me to break. I didn't. When I wouldn't talk, he planned to burn me alive. Had this whole big explosion planned. *I* had other plans." Now Cole retreated as he put a few careful feet between them. "I didn't break. *He* broke, though. I made sure of it." His chin lifted. "Right before I killed him and all the other bastards working with him."

A shiver slid over her.

One that his sharp stare caught. "Yes, I'm a monster. You knew that already, didn't you?"

"No."

"Yes." A slow nod. Then, voice low and rough, he added, "But I'm your monster, baby. The big, bad wolf who bows to your command. There is not anything in this world I would not do for you. That's why your brother originally called me back in. He knew that truth. Knew I would protect you with my life. Knew that I would trade my life for yours in an instant."

About five feet separated them. Chill bumps covered her arms.

Cole lifted up *his* arms. Stared at the tattoos. "I was going to be covered by small white scars. Courtesy of that bastard's knife. I didn't want to live that way. I didn't want to carry his marks on me for the rest of my life."

The tattoos were beautiful. Dark and swirling. So many designs. So many—

"So I decided that I'd choose what I carried. I'd choose what the world saw. I picked out every tattoo. And you know what the very first one was?"

She swallowed.

He yanked the T-shirt over his head. Dropped it to the floor.

"Your name," Cole said simply.

She saw the careful cursive lettering over his heart.

"Because *you* marked me, Evie. You took my heart, and for the rest of my life, I knew it would always be yours. I don't love easily. *I'm* the one who doesn't let others get close." A pause. "You were the best thing that ever happened to me, and I wanted something good on me. Not scars from that prick's knife. *Something good.* So I started with your name."

She blinked quickly.

He cursed. "I'm fucking this up. That's a trend I have with you."

He wasn't fucking anything up.

"I don't expect you to love me. I get that I screwed the pooch on that one the first time around. But when this is over, can you give me a second chance?" His hands were tight fists at his sides. "Can we start over? Let the past go and just see what might happen? You know, when I'm not being an asshole and you're not in danger, and we're just two normal people?" His lips twisted. "Though I'm sure Chase would say it's impossible for me to *not* be an asshole, but he doesn't know me like you do."

She was just staring at him.

"Evie?"

She should speak. She should say something. It was just hard. Shock was rather hard to deal with when it came and slapped you across the face. You didn't expect the blow, so you kind of stood there, all stunned.

"I see." A nod. "I...I'm glad I got to tell you how I felt. I promise, I wasn't trying to force you

to take me back. That's not what this was about."
He turned away. "I—"

"Stop." The word burst from her. Angry. Because she *was* still angry. Angry at him. Angry at Harrison. Angry at herself.

Gia was missing. The nightmare was wrapping tighter and tighter around them. And Cole—Cole was telling Evie that he loved her.

"You spoke. Now it's my turn." She had the damn metaphorical talking stick.

He squared his shoulders and slowly angled toward her. "Fair enough." He waited. His expression told her that he didn't expect to hear any good news from her.

"Your timing is horrible."

He nodded. "Yes, I, uh, get that."

"A woman was kidnapped. Bad guys are lurking everywhere I turn, and you decide—*now*—to tell me that you love me."

Another nod. "I can see where this might not be the optimum moment."

Her eyebrows lifted. "You can? Not optimum?"

He tensed.

"You know what else isn't optimum?" Evie pushed. "You dying for me. That's not optimum." She took one hard step forward.

"I—"

"You standing there, telling me that some crazy psycho cut you over and over again— tortured you—and I didn't know. That's not optimum." Another hard step.

"There was no point in telling you. You would have only felt sorry for me. Pitied—"

"I feel many things for you, Cole. Be certain of that. But I have never pitied you." Is that what he thought? That she would stare at him in pity? "I can hurt for you, I can want to hurt the bastard who injured you, but I don't pity you." *I hate that you were in pain and that I wasn't there.*

He looked down at the floor. "You weren't the only one to wake up yelling from nightmares. When I did, I called your name."

She stiffened. "*Not optimum.*"

His head snapped up.

"It's not optimum that I hear about this now." A third step. She'd almost closed all the distance between them. "Now, when everything is still crazy. When we have to catch the bad guys. When my brother is about to risk his life. It's not *optimum* that I hear all of this *now.*"

"Sorry." Cole cleared his throat. "If we catch the perps tonight, I thought you might want me out of your life. Seemed like I needed to tell you all of this while I had the chance."

Her eyes narrowed to slits. "You put my name on your heart."

A shrug. "Seemed to make sense. Considering you own it."

Her lower lip was trembling—a stupid quiver—so she pressed her lips together. She counted to five. Then ten. The counting trick didn't work. She still wasn't calm. "What did you think I would do?"

His head tilted. "What do you *want* to do?"

She wasn't going to tell him. But she'd show him. What did she want?

Simple.

Evie bounded forward and closed the last bit of distance between them. She grabbed Cole's head and yanked him toward her. Her mouth crashed into his as she kissed him with a wild, insane fury of need because that was exactly how she felt—crazy. Wild. Desperate. A million things.

Her right hand slid down to his chest. She put her fingers over his heart and felt that frantic beat. So powerful and strong. And hers.

He belonged to her. He had, all this time.

Only fair, really, considering that she belonged to him, too. "I want you," she said against his lips. "I want you right now. I don't give a damn if this is optimum or not. *I want you.*"

He kissed her, driving his tongue deep and making her whole body ache. She loved the way he kissed her. The intensity. The need. The hunger. Like he was frantic for her. Good, she was frantic for him, too.

And there was no way—no way—that she would give him up.

He lifted her, swinging Evie into his arms, and he held her with that easy strength of his. A strength that had always made her feel safe. A monster? No way, no day. To her, he was the hero of the story. If someone said differently, she'd just have to kick that person's ass.

He carried her back to the bedroom. Lowered her onto the bed. Kept kissing her. She kept kissing him, too. Sucking his lower lip. Making him growl. Dipping her tongue into his mouth.

"Don't tease, baby," he rumbled.

Oh, she wasn't teasing. Not by a long shot.

He tried to push her flat down on the bed. She twisted, spun her body, and pushed *him* down.

He bounced on the mattress. Stared up at her. Started to smile.

She crawled on top of him.

His smile froze. "Evie?"

"Don't worry. I don't intend to tease." Her fingers trailed down his chest, over the beautiful ink that would always make her heart ache. *I determine what marks me.* "I just intend to drive us both crazy." Her fingers unhooked the top of his jeans. Slid down the zipper.

"Fuck." He grabbed for the covers and fisted them.

She nodded even as she stared at her prize. "Absolutely. We will fuck so hard. But first, I get to do something else." She pumped the length of his cock. Long and hard and so thick. Evie licked her lower lip. "Didn't get the chance to do this before..."

"I will *not* last if you put your mouth on me."

Her gaze rose. Caught his. "I have faith in you."

His pupils flared.

"I pretty much think you can do just about anything. Even hold on to that control of yours while I put my mouth on you."

He growled again. She loved his rough, ragged growl.

"Let's see, shall we?" Her head lowered. She blew a light, easy stream of air over his cock and it jerked hard in her hold. She was smiling right before she licked him.

Then she stopped smiling. She just started feeling.

Her lips parted wide and she sucked his cock into her mouth. Her cheeks hollowed as she worked him. Her hand was still curled around the base of his dick as she pumped him in and out of her mouth.

She felt herself getting wet. *Wetter.* Every lick and suck made her want him all the more. His hips surged up against her mouth, and she took more of him inside. Even more. Her head slid forward, bobbing, then retreating, and her tongue snaked over the head of his erection as she tasted the saltiness that made her moan.

"Enough!"

No. It wasn't enough. She'd like plenty more, thank you very much. But he'd hauled her up. Trapped her beneath him on the bed. And now his mouth was between *her* legs. He wasn't being hesitant or slow. He was devouring her. Lashing at her with his tongue and thrusting his fingers into her. Licking her clit over and over again.

Her hips surged up against him. Her orgasm was so close and—

"No, baby, I have faith in you."

Her eyes flew open.

He licked his lips and smiled, as if he were savoring her taste. Why did that turn her on even more? A shudder slid over her.

"I have faith." He grabbed a condom from her nightstand. When in the hell had condoms been placed in her nightstand? She sure hadn't kept any stocked. "I have faith...that you won't come, not until I am balls deep in you."

"Then you'd better hurry," she whispered back. "Because I'm ready *now*."

He sank into her. Caught her hands with his. Threaded their fingers together and pushed them back against the pillows. Her head shoved back against the pillows, too, as she tipped up her chin and moaned his name. He filled her completely. Stretched her deliciously.

And she wanted more.

She wanted forever.

He withdrew, then slammed back deep. Her legs locked around him, and she heaved up, matching him thrust for thrust. He kissed her. Sucked her lower lip. She moaned his name. The bed surged beneath them. His hold tightened on her hands.

Evie could feel her orgasm growing. Building. Their bodies moved faster. The thrusts grew more frantic. Primitive and hard.

"I love it when you come," he rasped.

Yes, she pretty much loved it, too, and—*she was coming*. Pleasure blasted through every cell in her body as she stiffened beneath him. The waves rolled through her, stealing her breath and making her eyes squeeze shut.

He came with her. Surged deep and shuddered. He roared her name and drove his hips against her.

Her sex kept squeezing him. Hard, tight aftershocks of release pulsed through her. She didn't want the moment to end. If she had her way, they'd stay exactly like this. They wouldn't move. They'd be together. Everything would be perfect.

But...

The world wasn't perfect. She'd learned that long ago.

And you couldn't just hide from the bad things out there.

Evie slowly lifted her lashes. She caught him staring down at her, and in that one moment, his expression was unguarded. So tender. Filled with so much love.

He loves me. It wasn't some smooth line. Cole wasn't really the type for smooth lines. He truly loved her.

He bent his head and pressed a soft kiss to her lips. "How's your throat?"

How was what? Oh, right, her throat.

He withdrew. Reluctantly, Evie lowered her legs back to the bed. He eased away from her as he rolled to the side of the mattress and sat up. When she didn't answer his question, though, his head swung back to her. "Evie?"

"I forgot it was even injured." She was sure she could take off the bandage. It had barely been a wound at all. So small. Her little injury hardly seemed important.

Cole was cut. Over and over again. And he'd said that he woke from nightmares, crying out for her. "I'm sorry I wasn't there."

His brow furrowed.

"When you called for me," she added. "I'll be there next time." Because next time, nothing was going to keep her from him. Nothing. No one.

He smiled at her, and the smile was warm and slow, and it made her smile back at him. Despite what was happening, she felt happy.

"Hold that thought." He leaned forward and pressed his lips to hers. "I'll be right back."

He probably needed to ditch the condom. *Check.* She watched him walk away, admired the view, and called, "You'll have to tell me how condoms wound up in my nightstand. I'm super appreciative, but...also, assume much?"

He froze at the bathroom door. "I thought you put them in there." His shoulders stiffened.

"Nope." She hadn't exactly had time for a condom run.

"Chase," he groaned.

Her eyebrows climbed. "Chase?"

"I'm sure the dumbass thought he was being helpful."

She considered things. He *had* been helpful. And all up in their business. But helpful. So, ah— her phone rang, distracting her. It vibrated on her night stand. She grabbed it and automatically checked the screen. "It's Leo." Evie winced. Oh, crap. She knew he'd been somewhere in the crush of people at the charity gala, but she hadn't talked to him. He was always a social butterfly at those things. He thrived on attention while she tended to wilt.

She was sure he'd heard the story of her abduction. "I should talk to him." Leo in panic mode wouldn't be good.

Cole nodded before he headed into the bathroom.

Evie put the phone to her ear. "Leo, I'm fine. I promise."

"What in the hell happened? I heard you were kidnapped!"

She winced. "I'm sorry. I should have called you."

"Damn straight you should have called me! I think I lost five years of my life worrying about you!"

"I'm okay. I was taken last night, but Cole tracked me. I'm good."

Silence.

"Uh, Leo?" He was *never* silent.

"He saved the day, huh? Good old hero."

He didn't sound excited—or impressed. Her shoulders stiffened even as she yanked up the covers. Suddenly, being naked didn't feel so awesome. "He did save me."

"I read in the news that he shot the guy who'd taken you. Your Cole *killed* him."

"The man was going to kill me."

His shuddering breath filled her ear. "Evie...I was starting to be team Cole, too, but I've been told some things..."

Everyone always gave Leo the best gossip. And, sometimes, the worst. "You know you can't believe everything you hear."

"I'm worried about you," he added.

Some of the stiffness eased from her shoulders. "I'm okay. Really. I'm safe. Cole is here."

As if on cue, Cole walked out of the bathroom. Stood in the doorway.

"Here...as in...he's there right now?"

Why did Leo sound so worried?

"Yes, he's here now."

"Evie, do not tell him what I say next."

What?

"*You're in danger, Evie.*"

Well, yes, she knew that. Thus the protection detail from Cole and the other Wilde agents—

"*He's* dangerous."

Now her shoulders were tense again. "You don't know him. He would never hurt me." *And I don't know who has been giving you this gossip but—*

"Shit, shit! Can he hear you?"

He could. Cole was frowning at her.

"*Do not tell him what I'm saying! Did I stutter on that line before?*"

Leo sounded desperate. He wasn't the desperate type.

"I got information last night at the gala. Cole has been stalking you."

What?

"For at least a year. Maybe longer." His voice was hushed. "He was recognized at the charity gala. He's been coming to your shows. He's been watching you from a distance. And, word is, he swore to do *anything* necessary to get you back."

Her skin felt cold. No, icy. "I don't understand."

"We need to meet," Leo told her flatly. "I have to talk to you about this in person. *Without* Cole watching everything that you say or do."

Cole was watching her right then. He'd pulled on a pair of jeans, and a faint line cut between his eyebrows as he frowned at her.

"You were misinformed," she told Leo carefully. "I appreciate your concern, but you're wrong—"

"Robert Demakis isn't the type of guy to be misinformed," Leo threw back as his voice hardened with intensity and worry. "I've worked with him plenty before. Robert is one of those tells-you-like-it-is types. He said he recognized Cole because Robert had seen him at a few of the shows you worked on. Robert was certain of it, and he was worried about you. *I'm* worried about you."

Her hold tightened on the phone.

"We need to meet," Leo said again, voice urgent. "Robert even has proof, if you want to see it. He has photos that some paparazzi took when you were doing a show last December. He can show them to you."

"I have to go now, Leo." *Go straight to the source.*

"But—"

"I'm good. I'm safe. I promise." She hung up. Evie sat there a moment, still holding the phone and with the covers still tucked under her arms.

The silence in her bedroom seemed far too heavy.

"Your friend is worried about you."

She nodded. *Okay, just say it. Blurt it out.* "It's...a little more than that." She put the phone down on the covers and tipped her head back so that she could meet Cole's bright gaze. "It's crazy, really, but..."

He waited.

It seemed almost silly to say because this was Cole. "You haven't been stalking me, have you?"

CHAPTER FOURTEEN

I am so screwed.

Cole didn't even blink when Evie asked her breathless, nervous question.

He also didn't reply.

She laughed. The sound was high and, just like the question, nervous. "I know, it's ridiculous." She rose from the bed and pulled a sheet with her, wrapping it around her delectable body all toga-style. "But Leo was told that you had been stalking me for, like, the last year." She shook her head, sending her blond locks sliding over her cheeks. "Which is absolutely ridiculous because you've been working for Wilde and they are based down in—"

"Atlanta."

A nod from her. "Right. Atlanta. Not like you were flying back and forth to see me."

But he *had* worked cases in New York. Plenty of them. "Where did Leo get his intel?"

She nibbled on her lower lip. Of course, that small movement drew his attention right to her mouth and made him remember all of the amazing things that she could do with her lips and tongue.

Dammit, dumbass, focus.

"Where?" That question came out too rough. Cole tried again as he cleared his throat. "Sorry, um, where did Leo hear that story?"

She pushed back her hair. "From one of our chief suspects. Can you believe that?"

"No." Yes. Dammit.

"Robert Demakis told him. Robert said that he'd seen you at some of the shows I choreographed. That he even had proof if I wanted to see it." She advanced toward him, and the back of the sheet trailed behind her like the train of a wedding dress. It slithered ever so softly over the floor. "Some paparazzi photo that was supposedly taken last December."

"Last December, huh?"

"Yes." She stopped in front of him. Stared up at him.

Cole swallowed.

Her right hand lifted and slid over his cheek. His stubble probably felt like freaking sand paper to her, and he made a mental note to shave ASAP. When he had his face buried between her legs, he didn't want to scrape her.

"I don't believe the story." She smiled at him. "But I figured I'd go straight to the source so you'd know what was being said."

His chest squeezed. "You trust me."

"Well, of course." She offered him a sunny smile. "I love you. Can't very well love you without trusting you. That would just be weird."

I love you.

She brushed around him and maneuvered for the bathroom.

"*Stop.*" His voice was hoarse. Ragged.

She paused. Glanced back with a raised brow. Only mild curiosity showed on her face.

"You said you loved me." He needed to confirm her statement in case he'd had some crazy-ass auditory hallucination.

She nodded.

No auditory hallucination.

"And you...trust me."

Another nod.

"*How?*" It was hard to breathe. Much less talk. "Before, you didn't say—"

She huffed at him. "Really, Cole. Don't you know me better than that?"

He...maybe?

"Did you think I'd have wild, incredible, screaming sex with you if I didn't love you?"

Well, a guy could certainly hope but—

"Did you think I'd be able to let myself go that completely, if I didn't love you?"

Again, he'd been hoping, but she hadn't said—

Evie turned fully toward him. "Did you think I would have ever let you back in my life if I didn't still have feelings for you?"

His chest burned. The ache centered right beneath the tattoo of her name.

"There are other bodyguards," she told him softly. "But there is only one you."

"And there's only one Evie." *My Evie.*

"We can't control how we feel. The minute I saw you again, I knew that I was going to be in trouble. I could either slam the door in your face..."

"Sweetheart, you *did* do that." Had she forgotten?

Her smile made the ache in his chest grow even more. "You deserved it."

Okay, yes. Guilty.

"But then I opened the door again." A wave of her hand. "Literally. Figuratively. Whatever you want to call it, I did it."

His hands were clenching and releasing. Over and over again. He was fighting the urge to grab her and not let go. Not ever.

"I knew when I opened the door again that one of two things could happen."

He shouldn't ask. He should take the miracle he'd been given and run with it. But he sucked so he asked, "What two things?"

"One, you'd break my heart all over again. But I figured I survived it once. I could do it again. Sometimes, pain is worth the ride, know what I mean?"

"I never want you in any pain."

Her lashes lowered to hide her gaze. "Or the other thing could happen."

His hands clenched. Released. "What other thing?"

"This time, you'd fall helplessly in love with me, too, and we'd stay together. We'd try to make things work."

"I am helplessly in love with you."

Her lashes lifted.

"Helplessly and completely."

She smiled at him. God, did the woman get that she owned him with her smiles?

She dropped the sheet.

Fuck. *She dropped the sheet.*

"I need to shower. I'm dirty."

Fuck, fuck, fuck.

"Or, I'd like to be dirty," she murmured, "if you want to join me?"

He nodded quickly. "I will be right there."

She turned and took her time strolling into the bathroom. He took his time admiring her ass. But as soon as the bathroom door closed...

Cole yanked out his phone. He marched into the den and shoved that phone up to his ear. It rang once. Twice.

Come on, Chase. Pick up the freaking phone.

"Yo." Chase's low voice. "Missing me already?"

"I want eyes on Robert Demakis."

"Dude, what the hell? Are you psychic?"

"What's that supposed to mean?"

"I was just about to call you regarding Demakis. The Wilde techs got hold of video footage from Gia's place. Wanna guess who paid her a visit in the middle of the night? By middle of the night, I mean three a.m.?"

"You are shitting me."

"I shit you not," Chase assured him. "And rumor is—well, the rumor that I just pried out of Gia's very friendly neighbor Martha—Robert and Gia liked to meet up, quite often, in the middle of the night. The affair seems to have been going on for months."

Tension knotted at the base of his skull. "I want to talk to Robert Demakis."

"Yep, thought you might."

"But I don't want Evie near the guy. I don't trust him close to her." A pause. "Let's get James. Have him stay with her, then you and I can interrogate Demakis." His gaze lifted to the framed artwork in front of him. He swallowed as he stared at the careful strokes that formed the lighthouse. "Get him over here as fast as you can."

"On it."

Cole kept the phone to his ear. His gaze stayed on that lighthouse.

"I told you..." Evie's voice came from behind him. "My ex-boyfriend did the art."

He slapped the phone down on a nearby table and spun toward her. She stood in the doorway, a robe covering up her body, and one shoulder propped up against the wooden door frame.

How long had she been there? How much had she heard?

Was he losing his freaking edge? He should have been aware of her approach. But...

I was furious at Demakis.

And...*I was trying to cover my ass before Evie found out too much.*

Cole squared his shoulders. "The artwork is shit."

Her lips curled. "I think it's quite good."

"Your ex is an ass."

"Yes. You are."

He licked his lips and cast a glance toward the series of lighthouses. "Did you know they were mine...when you bought them?" When he'd walked into her place the first time and seen those paintings, he'd been floored.

And desperately hopeful. If she had the paintings, if she knew they were his, then—

"At first, no, I didn't. My friend Piper has a gallery in Atlanta, and she brought one of them up here when she did a show a while back. I fell in love with the piece and asked her if she had more."

His breath eased in and out. He looked down at the tattoos on his arms. Designs that he'd made. In another life, he'd loved art. But he'd had a choice to make, and he'd joined Delta Force. Battles had been his business. Until...

Until they weren't.

Until he'd found himself with a hole where his soul had once been, and Piper—who happened to be the wife of his boss, Eric Wilde—had suggested that he try painting. She'd said it could be therapeutic for him.

So he'd started doing damn lighthouses. The shelter in the storm.

And he'd thought about Evie.

"If you knew Piper, then you...you knew about Wilde before I arrived on your doorstep."

"Piper kept her maiden name for a while. Still uses it sometimes, and we aren't exactly super close friends. Not like I was invited to her wedding and met the Wilde team or anything." A faint shrug. "The name Wilde was familiar to me, though, and when you mentioned Eric Wilde, it just took me a few moments to put everything together in my head."

She'd bought his art and put it on her walls.

"The paintings were just signed with a V."

"V for Vincent," Cole muttered.

"I figured that out. Right around the same time that I realized you were the artist."

His hands were doing that clenching and releasing thing again. They did that every time he wanted to hold her. Which was a lot. "How?"

She pushed away from the door frame. "I went to Piper's gallery in Atlanta one day. I was speaking at a theater conference, presenting a workshop on choreography for kids, and when I swung by the gallery, I saw you."

He swallowed. *Piper didn't tell me!* But then, he'd never told Piper about Evie, either.

"You were dropping off a piece to Piper. I bought the piece right after you left."

"But you...you were there, Evie." He closed the distance between them. Stared down at her. "Why didn't you say anything to me?"

"I didn't think you wanted to see me. And how sad did it seem that your ex was buying your art? Talk about stalker-like."

"*No.*" The word came out as a snarl. He immediately tried to soften his voice. "That's not what you are. It's not what you ever could be. I did that art for you. You didn't know it, but it was always you. *You* are my shelter when the world is shit. You are the light I look for to get me through the dark."

Her eyes widened. "You paint..." she whispered. "And I think you were just poetic, too. Be careful, Cole, or I'll start to suspect that you're the romantic type."

"I'm any fucking type you want me to be."

Her smile came again. "You're the type that I *thought* would be joining me in the shower."

God, he wanted that. But..."James is coming over."

Her eyes widened. "When?"

"Probably...hell, fifteen minutes?"

She nodded. "That gives us time."

His heart slammed into his chest. "Don't tease."

She reached for his hand. "Wouldn't dream of it."

***

Cole yanked open the front door.

James blinked at him. "Well, hello, sunshine."

Cole glowered at him.

James winked. "Did I get here fast or what?"'

"You could have taken a bit longer. Wouldn't have killed you."

James cocked his head. "Your neck is red."

"Is it?"

"Your hair looks like you just stepped out of a hurricane."

Evie liked to run her hands through his hair. "Thanks for the fashion tip."

"You're flushed."

"Are you just making a list of insults right now?"

"Your breathing is labored."

"Because I'm having to put up with *you*."

James's gaze darted over Cole's shoulder. "Where is Evie?"

"Showering." Truth. They hadn't exactly gotten to the shower together part of the agenda. Mostly because when she'd told him that they had time, he'd pretty much instantly fucked her, and it had been *amazing*. He coughed. "She'll be right out." He'd hauled on his clothes seconds before James had pounded at the door. Because James had arrived within *ten minutes*. Not fifteen.

Cole backed up so that James could enter Evie's place. Then he shut and secured the door, and Cole checked his weapon.

"Chase is waiting downstairs," James informed him. "You two think this Demakis guy could be behind Gia's abduction?"

He tucked the gun in his waistband. "I think he's a problem." One that Cole would fix.

A nod. "Our tech agents still monitoring Harrison's phone lines?"

"Yeah, but there's been no call yet."

The bedroom door opened. His head swung toward it, and he saw Evie. Wet hair combed back. Face scrubbed clean. Skin gleaming. She wore faded jeans that hugged her legs, a loose top, and her black ballerina flats.

So fucking beautiful.

James cleared his throat. "Hate to tell you about your business, man, but you just stared at her for one solid minute without saying a word."

He had not.

Wait, had he?

Dammit. "Evie, this is James." He motioned toward the guy who was often his partner at Wilde. "He can be a dick, but he's also one of the deadliest bastards I've ever met."

Her eyes swept assessingly over James. "Is that...a good thing?"

Cole strode toward her. "Under these circumstances, it's the absolute best thing in the world." He caught her hand in his. Squeezed it. "He'll keep you safe. No one is going to get past James."

Her gaze searched his. "Why can't I come with you? I'd like to question Robert, too. And I know him. I can read him better than you can."

She *had* overheard part of his conversation with Chase. "It's not safe, baby. He could have fed that intel to Leo hoping to draw you out. Until the situation is contained, I have to keep you covered." He squeezed her hand. "Your safety matters most to me." Nothing was more important than her staying safe. *Alive.* "I'll be back before you know it." He leaned forward and brushed his lips over hers.

Cole turned away from Evie and headed for the door. He inclined his head toward James. "Guard her with your life."

"You know I will," James promised.

***

It was way too quiet.

James had shut the door and turned the alarm on right after Cole vanished. Now he was studying her in silence. His gaze swept over her slowly, and he looked oddly pleased with himself, as if he'd just solved some kind of puzzle.

"Um..." She cleared her throat. "So, were you Delta Force, like Cole? Former military, then you joined Wilde?"

He burst out laughing. "Oh, dear Lord, no." A pause. "I was an assassin."

Her lips parted. She couldn't quite manage a response. Was there a polite response to a statement like that? *Good for you* didn't seem appropriate.

He smiled at her. "So don't worry. If any perps try to get you, I'll stop them. I'm very, very good at killing."

"That is..." She choked down the lump that had risen in her throat. "Great to know. Thanks so much."

"Does that make you feel better?"

"Is it supposed to?"

He shrugged. "Figured it couldn't make you feel worse."

Fabulous.

***

"You can't barge in here!" The assistant—a young guy with lots of hair gel and a pressed suit—shoved his hand against Cole's chest. "Mr. Demakis has a meeting scheduled soon, and you cannot just burst in and—"

"It's okay, Clyde." Robert Demakis rose from his desk. He tapped his white ear piece and seemingly ended a call as he stood. "I can handle them."

Chase smiled. "Thanks, Clyde. You go have a nice day."

Clyde glared, but hurried from the office.

Robert surveyed first Cole, then Chase. "Hello, gentlemen. I'd like to pretend that I'm surprised to see you, but...I'm not. After last night's events, I figured you'd be paying me a visit." He lifted his hands and held them, palms out, in front of his body. "But let me begin by saying I had absolutely nothing to do with Evie's abduction. I consider her a friend, and I would never do anything to hurt her."

Chase and Cole exchanged a long look.

"Good to know," Cole assured him as he focused back on Robert. "But what about Gia Eastman?"

"Yes," Chase pushed. "Is she a friend, too?"

"Gia? Why, yes, she is." Robert lowered his hands.

Chase nodded. "A friend with benefits? Is that what you'd call it?"

Robert's cheeks puffed out. "I don't know what—"

Chase slapped a large, brown envelope onto Robert's desk. "Security photos from last night. You paid Gia Eastman a visit around three a.m."

Robert didn't look down at the photos. Instead, his stare burned into Cole. "Do you want me to produce photos, too? Is it show and tell time already?"

Cole didn't respond to the taunt. Not so much as a flicker of his expression.

But he felt Chase's gaze sweep his way. "Am I missing something?" Chase wanted to know.

"The only thing that's missing is Gia Eastman," Cole responded flatly as he kept his gaze glued to Robert Demakis. "So why don't we stop the games? Tell us where she is."

Surprise had Robert's eyes flaring. "Gia is missing?"

"Yes, and seeing as how you were with her in the middle of the night, you can see why you look suspicious as all hell."

"But I didn't do anything to her!"

Cole was so not in the mood for BS. "*Where is Gia Eastman?*"

CHAPTER FIFTEEN

There are things I wish Evie would never know.
Sometimes, not knowing is better. Easier, right?
Dammit. I'm screwed.

"Gia was fine when I left her." But sweat beaded Robert's brow. "Look, she was shaken up by what happened to Evie. She didn't want to be alone. Cops were questioning us like we were suspects!"

"That would be because we pointed the cops your way," Chase offered, ever helpful. "Due to the fact that you and Gia happened to be at the top of our suspect list."

Robert's jaw dropped. "What?"

"Someone is after Evie again. Obviously." Cole didn't let any emotion enter his voice or show on his face. "You've worked with Evie."

"Well, yes, sure, but—"

"You let her think you were her friend."

"I *am* her friend—"

"Only you never mentioned to Evie that her step-father bankrupted your parents."

Robert blew out a long breath. "What would have been the point?" His shoulders sagged. "You know Evie," he mumbled. "Her heart is too freaking big. On the sets, I've seen her sit and hold the hand of an actress who's getting hit with stage fright. I've seen her stay and rehearse for hours and hours—extra time, nothing she's getting compensated for—just because she had a dancer who was afraid she didn't have the steps down. I've seen her take freaking soup to sick stage hands. Evie tries to help everyone."

Yeah, I know Evie.

"If I'd told her about my parents, she would have felt guilty." Robert's gaze lifted. "She had nothing to feel guilty about. Evie wasn't involved in that mess. Was her step-father a creep? A cold-blooded bastard? Hell, yes. He ran shady deals all the time, and my dad fell for his lies. *That didn't involve Evie.* She was sixteen when that mess went down."

The guy seemed truthful enough, but Cole knew appearances could lie. "You're not angry at Evie, but what about her step-brother? How do you feel about Harrison?"

"He can be a dick, too, but he can also surprise you sometimes," Robert admitted the last part grudgingly. "Who do you think gave me the money I needed to open my first show?"

Okay, now this was surprising. "When we investigated, we didn't learn that."

"Well, yes, because Harrison didn't want anyone to know. He came to me, said he'd learned what happened to my parents, and he wanted to make amends. The money was supposed to be untraceable—he worked some kind of magic with that, don't know if he set up a fake corporation or whatever the hell he did—but he gave me what I needed. He set me up to succeed. And he never asked for a dime back."

Interesting.

"So I don't have a reason to hate Evie or her brother." Now Robert's shoulders rolled back. Straightened. He focused on Cole with grim determination. "In fact, it's quite the opposite. I want to protect them from people who might try to hurt them. People like you, Cole Vincent."

"Uh, yeah, buddy," Chase interrupted. "You've got this all wrong. He's her bodyguard. He's not here to hurt her—"

Robert reached into his desk drawer.

Cole tensed. If that guy went for a weapon—

Instead, Robert tossed photos onto the desk. Big, glossy color photos. Of Cole.

And Evie.

"My turn for show and tell," Robert announced as his hands went to his hips. "From what Leopold told me, you *just* started working as Evie's bodyguard. So why in the hell were you tailing her for the last year? Just how obsessed with Evie are you?"

Cole reached for one of the photographs. The photo was a close-up of Evie as she laughed with a man in a black suit. And in the background...

I'm there. Watching her.

"Are you so obsessed..." Robert continued doggedly. "That you were willing to do anything to get back in her life?"

"Dude, I don't like the tone," Chase snapped. But he poked at the photos.

Robert ignored him. He pointed at Cole. "Were you so obsessed that you faked attacks on Evie so that you could get back in her life? Just so she would need you again?"

***

"I don't trust that guy as far as I can throw him." Chase lifted his hand and pretended to heave a football. "And I was a player back in the day. You should have seen my arm..."

Cole's gaze swept the perimeter as they left Robert's office.

"Uh, Cole? You with me? You didn't buy his lines, did you?"

"The photos were real."

"Well, sure, because you're a lovesick jackass."

Cole's head snapped toward him.

Chase shrugged. "You think I didn't know about the side trips up here? Hell, James was the one who first tipped me off on them. Said you were moony-eyed over your ex."

"I am not *mooney-eyed*." Seriously?

"Huh."

"Do not pull that 'huh' shit on me—"

"You're not mooney-eyed now because you have her back, but you were. I mean, you were obviously hung up on her. When we hit the bars in Atlanta, you never flirted with anyone. You mostly just glared at any poor woman who came too close. Then you get around Evie, and you start lighting up like a Christmas tree."

He stalked away from his friend and hurried for the elevator. "I am not a damn Christmas tree."

"Sure you are." Chase entered the elevator with him and stabbed the button for the ground floor. "But I've got to say, one thing about that meeting really bothered me."

Only *one* thing?

"Was it me or did the guy not seem to give a shit that Gia Eastman is missing? Just said she was fine when he left her, but Robert barely had any interest beyond that. He immediately changed the topic to Evie." He rubbed his chin as the elevator descended. "Now, call me crazy..."

"Because you can be," Cole agreed.

"But if I find out my fuck buddy is missing—"

"Jesus, man, you *don't* call them that—"

"Fine, if I find out that my late night hook up, booty call, sexy party partner—whatever—is missing, then I don't just immediately turn the conversation to another woman." His words were mocking, but his gaze had gone flat and cold. "I demand answers. I ask as many questions as I can. I try to help."

Robert hadn't done any of those things. "He knew more than he was saying."

"He's not worried about Gia. Not even a little." A pause. "Why?"

Excellent question. The elevator doors opened when they reached the ground floor. They walked out—and Cole almost walked right into Stephen Lowe.

"This is sure one hell of a coincidence," Cole muttered. "What are you doing here?"

Stephen blinked a few times. "I-I have an appointment with Robert Demakis."

Cole lifted his eyebrows.

"I have to tell him that I can't help sponsor his new show. Not exactly cash fluid right now." He surged past Cole and threw out his hand. "I need that elevator!"

Cole and Chase watched him hurtle into the elevator.

"Huh," Chase said.

"Fucking exactly," Cole agreed.

***

"We think we know where Gia Eastman is."

Evie leapt to her feet when Cole came in and made that announcement. She'd been trying to make exceedingly awkward conversation with the guy who claimed to be an *assassin*... conversation that went like...

"So...you kill lots of people?"

"Um..."

"So...you, ah, do anything for fun?"

He'd stared at her.

Then winked.

Now though, Cole had returned, and she focused totally on him. "Did the kidnappers make contact?"

"No, but Gia's cell phone turned on for a bit, and Wilde was able to track her location. We've got it triangulated down to a small sector of town, and we're going to do a perimeter check until we find her." A brisk nod. "Chase and I are going in with a team. We'll get her back."

She remembered being trapped in the closet. Hoping desperately for some sort of rescue.

Gia had to be feeling the same way.

"We'll have two Wilde members stay with you. A guard is downstairs, and another is going to tag out with Ghost—um, James here."

Ghost?

"James is very good at getting in places undetected," Cole added. "Since we don't know what might be waiting on us, we need every advantage we can get."

Absolutely. She understood that.

James and Chase huddled together.

Cole closed in on her. He stared down at her, and there were so many emotions swirling in his bright gaze. "We need to talk," Cole told her softly. "Put everything on the table."

"I thought we already did that." He'd said he loved her. She'd said she loved him. They were going forward.

"No secrets," he murmured. "Because they will just come back to bite us in the ass."

She didn't particularly want anything biting her in the ass. "I don't have any secrets from you."

"When I get back, I'll tell you everything."

Does that mean you're keeping secrets from me? Now her stomach twisted. "Why does this sound so bad?"

His lips thinned.

Oh. Because it is bad.

"Your brother is on his way over. I briefed him. I didn't want to go with the retrieval team. I wanted to stay with you while the others went after Gia, but Harrison begged me to—"

"No," she cut through, adamant. "You go with the team." Because, yes, the others were good. Absolutely. *But I trust Cole.* "You get her back. Then you come home to me."

His eyes glittered. "I don't want you unprotected."

"You're putting two guards on me, *and* my brother is on his way over." A pause. "Don't forget, I can also protect myself. Besides, I won't be leaving this building until you get back. No one is going to get me."

"They'd fucking better not." He turned away.

She grabbed his arm and hauled him right back toward her. "No one had better hurt *you*, either." Evie yanked his head toward her and planted an open-mouthed, passionate kiss on him. The kind of kiss that made her want to hold tight to him and never let go.

But I have to let go. Only for now. Just now.

"You stay safe," she commanded against his mouth. "Don't you dare come back with so much as a scratch on you."

He eased back and nodded. "I'll have those perps tossed in a cell before you know it. They won't threaten you or anyone else again."

She tried to smile for him. Worried it was a very feeble effort. *Stay safe, Cole. Stay safe.*

"Then I will be back. I'll tell you everything, and maybe you'll let me stay."

What?

But he was striding for the door. When he opened it, another Wilde agent hurried inside. Cole made the introductions.

Harvey Radcliff. A tall, athletic man who wore faded jeans and a pale blue T-shirt. He inclined his head toward her. Stood all easy and confident with an I-can-kick-ass air about him.

Then the others were leaving. She watched them go as the knots in her stomach just got worse and worse.

When it was only her and Harvey, Evie released the breath she'd been holding. The silence seemed suffocating. "You're not a former assassin, are you?"

A ghost of a smile teased his full lips. A half-smile, not a full one. "No, ma'am," he assured her as the faintest drawl slid beneath his words, warming them. His ebony gaze held hers. "But I was a SEAL and DEA, so I've certainly seen my share of action. Don't claim to be perfect, not by a long shot, but you can count on me."

She took his measure. The carefully cropped dark hair. The casual readiness of his body. The easy strength of his build. The steadiness of his gaze.

Some of the tension eased from her. "Can I get you a coffee, Harvey?" She turned from him.

"Not much of a coffee drinker, but I could kill for some hot chocolate."

She swung back around.

He flashed her his half-smile. "Too soon? Sorry. Since you'd just been spending time with Ghost, I couldn't resist."

Ghost. That name again. She needed to get the story behind it. "You're going to be trouble, aren't you?"

"The best kind."

***

"Your typical no-tell motel," Cole said. They were on the edge of town. Far away from the pulsing energy of the big city. Tourists wouldn't usually stumble this way. Not if they were smart.

He peered through binoculars to get the lay of the land. Two cars in the parking lot. Business was not exactly booming.

"Talked to the clerk inside," Chase said as he sidled next to Cole. "A woman paid cash for room one-oh-six first thing this morning. He hasn't seen her since then."

Hello, room one-oh-six.

"He can't say if anyone else was with her, mostly because the guy was as high as a freaking kite and I'm lucky I got the info that I did."

Cole lowered his binoculars. Nodded as he considered things. "You and I will go in the front door." He inclined his head toward Chase. "We'll go in hard and fast and armed."

They weren't alerting the cops because the caller had been very specific. *Cops will get Gia killed.*

Besides, his team could handle things on their own. It was what they did.

"You go in the back," Cole directed James. There wouldn't exactly be a back door at a place like that, but they'd done a full area search and realized that each room had a bathroom—with a window. Breaking the lock on the window and getting in would be child's play for James.

Before they could move, though, Cole's phone vibrated. He hauled out the phone and looked down at the text from Harrison.

Just got another call. Was Gia. She begged for me to meet her at the Fiesta Motel. I'm on my—

Cole sent back his text. *We are in position outside the Fiesta Motel right now. Told you—we have this. Go to Evie. Will contact you when Gia is safe.*

He shoved the phone into his pocket. Pulled out his weapon.

"We take the perps down," Cole told his team. "We end this."

The other two men nodded.

No one was going to threaten Evie again. This was ending.

Silently, they attacked. They flew across the parking lot, sticking to the shadows. James disappeared behind the motel. Cole and Chase headed for the door of room one-oh-six. Cole paused only a moment before he motioned with his hand.

Chase nodded.

And he kicked in that door.

The door flew against the wall even as Cole burst inside.

A woman was screaming. Her voice was wild and hysterical and—

Cole aimed his weapon.

...At Gia Eastman.

Because there was no one else in the room. Just Gia. A Gia who was wearing sexy lingerie, with red rose petals sprinkled all round her, and champagne chilling on the chipped nightstand beside her.

"Stop screaming," Chase ordered her. "Can't you tell that we're here to save you?"

But save her...from what?

Gia stopped screaming, but her mouth hung open.

At that moment, James burst in from the bathroom.

She screamed again.

"Stop!" Cole lowered his gun and charged toward her. "Gia, what in the hell is happening?"

Her eyes were huge. "Where's Harrison?"

"He's safe, and you are, too."

"*Uh, yeah, buddy,*" Chase muttered. "*I'm getting the feeling she was always safe.*" He inclined his head toward Gia. "Nice bustier. It matches your eyes."

She snatched up the covers. "Harrison was supposed to come here. He was going to trade his life for mine." She bit her lower lip. "Where's Harrison?" Gia asked again.

For the second time, Cole told her, "He's safe." But he added, "He sent us to rescue you."

One bare shoulder rolled in a little shrug. "But I wanted Harrison." Her lower lip pulled into a pout. "He was going to prove that he still loved me."

Cole's temples throbbed.

"You have got to be fucking kidding me." James sounded disgusted. "Hey, lady, over here." He waved his hand.

Her stare whipped to him.

"Answer my question. Did you *fake* your own kidnapping?"

"I..."

"Yes or no."

"Y-yes..."

"Fuck me." James squeezed his eyes shut. "Why the hell would you do this? *Why?*"

"Because—because he would pay anything for Evie!" She jumped out of the bed. Wrapped the sheet around her body. "He would do anything for her, but I'm the one he was supposed to marry! If he still cared...he'd have to come to me." Tears spilled from her eyes. "But he's not here..."

Cole pulled out his phone and fired a quick text to Harrison. *Gia is safe. Whole thing was fake. She wanted you here. Found her wearing a bustier and with champagne chilling.*

He looked back at Gia. "Do you have any idea what you've done?"

"Uh...what?"

"Evie is in danger. You took guards away from her while we tried to locate you. You screwed up our investigation because we were looking for *you.*"

CHAPTER SIXTEEN

I will lose my mind without her.

Evie's phone vibrated. She looked down at the text from Cole.

Gia is safe. Kidnapping was a hoax. Will explain all soon.

Her breath left in a startled rush. When she glanced up, she saw that Harvey was looking at his phone, too. He'd probably gotten the same note.

Before she could speak to him, her phone rang. The familiar ring tone blared as her brother's face flashed across the screen. She swiped her finger over the surface and put the phone to her ear. "Harrison." Relief surged through her. "Did Cole tell you? Gia's safe."

"I'm not." His voice was funny. Thick. Nervous.

She frowned as she paced toward her bedroom. "You're not what?"

"Safe."

What? "Harrison?"

"Is anyone with you?"

She looked over her shoulder. Harvey happened to look up at the same moment. She gave him a quick smile then motioned toward her bedroom. *Be right back,* Evie mouthed. Evie hurried to the bedroom and shut the door behind her.

"I'm alone." Technically, alone in her bedroom, not alone in her home. "What's happening?"

"I'm in trouble, Evie." His voice was so low. "I think he's going to kill me."

***

"This is so embarrassing," Gia moaned. She'd dressed. Finally. And she was currently being led back to Chase's vehicle. "God, I can't believe I listened to him."

Cole had just opened the SUV's rear door. At her words, his attention sharpened on her. "Listened to who?"

She winced. "A friend. This stupid idea wasn't mine. He's the one who said that if I did this, if I managed to lure Harrison here to me, then everything would be fine between us again. I'd have proof that I came first in Harrison's life." She sniffed. "But I guess the only thing he proved was that Harrison was in love with his—"

"He's not fucking in love with Evie, I am," Cole corrected flatly. "And she's in love with me. So that BS story needs to end. Now."

She gaped at him.

"And, of course, Harrison wouldn't come get you on his own. Harrison White isn't equipped to handle kidnappers, and he damn well knows it. If he cared about you, he'd protect you by sending in the best to do the job."

From his position near the front of the vehicle, Chase cleared his throat. Then he pointed to his chest. "We're the best. That'd be us."

Her gaze darted to him. Then back to Cole. "So Harrison...does care about me?"

"I have no fucking idea." And Cole didn't want to know. The last thing he wanted was to get involved in Harrison White's sex life. "I don't care, either. I just want to know what *friend* came up with this idea." Though he had a suspicion, one that was sending every conceivable red flag flying through his mind.

A sigh blew from her lips. "Robert Demakis. He came over to my place pretty late, and maybe we had a drink or two and he was all like..." She waved one hand in the air, doing a little circle with her fingers. "If Harrison thinks you're in danger like Evie, then you can see how he really feels..." Her voice trailed off. Her hand stopped waving.

Cole's body tensed. "Robert Demakis told you to fake the kidnapping."

"Could you stop using the word 'kidnapping' when you talk to me? Please? I like to think that this was just some creative role play, you know? And—"

"Robert Demakis convinced you to call Harrison and tell him that he had to exchange his life for yours."

"Well, yes, but—"

There was no but. Cole and Chase had both gotten a bad feeling after they talked with Robert. This news made that feeling about ten times worse. "Harrison got a call from the kidnapper. Guy used a voice distorter."

"That was an app that Robert downloaded on the phone," she said miserably. "Told me it would sound more realistic."

"Oh, it sure as shit did." It had sounded far too realistic. So realistic that they'd gone hunting for Gia. "The call Harrison received—"

She looked even more miserable. "Robert gave me the phone to use. Said I couldn't use my own. He had the app on it."

James edged closer. He'd been silently watching the exchange the whole time.

"I want an interrogation with Demakis," Cole said, voice hard. Tight.

James nodded. "Sounds like a damn good plan to me."

Chase pushed Gia into the backseat.

"And I think we need to talk to Harrison White," Cole added. "Right the hell now." Because he needed to understand that Robert was involved in this mess all the way up to his freaking neck.

***

Harrison hadn't answered his phone, and Demakis had seemingly vanished. Chase was taking care of Gia—taking her to the police station so that she could explain her disappearance. When she'd learned that the cops had been notified, Gia had almost passed out in the back of the SUV.

Cole hurtled through the city, maneuvering as fast as he could on his motorcycle. Both Cole and James were using motorcycles, courtesy of Wilde and the company's seemingly never-ending resources. They could cut through traffic one hell of a lot faster on the bikes. James was heading to meet with the agents searching for Robert, while Cole—

I need to get to Evie.

Every instinct he had screamed for Cole to get to her. The situation with Gia had been a ruse. An attempt to lure away some of the guards who'd been around Evie, he was sure of it. Divide and conquer. The oldest trick in the book.

And they'd fallen for it.

Fuck.

The motorcycle's wheels screeched as he took the turn up ahead. He could see Evie's building. Hell, yes, he was almost there.

He'd called on the way and ordered Harvey to make sure that Evie didn't get out of her home. Harvey had assured him that Evie was in her bedroom, resting.

He braked. Tore upstairs as fast as he could and rushed toward her door. Even as he reached for the handle—

The door wrenched open. "Where is the fire, man?" Harvey frowned at him. "Damn. What in the hell did you do? Run up all those stairs?"

Hell, yes, he had. Folks had been waiting for the elevator. There hadn't been time for him to stand around. "Evie."

Harvey jerked his thumb over his shoulder. "She's still in her bedroom. Look, I saw her go in.

She hasn't come out. You can take five seconds to breathe and tell me why you're freaking out."

"Because it was a trap." He didn't take five seconds. He rushed straight for Evie's room. He reached the door. Knocked lightly with his knuckles. "Evie?"

No answer.

Harvey crowded closer. "A trap? Who was supposed to get caught?"

Cole glanced back at him. "Me." He knocked again. Harder. Twisted the knob. It was locked. *The door shouldn't be locked. Why would Evie lock the door?* "He knew Harrison had sent me to rescue Evie. He figured Harrison would do the same thing for Gia. He wanted me out of the way."

"Who is this 'he' that you're talking about?"

"Robert Demakis. He wanted me away from Evie."

"Look, I hate to break it to you, but other Wilde agents are just as good at keeping people safe as you—"

Cole kicked in the door. The lock shattered. Wood chips flew. The door swung inward and bounced against the wall.

At first, he didn't see her. His heart stopped. Somehow, she'd gotten out or the bastard had gotten to her or—

Evie's bathroom door opened. She came out, her steps slow and uncertain. Her skin seemed too pale. Shadows lined her eyes. She took in the broken door. The way his body was all heaving and tense. Then her stare flickered to Harvey.

"Evie..." Her name tore from Cole.

"You broke my door."

"I will buy you ten new doors." He lunged toward her. "What's happened?" He could feel it, tell it—

Her lower lip trembled. "He said I had to sneak away. That I had to come to him." She shook her head. "But I have a whole team of agents waiting to help me. I have *you*. Why the hell would I go to him on my own?"

Cole hauled her into his arms. He buried his face in the crook of her neck.

"Harrison has been taken," she whispered. "I have orders to clear out five million dollars from his account. He said the bank wouldn't even try to stop me. Apparently, I'm listed as having full access to his money all the time."

His hold tightened on her.

"Whoever took Harrison, he told me to do it. Gave me all these instructions."

Cole forced his head to lift. Her sweet scent surrounded him.

"Harrison was talking to me at first, but then someone took the phone from him. The guy's voice was all distorted and robotic. I know he was disguising it." Her gaze searched his. "If he's hiding his voice that way, it means I know him, right? It means he thinks I'd recognize his real voice?"

Cole nodded. "I suspect you do know him."

"Do you think Harrison was blindfolded or something? Because he'd have to be. If he wasn't, if the guy let Harrison see his face..." Her lips pressed together a moment, then she continued, "He wouldn't let Harrison go. Not after I gave him the money." Her words tumbled out too quickly.

"That's what I kept thinking about. He's disguising his identity from me, but...is he disguising it from Harrison? Or does he just plan to kill my brother no matter what I do?"

Cole didn't answer her. Mostly because he didn't want to see the hope fade from her eyes. But...*Yeah, baby, I think he plans to kill your brother.*

He tenderly kissed her cheeks. "I'll get Harrison back for you."

She grabbed his hands before he could back away. "*We'll* get him back."

"Evie—"

"I waited for you, Cole. Just so you know, I could have gotten out." Her gaze flickered to Harvey. "No offense, and I'm not trying to insult you, but I could have gotten away."

Harvey's eyebrows climbed.

"I didn't, though. Because I knew that I needed you guys. But I'm not sitting on the sidelines. The kidnapper said he wanted *me* to drop off that money. Me or else Harrison would be dead the second he saw someone else there. So we have to come up with a plan—together—to make this work. One that involves saving my brother and none of us dying." She straightened her shoulders. "We can do this."

Cole exchanged a long look with Harvey.

"Piece of cake," Harvey muttered.

"I freaking love cake." Cole focused on Evie. "Something you need to know."

She waited.

"It's looking like Robert Demakis is the one we're after. He convinced Gia to do a whole fake kidnapping hoax. He even had Gia disguise her voice with a distortion app."

"You think he used the same app on the phone with me?"

"I think Robert is missing. I think he wants vengeance for what happened to his folks, and I think he is very, very dangerous."

***

"Harrison's so-called bodyguards have disappeared." Chase delivered that bombshell when he strolled into Evie's home two hours later. "Interesting, don't you think?"

Cole shoved the duffel bag that he and Evie had only recently filled onto the table and glanced at his friend. "Either they were taken out..." He let his voice trail away as he glanced toward Evie.

She frowned.

"Or they helped take your brother out," Chase finished. "My money says option two because guess who those guys worked for right *before* they became employed by Harrison White?"

Cole knew where this was going. "Robert Demakis."

"Bingo."

All the pieces were shoving together. Robert was looking guiltier and guiltier by the moment.

Evie's fingers toyed with the handles on the duffel bag. "Are we set to go?"

Pretty set. In that bag, five million dollars waited.

Chase whistled. "Oh, shit, is that the cash? Like, you just have it right here?" He moved closer and poked at the bag. "Can I see it?"

Cole swatted his hand away. "No. Dammit. In addition to the cash, we've got a tracker in there—one that is carefully hidden—and I don't want you screwing with it."

Now Chase huffed. "I wasn't going to screw with it." He paused. "Maybe I was."

Cole could only shake his head.

"What's the battle plan?" Chase motioned toward Evie. "I see that she's wearing her special bling-bling. Good job, Evie. That way, we can keep track of you no matter what."

Evie lifted her wrist. "It's my new favorite accessory. Never leave home without it."

They didn't know where the drop would be yet. They hadn't heard back from Harrison or his kidnapper. But Cole knew the call could come at any moment.

James and Harvey were outside of Evie's building. Wilde tech agents were scouring traffic cams and searching online databases for any intel that they could use.

As far as the team could tell, Harrison had gone down to his parking garage with his two bodyguards.

Then they'd all vanished.

As fate would have it, all security cameras in the parking garage and all nearby street cams had been on the fritz. A very convenient fate that Cole was sure the bad guys had arranged.

"The battle plan…" Evie cleared her voice. "The kidnapper tells me where to make the drop. I do it. Hopefully, he gives me Harrison in return."

Cole didn't have that high hope. The exchange was *not* going to happen that easily.

"Then I walk away with Harrison." Her fingers fluttered over the large duffel bag again. "That's when the Wilde team swarms." She gave a brief pause. "We call that Plan A."

"Huh." Chase's head tilted to the right.

"For Plan B, he gets away before Wilde can swarm. In that case, the kidnapper takes the money. He doesn't realize that a tracker is inside, so we all follow him. *Then* Wilde agents swarm."

Chase tapped his chin. Cole was pretty sure the man was using all of his strength to hold back another "huh." Very unlike him.

Chase must know that if he said anything else, he would terrify Evie.

The guy had better keep his mouth shut. The last thing Cole wanted was for Evie to be more afraid. She was holding onto her control. Impressing the hell out of him. But then, she'd always impressed him. Charmed him. Addicted him.

Evie's phone rang. Wilde agents had already set up tracking on her phone, so they would be trying to follow the call, triangulate the other phone's signal, and run the bastard down. Cole had instructed Evie to keep the perp on the phone as long as possible.

When she saw her brother's number on the screen, Evie's gaze lifted.

Cole gave a small nod. "You've got this, baby."

She swiped her finger over the screen, turned on the speaker so that he and Chase could hear the call, and said, "I have the money."

"Evie." Harrison's voice. Rough. Worried. "Thank Christ!"

"Harrison? Harrison! Are you okay? Has he hurt you—has he—"

"I'm okay." He didn't sound it. "Evie, I'm sorry."

"You don't have to be sorry," she rushed to tell him. "This isn't on you. I have the money. I'm going to make the exchange. Everything will be fine."

Silence.

"Harrison?"

Cole saw the fear flash on her face.

"That was your proof of life," a robotic voice said.

Evie's body shuddered.

"He'll stay alive as long as you—and only you—bring the money to me. That means you leave the boyfriend at home."

Evie's gaze locked with Cole's.

"If we see the boyfriend, your brother will die. I will put a bullet in his brain, and you'll be all alone, Evie."

"Don't hurt him!"

"Then bring me what I'm owed. Five million." He rattled off an address.

Chase wrote it down quickly and fired off a text, no doubt ordering the other agents to get in position.

"Take your car and come alone, Evie. Only you. I will have eyes on you the minute you leave your building. If you're not in *your* vehicle, if you're not alone—it's over. If I learn that Cole—or his asshole buddy Chase—are with you, then your brother dies. I'll consider his death the payment that I'm owed."

"Don't—"

He hung up.

Evie's breath sawed in and out. "You can't come with me, Cole."

"Baby..."

"If they see you, he's dead. He's my brother. The only family I have!"

Cole cut his stare to Chase. "Give us a minute."

"I'll make sure the agents are ready to roll." He slipped out.

Evie paced to the window. Stared out. "He's watching. He has people *watching* me right now. They know about you. They know about Chase." She spun toward him. "You can't get in the car with me."

Sweetheart, there is no fucking way I let you leave without me.

"I'll go alone." Her shoulders straightened. "I'll drive there alone. I'm sure other Wilde agents are already going to be scoping out that address. Tell them to stay back, a safe distance back. They can watch. They can be backup. But don't let them move in. Tell them to wait until I come out with my brother. After that, everything will be fine."

He slowly crossed to her. Cole lifted his hand, and his knuckles brushed over her cheek. "Baby..."

She stared at him with eyes that had never been so dark.

"The bastard wants you alone. He wants you alone because he has plans." Plans that Cole didn't like, but sure as hell suspected. "You go in alone, and we won't get your brother back. We won't get *you* back."

"Cole..."

"This shit has been going on for years, Evie. Years. This guy has planned and watched and waited. After all of this time, he's not just going to let you waltz in there, drop the money, and walk away. You know that. I know that."

Her lower lip trembled.

"If your brother saw the leader's face, then the guy is planning to kill Harrison." She needed to be prepared for this. "You may walk in there—"

"Please don't," she begged. "Don't say that I'll walk in there and he might be dead."

He swallowed and didn't say the words. Hell, hadn't he feared the same situation, so long ago, with her? When he'd been sent into that old, rundown building, he'd been afraid that Evie was already dead. He'd only had her pictures to see at that point. Her smiling pictures. God, she had the best smile.

As he'd walked through the darkness, a gun gripped in his hand, he'd known that when he finally located her, he might just be finding a body.

He'd been terrified that he'd find her too late. Because just from her picture, something about Evie had pulled at him. When he'd discovered the locked closet, when he'd heard the faint sounds coming from behind the door...

He'd broken that bitch down in order to get to her. Damn near ripped it right off the hinges.

He'd grabbed her. Pulled her into his arms.

She's alive. She's safe.

He'd never felt that way on a mission. Never had that earth-shattering, personal connection before. As if...

As if I'd just rescued someone who belonged to me.

Now, he stared at Evie. Saw the paleness of her skin and the darkness of her eyes. The fear she tried to fight.

"You can't go in alone, sweetheart."

"I *have* to."

Over my dead body. He nodded. "I'll make sure your car is empty."

Suspicion flashed on her face. "Cole, no, this is my brother's life, you can't—"

"This is your fucking life, too, Evie!" *And you are my life.* "Don't think for a second that I am going to let you walk into death. I can't. I won't. You matter too much to me. Don't you get it? You *are* my life. You're worth more than five million dollars to me. You are worth more than everything else to me. I will do whatever is necessary to keep you safe."

Her breath hitched.

"That's my job, remember? Keeping you safe."

She shook her head. "It's not about the job."

"No, it's just about you." She needed to understand this. "I would kill for you in an instant, but I won't back the fuck away and let something happen to you. I've seen these situations before. I know how these bastards think. They break rules. They kill." His voice roughened even more. "If something happened to you, if someone hurt you, I would lose my mind."

"No, you wouldn't." Her head turned. She caught his hand. Brought it to her mouth. Pressed a tender kiss to his palm before she released it. "Not you, Cole. You're the strongest man I ever met. You can do anything."

Only when I have you.

"You survived torture. You don't need me. You can be—"

"You are the person I need most. You are the reason I survived torture. You are the reason I am still breathing."

Her eyes widened.

"You got me through it. When I thought of you, I got through it. I didn't feel pain because I focused on you. For the last two years, you've been what keeps me going." She was in his very soul. "I will do anything to protect you."

"I love you, Cole," she told him.

Love was way too tame of a word to describe how he felt about her—

"But you heard him. If he sees anyone else in that car with me, he will kill my brother. That *can't* happen."

If he sees anyone else...

His chin lifted. "Don't worry, Evie, I got this." The perps had screwed with the wrong man. The wrong team.

It would be their last mistake.

Because no one threatens Evie and walks away. No one.

CHAPTER SEVENTEEN

What if you lose the one thing you want the most? You ever wonder about that? About what would happen...after? Hell, screw that kind of talk. I'm not losing her. Not now. Not ever.

Evie slowly pulled her car onto the road. Truth be told, she didn't drive much in New York. Who did? Must easier to get around by foot or cab or subway, and she hadn't been in her car in ages. Her hands were shaking as she gripped the wheel. Chase had programmed in the GPS location of the ransom drop site for her before she'd left. She looked to the left and the right. Her heart wouldn't stop racing.

Everything is going to be okay. The money was in the passenger seat, and the duffel bag appeared so unassuming. Like it was just a workout bag that she'd tossed in with her. Strange to think that five million dollars could be put in a bag like that. It had taken a few hours for the bank to the get the cash ready for her. She'd sat in the little office, with Cole at her side, and sweat had covered her.

The bank manager had been courteous and helpful, even as he'd cast worried glances at Cole every few moments.

People tended to be nervous around Cole, and she didn't get that. When she was around him, that was when Evie felt safest.

She paused at the red light and glanced over her shoulder at the empty back seat.

You can do this. There really wasn't much of an option. She had to do this. Her brother was waiting on her. He was—

A phone was ringing.

Only it wasn't her phone.

The light was still red.

The phone kept ringing. It sounded as if it were coming from somewhere near the passenger seat. *Under* the passenger seat?

She surged to the right and angled down as far as she could go. Her seatbelt bit into her chest, and she growled as her fingers stretched and stretched and—

There.

She grabbed the phone. Not her phone. *Who the hell put this phone here?* But, even as her finger swiped over the screen, she knew.

The light turned green. She didn't move. "Who is this?"

"You're going to want to turn left at the light."

"My GPS directions say to turn right."

A car horn honked behind her.

Her gaze jerked to the rear-view mirror. She frowned at the flower delivery truck and the waving driver.

"Turn left," the robotic voice ordered. "There's been a change of plans..."

"I want to talk to Harrison."

"You already did that. Now turn left or I might just start shooting. I figure I could start with his leg and work my way up from there."

She cursed.

And turned left.

***

"Oh, hell." Chase clenched his fingers around the steering wheel as he hunched in the flower delivery truck. Evie wasn't going the right way.

And before she'd turned left, he'd clearly seen her bend down and pick up what had looked like a phone from beneath the passenger seat. His comm was on—all of the agents were using the Wilde tech to communicate on this mission—and he knew the other agents could hear him as he asked, "Was Evie's car searched before she got in?"

Harvey replied, "Yesterday, two guys did a full check to make sure there were no explosive devices or anything that might be dangerous in there."

"Yesterday? Shit, we should have checked again."

"The car didn't leave the garage and agents were watching the building the whole time."

Someone missed this. "A phone was put in her ride." He turned left and followed her. Not too fast, though, because Chase didn't want to look suspicious. "The meeting location has changed."

That was gonna be a pain in all of their asses because the majority of the team was already planning for a raid at the coordinates they'd originally been given. "I'm keeping eyes on her, but my van can't follow her the whole way. I'll need to switch out with someone—"

"I'll be there," James assured him through the comm link. "You just keep giving me directions as you go. You and I can switch out. Hopefully with our two different vehicles, we'll keep anyone from noticing the tail."

She turned right.

So did he.

Chase could see that Evie still had the phone clutched in her hand. She had it lifted up— deliberately, he was sure—so that it was near her head and in plain view for him.

He followed her in silence for a few moments, but his gaze kept darting to the speedometer. Was the woman speeding up? She was. Shit. He shoved down the gas. "Cole isn't going to like this," Chase said as he glared at the car ahead him.

"No." Cole's voice came through, very low and very, very angry. "He's not."

***

"Stop the car, Evie."

"But I'm in the middle of the road. There are other vehicles—"

"Stop the car. Open the door. And drop *your* cell phone onto the street. You don't need it, not after I've kindly given you a new phone."

She looked back. Saw the flower delivery van. Not too close. Not close enough to hit her.

"Do it now or I will shoot your brother."

She slammed on her brakes. Opened the door. Dropped her phone.

"Good."

He is watching me. Or...he had someone else watching her and reporting her movements to him. Because he couldn't be physically watching her and holding a gun on her brother, could he? No, that didn't make sense.

Unless...her gaze whipped around the interior of her car. If someone had put a phone in her car, maybe other things were in there, too. Like a small camera.

"Start driving. Head straight. I'll call you back when you need to turn again."

"But—"

"Why do you keep glancing back at that van?"

Oh, shit. There is a camera in here. He's watching the interior of the car.

"Don't worry. We'll take care of him. Keep driving."

He hung up.

***

A freaking garbage truck cut off Chase. Just pulled right out in front of him.

Hell, *no.*

He slammed on the brakes. Barely avoided a collision. "Fuck!"

"What's happening?" James barked from the shared connection.

"Freaking garbage truck just cut me off from Evie—"

"Yeah, well, go the hell around and—"

Chase's eyes narrowed on one of the men who'd just jumped from the side of the truck. The guy lifted up his hand, indicating that Chase was supposed to freeze. There was something about that fellow—

I've seen his picture. He was one of Harrison's missing bodyguards. What had been the guy's name? Tyler? Tony?

"Are you listening to me?" James demanded.

No, he'd gotten lost for a minute. Chase rattled off his location. "You close, man? You got her?"

"What is happening?"

"One of Harrison's bodyguards is moonlighting as a garbage truck driver. And he's coming my way."

"You need backup?" This question came from Harvey. He'd been listening the whole time.

Chase smiled. "No, I got the bastard. Just tell me real quick. The guard that Cole slugged. Was his name Tony?"

"Tommy," Cole growled.

"Gotcha. Thanks." Chase shoved open his door. Jumped out. "You need to move!" Chase yelled. "I got deliveries to make!"

"Just gonna have to wait, asshole," the fellow fired back. He kept his face partially averted. Like that was going to help. *Too late.* Chase had already recognized the guy.

"Got quite the bruise on your jaw," Chase announced. "Want to tell me how that happened, Tommy?"

The man's head snapped toward him as soon as Chase used that magic word...*Tommy.*

Seriously? Did you think Cole hadn't told the rest of the team about you?

"Oh, wait." Chase tapped his chin. "I know how you got the bruise. My buddy Cole kicked your ass."

Tommy let out a roar and barreled toward Chase. He bent his body low and slammed his shoulder into Chase's stomach, sending Chase hurtling back against the side of the flower delivery van.

***

She'd lost sight of the delivery van. Evie hadn't seen it for at least twenty minutes. She'd left the city, left the bright lights and buzz of activity, and with each mile that passed, the buildings showed more wear and tear.

Fewer people.

More decay.

"Turn right, then you'll head toward the old warehouse that's up ahead. The shipping doors are open. Drive through them. Park your car. Get the money and climb up the stairs."

"And you'll have Harrison waiting for me?"

Laughter.

The call ended. Again. The jackass liked hanging up on her.

"You're an asshole," Evie said angrily, deliberately raising her voice. "I know there's a camera in this car. I know you've been watching me the whole time." She was almost screaming. Again, deliberate. She wanted *him* to hear her. "So I'll drive into your stupid building. I'll park the car. I'll take the money and I'll climb up the stairs. But you'd better give me my brother. I've done everything like you wanted. *Everything.* You can see no one else is in this car with me. I came alone. *Now give me my brother!*"

She spun the car to the right. The huge shipping doors on the old warehouse were wide open. She drove forward. Slammed on the brakes once she was inside. Her breath heaved in and out. Then her hand flew over and grabbed the duffel bag. She jumped from the car. Shut the door. With quick steps, Evie headed for the old stairs. And as she climbed them, she saw the man waiting at the top. The man holding the gun.

Her steps faltered for a moment, but then he waved her forward.

As she drew closer, her gaze locked on his face. Lights were on in the warehouse, old, flickering lights overhead. "I...know you."

She'd seen him before. He was standing in front of a door on the second floor, and the first time she'd seen him, he'd been standing in front of another door then, too. Guarding it. *Guarding my brother's place.* "You work for Harrison." She struggled to remember his name. She knew Tommy. He'd been the one that Cole had fought, but this guy—he hadn't said a word. He'd been silent. Like a statue.

As she neared him, he laughed. "Don't really work for your brother."

Obviously.

"Gonna have to pat you down. Gonna need to make sure you didn't try to bring a weapon."

"W-would I do that?" The stutter wasn't faked. She was freaking terrified. "I just want Harrison."

His pat down was fast and hard. He grunted. "Glad you're not stupid."

She stared straight at him. *I can't say the same for you.*

"Boss is waiting. Go inside. I'm gonna get rid of your ride."

But...but if he got rid of it, how was she supposed to get out of there?

As she stared into his cold eyes, she knew...

I'm not. The plan isn't for Harrison or for me to leave.

Not going with Plan A.

Not going with Plan B.

That left...Plan C?

They really should have talked more about Plan C.

Plan C...time for Cole.

               ***

Every muscle in Cole's body was locked tight with tension. He was also fucking cramped as hell.

Plan C is a pain in my ass.

Darkness surrounded him. Thick and suffocating. His body was curled in on itself, and when he tried to stretch, he hit the metal above him.

He could hear Evie's words, seeming to echo in his mind.

"I know there's a camera in this car. I know you've been watching me the whole time. So I'll drive into your stupid building. I'll park the car. I'll take the money and I'll climb up the stairs. But you'd better give me my brother. I've done everything like you wanted. Everything. You can see no one else is in this car with me. I came alone. Now give me my brother!"

She'd shouted those angry words so that Cole could hear them...

As he waited in the damn trunk of her car. Not the most comfortable of positions, but screw comfort. The position had left him perfectly hidden.

The only worry he had...if there *was* a camera in the car, then it was possible the bad guys had seen him when he'd slipped inside. But...

He'd been careful. He'd come up to the rear of the vehicle, hadn't gotten anywhere near the front seat or doors. If the camera had been positioned to view the interior of her car, it would have missed him.

If it hadn't been positioned that way, though, he was seriously screwed. In the hard, rough, and very uncomfortable way.

He listened intently and heard the thud of Evie's steps as she headed up the stairs. No one came bounding back down to pop up the trunk and shoot him in the head, so Cole figured he might have gotten lucky.

If the camera couldn't see me, we are golden. But he'd be extra careful when he got out. Make sure that he stayed low until he was clear of the vehicle.

"You good, buddy?" James wanted to know.

Cole had his comm link in his ear. He'd been listening to the others the whole time. The team had tried to give Evie a comm link, too, but she had feared the perps would discover it if they searched her—and then they would hurt Harrison.

"I'm right outside of the building," James added. *"Ready at your order."*

"Any sign of Chase?" Because they'd lost their link to him after he'd started fighting that SOB Tommy.

"No. But I gave the others his location, and I updated them on where we are. They are en route, but it will take at least ten minutes before backup gets here."

He was already reaching for the trunk release lever that glowed so brightly in the dark. "I'm not waiting ten minutes." His voice was low, barely a breath, just as it had been before. "I'm moving now."

"Then I've got your six."

"She's on the second floor. She took the money up there. And I'm going to cover *her* ass."

"Damn straight."

He popped the trunk. Grabbed the metal before it could bounce up too high. He slid from the vehicle, then crouched behind the bumper as he lowered the trunk back into position. His gaze swept the area.

Guard upstairs. He saw the SOB.

And actually...

He's coming down here.

The lumbering fellow was heading down the stairs right then. That would make things much, much easier.

Cole disappeared into the shadows. He waited. Barely breathing.

He recognized the SOB slowly heading down the stairs. One of Harrison's bodyguards. The hulking figure who'd stood outside of Harrison's door and looked bored to pieces.

The guy headed for the driver's side door. He opened it. Reached in and pulled out something—something that he fisted in the palm of his hand. The camera? When had the jerks put the camera and the phone into Evie's car?

Shit. I know when. When we were out rushing to save Gia. When the Wilde guards switched out and our attention was divided.

Harrison had thought his new bodyguards would keep him safe. But all along, they'd had other plans. Tommy Marshall and Bruce Baker, those were their names. Cole had Bruce in his sights. *You're going down, big guy.*

Bruce walked slowly around the car, eyeing it with a smirk. Then he looked up toward the stairs, licked his lips, and gave a hard nod.

Bruce didn't even glance toward the shadows in that old place before he hit the steps. Hurried up the first one, the second, the third, the fourth—

Cole's hand flew out and grabbed Bruce's ankle. Cole yanked him back, a hard heave that sent Bruce falling and slamming his head into the steps.

The bastard was out cold in the next instant.

And Cole was silently rushing up the steps.

I'm coming, Evie.

Plan C was looking better and better by the moment.

CHAPTER EIGHTEEN

Secrets have a way of coming back to bite you in the ass. And those little bastards have really sharp teeth.

A few pieces of dusty furniture were scattered around the room. Overhead, dim lighting spilled down on her. Evie hurried inside, then spun around, lost. "Harrison?" No one was there. That didn't make any sense. She dropped the duffel bag. "*Harrison!*"

There was a thump from the right.

She spun. Stared at the closed door.

The thump came again. From behind the door. Memories swamped her.

When they took me, they locked me in a closet. I couldn't get out. I hit my fist against that door over and over again, but I couldn't get out.

She ran for the door. Grabbed the knob. Twisted it.

Locked.

She kicked at the lock, hoping she could break it or—

Fuck me! She hopped back. She'd almost broken her damn foot. That kicking trick had *not* worked. Cole did it all the freaking time, like it was nothing, but it was obviously way harder than it appeared. She stumbled back. Her gaze flew around desperately as she searched for something that she could use to force open that door. "Just hold on!" Evie cried out. "I'll find a way to open the door—"

The door opened. From the inside.

"Don't worry," Stephen Lowe told her with a smirk. "I've got it."

"Stephen?" She could only shake her head. "What are you doing?"

But, jeez, wasn't it obvious? He was at the ransom drop site. He was all smirky and smug. Cole and the Wilde agents had been convinced Robert was the perp they wanted, yet it was—

"What am I doing? I'm taking what's owed to me." He sauntered toward her. She realized that he hadn't been in a closet but, rather, he'd been waiting inside a smaller room.

She backed up.

He grabbed the duffel bag.

It was Stephen. Him all along. He unzipped the bag and peered inside. "You think it will look like more."

Her hands fisted at her sides.

"Because five million sounds like a lot, am I right?" Stephen glanced up at her. "But when it's all bundled into stacks, when you have piles of hundreds, it doesn't look like so much."

"It's all there," she assured him quickly. "Every single bit. I'm not trying to screw you over."

"Aren't you?" He zipped the bag. "What do you call your friend in the delivery truck? I told you to come alone, but you tried to bring a tail."

"He's not here."

"That's because Tommy took care of him. But since I have my money, I'll play nicely." He rose. The bag stayed at his feet. "This is your brother's warehouse. Did you know that? One of the many pieces of property that he stole from someone else."

She didn't move.

"He's paying the light bills." He glanced up at the faint lighting. "And he's paying for his own temporary jail cell."

That meant... "Harrison is here?"

A slow nod. "Go back down the stairs. You'll find your brother on the first floor of the warehouse. He's in a closet on the east side."

She whirled to go after him—

"I didn't want to hurt you, Evie. That was never part of my plan."

She caught sight of someone just beyond the doorway. The faintest of movements, the faintest glimpse of...

Cole.

Cole was there. Plan C was in effect.

She stopped and turned back to face Stephen. "If you didn't mean to hurt me, then why did you have someone attempt to kidnap me?"

Stephen rubbed his cheek. "I tried to talk to you at the gala. Did your boyfriend tell you that?"

"No."

"I was worried about you. I've noticed that you have a tendency to trust the wrong people."

No, she didn't. She trusted the perfect people.

"Like your brother, for example. He's a total douche, in case you didn't know. The guy sent a corporate spy to destroy my business. Like father, like son." He shook his head in disgust. "Good thing a friend had my back and told me the truth."

A friend?

"It's the same shit Harrison's dad used to do back in the day. Play corporate spy. Lie to allies. Trick people. Steal them blind. I mean, look what he did to Robert Demakis."

She rocked forward onto the balls of her feet. "Where is Robert?"

"How the hell would I know?" But...he smiled.

Her gaze darted around the room.

"*I* didn't try to kidnap you, Evie. I didn't want you involved in this mess at all. I know you're not like Harrison. You're not guilty of anything."

She took a slow step back, moving her body toward the doorway. Toward Cole. She knew he was out there. Waiting. Listening. She kept talking because she wanted Stephen's attention on her. "I'm supposed to believe you?"

"Why would I lie now?"

"Fine. If you didn't try to kidnap me, then who did?"

"Your boyfriend."

She laughed. It was just so ridiculous that Evie laughed.

Stephen's face hardened. "I'm trying to help you."

"You abducted my brother. You just forced me to bring you five million dollars—"

"And I have never hurt you. I won't. I really am trying to help." He nodded. Then he motioned toward a desk on the far side of the room. "There are pictures on that desk. Why don't you go take a look at them?"

She didn't want to take a look at them.

"Take a look, Evie." And, holy hell, but he had a gun in his hand. He'd yanked the gun from the back waistband of his perfectly pressed khaki pants, and he'd aimed it at her. "Now."

Her breath stuttered. "I thought you weren't going to hurt me."

He looked at the gun. "I...*go look at the fucking pictures!*" He pointed the gun at the floor, not at her.

Her steps were slow as she headed for the desk.

Then she looked at the photos. Saw herself. Saw...Cole?

"Robert told me that Cole would watch you all the time. He would come to New York without telling you."

She pushed the pictures across the desk, spreading them out and staring at them in shock.

"Remember when you were almost hit in New York a while back? That car? The hit and run? That wasn't me. It was your boyfriend. Or, rather, the stalker who wanted to be your boyfriend again."

Her stomach felt like lead. "You're lying."

"Pictures don't lie."

"They do when they're fake."

Stephen sighed. "Cole wanted a way back into your life. The best way? An excuse. He needed it to look like you were in danger. So he staged that attempted hit and run scene. He also arranged the kidnapping at the gala. He didn't want his hired help talking, telling you that it was all fake, so Cole Vincent—if that is even the guy's real name, highly doubtful, by the way—Cole shot him. He killed his accomplice because Cole didn't want you knowing what had really happened."

She balled up one of the photos. "No."

"Yes." Stephen nodded. "Actually, I kind of owe the man. Because, hell, where do you think I got this abduction idea from? I figured...hey, this shit would work with Harrison. I could take him and get what I was owed. Easy. Then Gia conveniently vanished and I had the perfect opportunity. I was waiting and watching, you see. I knew my time would come."

She dropped the balled-up photo. "Cole wouldn't do this to me."

His smile was mocking. "Haven't you noticed yet...that bastard would do just about anything *for* you?"

She would not look toward the door. She would not look toward—

"That's why he's standing outside the doorway right now, completely fixed on what I'm saying, and he doesn't know that my partner is waiting down at the foot of the stairs, with a gun aimed straight up at Cole's back." He winced. "And that's why I had to pull out my own weapon and force you away from the door. Didn't want you getting hit by a stray shot. See, I told you, I don't want you hurt."

Her eyes widened. "No!" Evie rushed for the door. *"Cole!"*

* * *

"That's why he's standing outside the doorway right now, completely fixed on what I'm saying, and he doesn't know that my partner is waiting down at the foot of the stairs, with a gun aimed straight up at Cole's back."

Cole whirled.

Robert Demakis had lifted his weapon. He stood at the foot of the stairs. A cold grin curved his lips.

Cole brought up his own weapon even as he ducked down to—

***

Bam. The gunshot blasted. The sound seemed to echo endlessly in Evie's ears. *"Cole!"*

She ran for him, but hard hands caught her from behind. Evie was yanked up against Stephen's body. "No, Evie," he gasped in her ear. "Give him a minute. I don't want you walking into gunfire. How many times do I have to say it? I don't want you hurt!"

He was such a lying bastard. And where was Stephen's gun? Had he dropped it or just shoved it back into his waistband? Either way, he wasn't holding it. Both of his hands were on her. *His mistake.*

She elbowed him as hard as she could. He grunted, and his hold loosened on her. She lunged forward and ran for Cole. She could see his sprawled form just beyond the doorway.

But Stephen caught her again, and this time, he hurled her behind him. She hit her knees on the floor, but Evie jumped up, ready to tear that jerk apart.

"He's gone, Evie," Stephen said as he turned toward her. "Can't you see that Robert killed him?"

Robert? Robert was a dead man, he was—

Cole was moving.

Stephen didn't notice Cole's movements because he was staring at her. He'd turned his back on Cole's sprawled form. Stephen sadly shook his head. "We needed a fall guy, Evie. Someone had to take the blame for this mess. Since Robert already had those photos of Cole, it's perfect. We'll be able to walk away. As for you—"

Cole leapt to his feet.

Unhurt, no signs of blood on him, he *leapt* to his feet. He grabbed Stephen.

No, first he grabbed Stephen's gun from the back of the guy's waistband in a lightning-fast move, then Cole whipped Stephen around to face him. "There is no fucking way I would ever leave Evie." Then he drove his fist into Stephen's face, a blow that had Stephen's head snapping back and the other man staggering.

When Stephen tried to surge toward him, Cole aimed a gun at him. Evie had no idea if that was the gun he'd taken from Stephen or if it was Cole's own weapon. Didn't really matter. The result was the same.

Stephen froze.

"Go ahead, come at me," Cole dared him. "Because we both know that if you so much as twitch toward me or Evie, I will pull this trigger."

Stephen didn't twitch.

Cole's gaze darted to her face. Then it raced over her body. "Baby, are you okay?"

She nodded, dazed. "I thought you'd been shot." Her words came out oddly calm. Way, way too calm. When what she'd wanted to yell was...

I thought you'd been killed! I thought I'd lost you! I heard a shot. I heard a thud. You were on the floor, and you weren't moving, and I think I went crazy because I had to live without you for two miserable years, and I don't want to do that again, not ever.

"I wasn't stalking you," Cole said quickly.

What?

"I know the pics look bad."

The pics. Right.

Stephen still wasn't moving.

Neither was Evie. She felt rooted to the spot.

"But I...I just came to see you. I missed you, and I just—I'd missed my chance with you, but I wanted to make sure you were happy. Safe. That's all. I swear it. I wasn't behind anything—"

"He's lying, Evie," Stephen snarled. "Robert and I haven't been behind any attacks on you, I swear it. We wanted you kept out of things. It was only about Harrison."

Her mouth dropped. "Does it *look* like I'm out of things? You pulled a gun on me!"

Cole advanced on Stephen. "I told you not to even twitch."

"But—"

Cole's punch sent Stephen sprawling on the floor. Cole followed up that hit with several more brutal blows. Stephen didn't put up a fight. His body went limp as he passed out. Cole grabbed him, flipped him over, and slapped cuffs on Stephen. Cole searched him quickly, but turned up no other weapons. Then he left Stephen in a heap, and Cole's stare flew to Evie once more. "Evie, I am so freaking sorry. I wanted to explain everything to you before—"

She ran to him. Threw her arms around him. "I love you, but I have to find my brother."

"Evie, wait, you...believe me?"

She paused long enough to stare into his eyes. "Are you asking me if I bought the line about you being a stalker who arranged for someone to kidnap me? If I believe that you did all of that so you could play hero for me?"

A muscle flexed in his jaw.

"First, you don't play hero. You are a hero." They needed to get that shit straight. "And second, hell, no, I don't believe him. I believe you. Because I love you."

Stark and savage emotion flashed on Cole's face.

"Now, I have to go and find my brother because he needs me." But she grabbed Cole's jaw and she pulled him down toward her. Evie pressed a hard, frantic kiss to his lips. "But hold whatever awesome thought just passed through your head, okay?"

Then she rushed to the doorway.

A groan had her looking down the stairs.

James was at the bottom of the stairs, and he had his gun pressed to the head of Robert Demakis. A Robert Demakis who was bleeding pretty heavily from an injury to his side.

"He didn't get the chance to shoot," Cole told her softly as he slid up behind her. "James had my six."

"Fucking assholes!" Robert snapped.

James raised his eyebrows at Evie and Cole. "Everything okay up there?"

"Stephen's cuffed and unconscious. I've got his weapon. And we've got Harrison's location."

James smiled. "I have this prick under control. The guard you knocked out earlier is cuffed and in the corner." He inclined his head to the right. "Additional agents will be pulling in any moment. Harvey is closing in with them. Of course, they missed the party. We've got these bastards."

Yes, they did. Evie bounded down the stairs, making sure to steer clear of Robert at the bottom.

"Bitch," Robert spat at her. "Your brother should have just given me the money I wanted for my next show. This shit would never have happened—"

Evie paused beside him. Stared into his face and saw the rage that twisted him. She pulled back her fist and plowed it into his nose. "Don't call me a bitch."

James whistled. "I think her right hook is better than yours, Cole."

She hurried away, with Cole at her side. Her heart was racing, and she needed to see her brother. The bad guys were caught, yes, but...

What if they'd done something to Harrison? That rage on Robert's face had been unmistakable. He *hated* Harrison. And maybe, God, what if he'd hurt or even killed Harrison before she arrived at the warehouse?

Cole slipped before her, keeping his weapon at the ready and checking the rooms as they entered. She knew he was worried there might be other hired goons around.

Then she heard the thumps.

Just like she'd heard upstairs.

And she saw the closed door.

Cole wrenched the knob. *Locked.*

"Harrison?" Evie shouted.

Thump.

That wasn't a yes, but..."Harrison, move back from the door!" Evie commanded.

A few moments later, Cole kicked at the lock and broke it on his first attempt.

"I love it when you do that," she praised him as he wrenched open the door. "But, damn, I know it's harder than it looks."

He frowned at her.

She shoved past him. Saw her brother. Evie's body swayed as relief poured through her. Harrison was on his knees in the back of the closet. He was gagged, his hands were bound behind him, and when she scrambled toward him, she saw that his ankles were bound, too.

She yanked the gag out of his mouth. His face was littered with bruises and his nose appeared broken.

"Evie," he gasped out her name. "God, I am so glad to see you."

She held him tight.

"And never thought...I'd be so...h-happy to see Cole."

"You're welcome," Cole announced.

She squeezed her brother tighter. "Do you need an ambulance?"

"I just...need to get the hell out of here."

She put her forehead against his. "That can be arranged."

CHAPTER NINETEEN

*The bad guys are in jail. Evie's brother is safe.
Do I get my happy ending now? Because I
really, really fucking want it. Correction. I want
her.*

Chase strolled into Evie's place with a bottle of champagne in his hand. "Celebration time!" He flashed a grin.

Behind him, Harvey and James shared a long look.

"What?" As if sensing their shared look, Chase cast a frown over his shoulder. "Come on, it's the good stuff. Evie's brother paid for it."

Then it was probably expensive as shit, but that didn't necessarily make it good. Cole rolled back his shoulders as he studied his team. Damn, but he owed these guys. These three—and all the others who'd been working behind the scenes. The bad guys had been captured. Harrison was at home, recovering, and Evie—Evie didn't have to worry any longer.

She was safe.

And that means she doesn't need me.

"I'll get some glasses," Evie said with a quick grin. She hurried toward the kitchen.

Cole closed in on his friends.

"Robert and Stephen are under arrest," Harvey told him quietly. "Locked away tightly, and nope, I wouldn't be counting on bail anytime soon for them."

"What about Robert's gunshot wound?" Cole asked.

James laughed. "Come on, do you really care?"

Not particularly. "Just making sure he's not in the hospital, about to slip past guards and cause trouble for Evie."

"He's not," James assured him. "That was a flesh wound. Guy's a bleeder. He's patched up and currently enjoying the high life in a lovely jail cell."

"And *that* my friends..." Chase grinned. "Means our work is done." He lifted the champagne. "How much do you think this stuff cost?"

"I'm not so sure our work is done." Harvey's voice was low. And he wasn't sporting any kind of grin. Not even the mild, half-grin that he sometimes liked to flash.

"Buzzkill." Chase's gaze flickered to him.

"When I left the PD, those two men were still swearing that they had nothing to do with any attacks on Evie. They were confessing to everything else, apparently ignoring the whole 'right to remain silent' bit and talking about how Harrison White had it all coming because he's such a bastard." Harvey's head tilted to the left.

"Over and over again, though, they kept repeating that they were never after Evie."

Cole glanced toward the kitchen. And Evie. She'd just put five champagne flutes on the bar top.

"What do you think, Cole?" James wanted to know. His voice was so low that Cole knew Evie wouldn't be able to hear his question.

"I think..." *I want her safe.* "I think I don't have a lot of reasons to trust anything that either of those jackasses say. Stephen threatened Evie with a gun. They beat the hell out of Harrison."

James nodded.

"But..." And that was it. The *but* part. "I'm not closing this case until I am one hundred percent sure Evie is safe. That means I want our intel group to keep digging. I want loose ends tied up. We still don't know who killed Evie's parents—"

"And we may never know." Chase muttered gruffly. "I hate to say it, but it's true. With the murder happening years ago, in a foreign country, and all the evidence basically gone—hell, finding the truth on that might be like finding a four-leaf clover on St. Patrick's Day."

It might be. "I never found the men who kidnapped Evie two years ago. I didn't tie up those ends, and I worried about them coming back for her. Every single day, I thought about them." He released a hard breath. "I have to be sure this is over. I need that." For her.

For himself.

I can't have Evie in danger.

"Glasses are ready!" Evie called.

The men headed to the bar. Popped the champagne, and though they wore grins for Evie—even Harvey had his half-smile in place—Cole could feel their tension.

They were all worried that they might have missed something. Someone.

And if they'd missed someone, would another attack be coming?

"Oh, God." Chase shoved his champagne flute back on the bar. "That tastes like shit."

***

"You didn't think it was me."

They were alone. The other Wilde agents had left, and Cole could finally say all the things to Evie that he needed to say. And, yes, the first thing out of his mouth was...

"When Stephen told you I was behind the attacks on you, you didn't hesitate. You didn't doubt me."

She was on the couch with her legs tucked beneath her. She wore a pair of jogging shorts, a loose T-shirt, and no shoes. Her hair was pulled back and secured with a clip.

He'd didn't think she'd ever looked more beautiful. Then again, every time he looked at her, he tended to have the same thought.

Maybe she just is more beautiful each time I see her.

Evie glanced up at him. "Of course, I didn't think it was you."

"But...the photos..."

"I told you that I saw you in Atlanta."

He blinked.

"When I was at Piper's gallery, when I went to get the second piece..." She waved her hand toward the wall. "I saw you, and I was glad to know that you were okay. Seeing you made me feel better." Her lips pressed together, and he could see she was gathering her thoughts.

He wanted to go to her. To pull her into his arms. To hold tight.

That bastard had a gun on her.

But he didn't move.

He'd been waiting on Evie for a very long time, and Cole thought that his wait might just be ending. There was no way he'd screw things up now.

She had to come to him. She had to make the choice.

"I wasn't angry with you. Wait, I was, yes, obviously. I think you got that when you first knocked on my door again." A ghost of a smile teased her lips. "But I also—I didn't stop caring. When we were apart, I wanted to know you were safe. So when I spotted you in Atlanta, it felt good to see you." Her hand pressed to her chest. "It ached here, but it also made me feel better." She stared into his eyes. "I figured it might be the same way for you."

"Nothing made the ache I feel for you any better." Brutally honest. "I missed you every single day. It was like I'd left a part of my soul behind when I left."

She sucked in a sharp breath, rose to her feet, and headed toward him with slow but certain steps.

He didn't move.

"The case is over now," she told him.

He wasn't so sure.

"Are you planning to leave again?"

Hell, no. Leaving her wasn't on any to-do list.

"Because, once, you told me that everything you and I had been through would be nothing more than a bad dream."

His brow furrowed. "I said that shit?"

"Yes. After you saved me in LA, but before you left me at Harrison's door. You said I'd go back to my life and it would be like everything was a bad dream." She swallowed. "Life without you is like a bad dream, and I don't want those nightmares anymore. I want you. I want us to have a real shot."

He wanted that, too. So badly.

Her gaze focused on his mouth. Her eyes gleamed. "Will you kiss me?"

Any fucking day of the week—

Her shoulders straightened. "I want *you* to kiss *me*."

Cole blinked. "That sounds familiar."

"Then you have a good memory. Because I once told you those same words. *Before.*"

Their night together. *Before.*

"To be crystal clear," Evie told him, voice becoming husky. "It's not because of adrenaline or confusion or because we locked up the bad guys. I want you to kiss me because I know how you taste, and I know I love that taste."

Sweet mother of—

"I want you to kiss me because I love the way your mouth feels against mine. I want you to kiss me because I want you to lose your control." She leaned toward him. Spread her hands over his chest, and he could feel the heat of her touch through the T-shirt that he wore. "I know you're strong. I know you're protective. I know you're intense and passionate, and I know that no one else makes me feel the way that you do. No one else can."

No one else had ever gotten to him the way she did.

"You're the only lover I want, Cole."

"Baby, you've been it for me since I first saw you."

She pushed up onto her toes. "Then what are we waiting for? The rest of our lives—that part starts right now."

Hell, yes, it did. He locked his hands around her waist. Lifted her up against him. Her lips were parted. Her mouth open and ready, and he kissed her. Kissed her tenderly at first, savoring her. Cherishing her. *Worshipping* Evie's mouth.

Then the kiss became harder. His tongue thrust past her lips. He tasted. And he took. And she moaned against him and curled her arms around his neck.

Evie wants me. Evie loves me.

He knew he was one lucky sonofabitch. No one would *ever* take her away from him.

He carried her back into the bedroom. Stripped her clothes away. She stretched out on the bed, completely open to him. That was exactly how he wanted her. He took a moment to simply stare at her. He'd long ago memorized every curve and dip of her body. To him, she was pure perfection.

And perfection should be touched.

He leaned over her. Trailed his fingers up her abdomen. Up...to the tip of one pert breast.

Perfection should be kissed.

He bent his head. Took her nipple into his mouth. Licked and sucked. His cock shoved hard against the front of his jeans.

She moaned. Arched toward him.

He kissed his way to her other breast. Gave it the same attention as she called out his name. He loved her frantic little pants.

Cole kissed his way down her body. Slid his fingers between her legs. She felt so good. Wet and tight, and he stroked her over and over again.

Inside his head, Cole heard a voice roaring for him to *take*. To *take* and *take*. To own her. To claim her. To go wild with her.

But this time, he was going to be different. This time, he would treasure her. Because she was the person who mattered most.

She owns me. Has for so long.

He put his mouth between her legs. Her first orgasm came while he was licking her. Her whole body shuddered around him, and she screamed out his name. He liked her scream. Wanted to hear more. So he didn't let her come down from the first wave of pleasure. He strummed her clit with his fingers, then he drove his tongue into her. He kept his touch careful. His mouth and his fingers. He gave her exactly what she wanted and what she needed.

He wanted to taste her second orgasm on his tongue.

And he wasn't going to stop until he did.

A growl tore from him, but when his hands clamped around her hips and lifted her up, positioning her so that he could work her over and over with his mouth, he made sure his touch wasn't too rough. He held back his strength. Kept his control.

He made sure she came again. She didn't scream his name the second time. She moaned it.

Only then did he let her go. Only then did he strip and grab a condom. He rolled it on in record time. Only then did he—

Evie shoved him onto the bed. She straddled him. Rubbed her core over him. Slick and ready. Her eyes gleamed. Her cheeks flushed a soft red.

So beautiful.

"You have a lot of catching up to do," she told him. Her voice was sexy as fuck. "Better get started."

She sank down on him. Took him in balls deep.

Her head tipped back. Her hands splayed over his chest. "I'm...two ahead of you..." Evie gasped out.

"You're about to be three," he promised.

Her eyes widened. "Cole—"

His hands were around her hips again. He lifted her up, then dragged her back down onto him. Again and again. And he got that third orgasm from her. Pleasure washed over her face and made her gorgeous gaze flash, and only then did he let go.

Only then did his thrusts get harder. Wilder.

He erupted into her with an orgasm so strong Cole was surprised they didn't break the damn bed with all the body heaving and twisting and shuddering. As it was, he let go of her so that he could grip the sheets. He was afraid he'd bruise her as the climax surged through him on wave after fucking shuddering wave.

The best sex of his life...always, with her.

He pulled in a breath. Then about ten more. His heart thundered in his ears. Cole forced his hands to let go of the sheets, and he slowly withdrew from her.

She smiled at him. Yawned. Looked freaking adorable.

He hurried to the bathroom. Ditched the condom and returned with a warm cloth. He liked sliding it between her legs. Liked stroking her with his fingers and the cloth because she gave the sweetest little moan with his every touch.

Don't pounce again. The problem was that he always wanted to pounce when it came to Evie.

But he could be a fucking gentleman. And he could pounce tomorrow. And the day after that. And all the days to come. Because now they had time.

He got rid of the cloth. Slid into the bed with her. She rolled toward him, tucked her body against his, and *fit* him. God, yes. She fit.

Her hand smoothed over his heart. "I like your tattoo."

He'd turned off the lights before he climbed into bed—well, all the lights except her lamp—and now he smiled at the ceiling. "Just the one? You have a favorite?"

"I love them all." Her voice was definitely sleepy. "But I have a favorite."

"So do I." He pressed a kiss to her head.

He thought she'd drifted off to sleep, but then she said, "Cole?"

"Yes, baby?"

"Thank you for saving my brother."

And, God, he remembered another time. Another place. LA. Because that time—that conversation was burned into his memory. He had to swallow twice before he could speak, and his Adam's apple clicked before he said, "Did you just give me thank you sex?" Because those had been the words—his words— to Evie so long ago. Right after they'd had sex for the first time, and she'd thanked him for saving her.

Cole held his breath, and he waited, hoping she would give him the words that he needed. The words that had gotten him through hell and back to her. When he'd once asked if she'd given him thank you sex, Evie had said—

Her soft breath sighed over him. "Don't be an idiot."

His heart thudded hard in his chest. *She remembers. She—*

"I had sex with you because I'm in love with you."

The words he needed to hear. The woman he wanted.

He was finally fucking home.

CHAPTER TWENTY

So how do I ask her to marry me? Needs to be something flashy. Unforgettable. Romantic as hell.

"Thank you for saving me." Harrison stood beside his desk. There was no sign of his usual arrogance. He was pale and bruised, and he had what looked like white tape on either side of his nose. "Without you, I'd have been screwed."

Evie smiled at him. She was so glad he was safe. "It wasn't just me, you know. It was completely a team effort." She lifted her hand—the hand that was threaded with Cole's. "Actually, I'm pretty sure Cole did the heavy lifting."

"Bullshit," he immediately told her. "You are the one who got the five million, who drove like a freaking boss to the drop site, never letting on that I was in the trunk—"

"Uh, you were where?" Harrison squinted at him.

"And, Evie, you marched up those stairs to confront Stephen. Did that shit like a total badass." He brought Evie's hand to his lips.

Kissed her bruised knuckles. "You used your killer right on Robert."

A warm glow spread through her.

"You don't mess with Evie Lake." Cole's gaze caressed her face.

"No," Harrison agreed quietly. "You don't, and you sure as fuck shouldn't try to come between her and the man she loves."

Evie felt her eyes widen. Her heart thumped hard in her chest. "That your way of saying you're about to welcome Cole to the family?"

"It's my way of saying that I'm an asshole. And I'm so sorry. I will apologize to you both for the rest of my life. While I was in that freaking closet, I had plenty of time to think—and I, uh, came to the conclusion—"

"That you're a giant dick?" Cole finished smoothly.

"Yes." Harrison's shoulders sagged. "And I know you owe me that ass kicking, but could you please wait until my nose heals, at least?"

"Maybe," Cole allowed.

Harrison exhaled. "I owe you so much, Cole. God, I will pay forever."

"I don't want anything from you." Once more, Cole's gaze tenderly swept over Evie's face. "I have everything I need."

And so do I.

Harrison cleared his throat. "Thank you, Evie, for saving me, and Cole, thank *you* for saving me, too. I will be forever grateful to you both and I—"

Gia Eastman burst into the room. "Harrison!"

Evie blinked. "What in the hell is she doing here?"

"I have zero clue," he retorted.

Gia ran across the room. "I'm here because Harrison needs me!" She grabbed him. Held on tight. "I came over last night and stayed."

She'd been there the whole time?

Harrison coughed. "I, uh, couldn't sleep. I called Gia because—"

Gia took his hand in hers. Straightened her shoulders. Her huge, designer bag hung from her shoulder. "He called me because Harrison and I have been a package deal—on and off—since you were sixteen years old, Evie. We dated in college. Would have stayed together then, too, but...he had to raise you."

Evie stiffened.

"It's always been you in my way," Gia added. For a moment, her eyes narrowed on Evie. But then she glanced at Cole. Smiled. "Only you won't be in the way anymore. Now you have your own life." She sidled even closer to Harrison. "And we finally have ours."

Okay, her head was spinning. Harrison had called Gia last night? "You faked your own kidnapping." Shouldn't she be in jail?

Gia fluttered her hand. "That was all Robert's idea! He used me. He's evil and twisted, and I never saw it." She gazed adoringly at Harrison. "I'm sorry for what he did to you. He's a bastard, and I hope he never gets a breath of freedom again."

Evie cut a quick glance at Cole. He was frowning at Gia. Evie was pretty sure a permanent frown was on her face, too.

What is happening here?

"I love Harrison," Gia announced flatly. "Always have. I won't step aside any longer. From here on out, I'm going to fight for him."

Her words sounded like a declaration of war. "I'm...not going to be in your way."

Harrison swallowed. "Evie, Cole, *thank you* both. You saved me from hell, and I can't—"

"I just hope he doesn't have nightmares," Gia cut in quickly. Her face flashed with worry. "Like you did, Evie, after you were held in that terrible closet in LA. I mean, they tied your hands and feet and stuffed you in that tiny closet. It must have felt like a coffin." She lifted Harrison's hand and made an actual *tut-tut* sound as she stared at the bruising on his wrists. "They tied you up just like they did Evie. Those sick bastards!"

Cole stiffened.

And so did Evie. She blinked at her brother. "You...told her that they put me in a closet?"

He frowned. "Uh, no." He cocked his head toward Gia. His expression had tightened. "I didn't even tell you that they put *me* in a closet."

Gia's lips parted. "But...of course, you were in a closet. Where else would you have been?" She pulled away from him. Waved toward Evie. "And if you didn't tell me about her, then I must have seen the info on a news story or something."

But Evie shook her head. "That part was never revealed in any news story. The Feds wanted to keep certain details quiet so they could use them against the perps." *In the event that they ever caught the perps...*

"But it's so *obvious*." Gia huffed out a breath. "I mean, you're going to be tied up. You're going to be stashed in a closet. It's like kidnapping 101."

Kidnapping 101. How could the woman be so flippant? And...

"*Harrison*." Cole's voice was hard. Cold. "You were dating Gia before you father was killed?"

"I..." He frowned at Gia. Blinked at her.

"Yes, we were dating." Gia's chin notched up.

"My dad didn't like her," Harrison suddenly said. He caught himself. Shook his head. "Fuck, Evie, am I as much of a controlling dick as he was?"

She didn't answer.

Harrison's gaze turned distant as he added, "Quint...he told me I shouldn't settle down. Told me that I had to earn my own way. Prove myself in this world before I got married."

Gia glanced away. Her hand shoved into her purse.

"Then he died," Harrison said. "And I didn't have to earn anything anymore."

"Because it was handed to you on a silver platter," Gia snapped. "*My* platter."

Harrison stumbled away from her. "Gia?"

She yanked a gun out of her bag.

Holy hell, Gia Eastman had just yanked a gun from her designer bag.

"Shit," Cole muttered. "I knew this case wasn't done." He slid his body in front of Evie.

What in the hell?

He'd moved his body in front of hers. No. She shoved against him.

He didn't budge. Not an inch.

"Cole, don't do this," Evie hissed.

And she realized that he had a gun tucked into the back waistband of his jeans. She could just see the edge of it. And she remembered the way he'd taken the gun from Stephen. Such a fast, quick move.

Her breath eased out.

"*It won't fucking end!*" Gia yelled. "I thought that I was finally going to get what I had coming to me—but it just won't end! You people are screwing everything up!"

"Gia," Harrison began.

"He tried to buy me off! Did you know that shit? Your dad offered me ten grand to stop seeing you. So I took that money, and you know what I did with it?"

"Oh, God." Harrison's voice. Shocked. Broken.

"My mother's family was from France. I had connections there. I used them. And then your asshole of a father was gone."

His father. Evie's mother.

Evie reached for Cole's gun. Her hand was rock steady.

"You got all the money, and you turned away from me!" Gia's voice rose even more. "Told me you had to help that freaking sixteen-year-old brat! So I was like—what the hell ever. He'll come back to me. You *always* came back to me."

Evie peeked over Cole's shoulder. She saw Harrison edging away from Gia as he gaped at her in shock and horror.

"You kidnapped Evie," Cole accused. "Back in LA, you were the one behind it. You knew she'd be at that hotel. You arranged everything."

Gia's head snapped toward him. "I didn't just want to kidnap her. I wanted to kill her! But those idiots I hired thought they could get more money from Harrison than from me." A roll of her shoulders. "But when the kidnapping went wrong and *you* showed up, they realized they should have freaking listened to me and stuck with the original plan. Everything would have been perfect then. Am I right?"

No, nothing about her was *right*.

"It was you that night, in the ladies' bathroom," Evie realized. "You...you had some goon waiting in there for me."

"Same guy I used before. Didn't even recognize him, did you?" Gia smirked. "I made sure no one else was in there *and* that your boyfriend was distracted so my man could make the grab. Then wham, you were out of the picture, again."

"Gia, put down the gun," Cole ordered.

Evie was on her toes. She could see over Cole's shoulder. She also had his gun in her hand.

Gia looked at her weapon and shook her head. "If I drop it, you'll do something stupid and heroic like charge at me. That can't happen." She bit her lip. "There are bodyguards outside. How am I going to get past them?"

"You're not," Cole told her. "You're not getting out of this room."

She swallowed. Her hand moved as she aimed the gun right at him. "I have to shoot you first. I'm sorry, but you're the threat. I'll shoot you and—"

"And the bodyguards outside will hear the sound," Evie cut in desperately. *You will not shoot, Cole. Oh, hell, no.* "They'll run inside and that will be the end. You'll go to jail, and you will never get out."

Gia wilted. "I don't want to go to jail." Her gaze flickered to Harrison. "You won't let me go to jail?"

He stared at her in horror...and disgust.

"But I love you. I did *all* of this for you. I got you money you needed, no strings. I was going to get your sister out of the way. I was going to make you free so that we could be together again!" Her breath heaved. "But those idiots Robert and Stephen took you! They screwed things up! It should have been easy, it should have been—"

Harrison lunged at her.

He grabbed for the gun, but Gia fired.

She screamed when he staggered back. Evie could see the spray of blood on his white shirt.

"Harrison!" Evie yelled. She tore from behind Cole.

Gia's head whipped toward Evie. "This is your fault!" She raised her gun—

Too late. Evie fired at her. She squeezed the trigger, and the bullet tore into Gia's shoulder. The gun fell from Gia's hand even as she screamed over and over again.

Cole rushed to her and kicked Gia's weapon away.

The bodyguards outside burst in.

"Call nine-one-one," Cole shouted at them. "Now!"

Evie shoved her hands over Harrison's side. His blood seeped through her fingers. "You're going to be okay," she told him, frantic.

His terrified gaze met hers.

"It's just a flesh wound." She had no idea if it was or not, but people said stuff like that on TV shows all the time.

Cole eased beside her. He lifted her hand. Studied the wound. "It really is a damn flesh wound."

Evie's breath left her in a relieved rush.

"And, Harrison," Cole added roughly, "you have some serious bad taste in women."

Harrison groaned in pain.

"You'll also be spending the next fifteen years apologizing to me, got it? Because I am like a *dream* family member compared to the woman you were dating."

Another groan.

But Harrison also nodded. "S-sorry..."

***

"Your brother will be fine," the doctor promised Evie. "He's stitched up, secure, and he'll be released by tomorrow. We're just keeping him for observation."

"Observation." Chase lifted a brow and nodded. "Because the guy's crazy ex-girlfriend tried to kill him."

"Thank you, doctor," Evie replied quickly. "Can I go see him?"

"Of course." But he frowned at Chase. She'd noticed that most people tended to frown at Chase.

They were in the waiting room. She'd been pacing like mad for the last hour.

Chase and Cole had been watching her.

After one more frown at Chase, the doctor hurried away.

Chase waited just a few moments then... "So...she did it. She was our missing piece. She killed the parents—Jesus, sorry about that Evie," Chase added quickly. "I know that must be hard as hell for you to handle."

"Hard isn't quite the word I'd use." *She hired someone to kill my mother and step-father. She wanted me dead. She shot my brother.*

Cole's gaze stayed on Evie. "Gia confessed. Wilde is pulling more evidence on her, too. Once we start digging, we don't stop. She'll be going away to prison for a very long time."

Not like that would bring Evie's mom back.

I miss her so much.

As if sensing her pain, Cole took a step toward her. "Baby..."

She swallowed.

"What can I do?"

Those four words tore right through her. She'd been trying to keep her shit together, been trying to keep her chin up and her spine straight in the waiting room, but now... "Take me to my brother."

He nodded. Without another word, he took her hand and guided her down the hallway.

A tear slid down her cheek. "Gia hurt so many people."

He stilled, then turned toward her. "She will never hurt you again." His left hand rose and brushed away the tear. "No one will, I swear it."

A weak laugh slipped past Evie's lips. "You can't protect me from the world."

"Can't I?"

"Even you're not strong enough to do that."

His face was dead serious. "I will protect you from every threat, and I will gladly do it for the rest of my life."

Her breath caught. "You put yourself in front of me. When Gia pulled her gun, you moved in front of me."

A nurse bustled past them. Chase had stayed in the waiting room. Thankfully.

Cole nodded. "Damn straight, I did. You think I'd let a bullet hit you?"

She yanked her hand from his and jabbed her finger into his chest. "Don't you ever do that again!"

His eyes widened. "I'm the bodyguard, Evie, it's my job—"

"No."

Now his brows shot up. "It's...not my job?"

"Your job—" God, she was going a little crazy. Or a lot crazy. "It's not to die."

"Okay."

Okay? Good. "It's not to get hurt."

"How about I just hurt the other people? The bad people?"

A passing doctor frowned at him.

Evie ignored the doctor and jabbed her finger into Cole's chest again. "Your job is to stay alive. To stay safe. And to always love me."

"Oh, that's easy. I will love you until I die."

"You will not die!"

His hand curled around her jabbing finger. "I love you." His expression had softened.

"I love you, too." With every bit of her heart and soul.

He smiled. "You ever think about getting married?"

What?

His smile slipped. "What I meant to say was...Will you marry me, Evie?"

She couldn't speak.

He cursed. "This...is not how I was planning things."

Her chest felt tight.

"It was going to be way more romantic. I was going to get some of that champagne that you seemed to like but Chase thought tasted like shit..."

Yes, she remembered that champagne. She'd hated it.

"And I was going to get on one knee."

Cole dropped to one knee.

"And I was *not* going to do it in the hallway outside of your brother's hospital room."

She swallowed.

"But we kind of had a whole heat-of-the-moment thing going on there. And I just looked at you and thought about how every part of my world is better when you're in it, and the 'marry me' part slipped out."

Okay. She licked her lips. "Do you want to take it back?"

He shook his head.

Good.

He paused. Then asked, "Do you want to marry me?"

"Yes."

"Yes?"

"*Yes.*"

He shot to his feet. Hauled her into his arms. Held her tight.

A throat cleared. Very close.

Her head turned. Harrison was poking his head from the hospital room. He smiled at her. "Congratulations, Evie, and, ah, thanks for shooting my ex."

Thanks for—

"You proposed in the hospital?" Chase asked as he propped his shoulders on the wall close to Harrison's head. "And she said yes?"

Evie turned her gaze back to Cole. "She said yes," Evie responded definitely.

"Huh."

James and Harvey strolled down the hallway. James frowned at them. "What did we miss?"

"The good part." Evie kissed Cole. She didn't care who was watching in that hallway. Even though, it was apparently now a full crowd.

"Do you even have a ring, bro?" Chase pushed.

Okay, she was going to hurt him.

Cole eased back. "Of course, I do." He reached into his pocket and pulled out a small, blue box. "I've had it for over two years and six months..."

He opened the box. The diamond flashed. "But who's counting?"

"I am," Evie whispered. And *he* had been. She knew that now. He'd never forgotten anything that happened between them, and he'd never stopped caring for her. "I love you, Cole."

"And I love you, Evie. Forever."

Forever.

EPILOGUE

I will be needing vacation time. Or, Evie time.
Lots and lots of Evie time.

"I am officially on vacation. Honeymoon paradise, here I come." Cole smiled at his boss. "Thanks for the wedding gift, by the way. Tell your wife that Evie loved the art work. Turns out she is a super fan of the artist in question."

Eric Wilde just shook his head.

"Ahem."

Cole glanced over his shoulder.

"What about my wedding gift?" Chase wanted to know.

"Yeah, that champagne tastes like shit. Do not send anymore to us."

Chase grinned at him. "The office is gonna be quiet without you."

"Don't worry, I'm not going far."

"After your honeymoon, you're going to be based in New York. That's far. This is Atlanta. I will have to fly up to visit your crazy ass."

"Yeah, but you can always see a show while you're in town. I know a lady who can get you the Broadway hook-up."

Broadway. Cole shook his head. That was actually one of the fucking sticking points of Evie's case. Robert Demakis had hatched his scheme to kidnap Harrison just because he'd wanted money to start a new show. Harrison had refused Robert's first attempt at getting the additional cash—Harrison had said that he'd already paid back the original money owed to Robert's family years ago.

Paid it back, with plenty of interest.

Robert hadn't been in the mood to accept a no response from Harrison. He'd been frantic to get the money for the new show. And Stephen Lowe had been ready to make Harrison pay for stealing the last bid in their business rivalry...All that had combined to make...

The perfect storm.

Especially when you added cyclone Gia Eastman to the mix.

But that storm was over. The perps were all facing charges. Evie was safe.

And we're getting our happy ending.

"Don't worry, Chase," Eric announced. "You'll be so busy that you'll hardly notice Cole is gone."

Suddenly appearing far more enthusiastic, Chase hurried toward Eric. "Oh, really?"

"Um." Eric tapped a file on his desk.

"What's in the file?" Chase asked eagerly.

"You'll need to go in undercover."

"Oh, done. You know I can do undercover work in my sleep."

"You'll have to get very close to the target."

"Close is my middle name," Chase instantly responded.

Cole shook his head. "No, it's not. Your middle name is Melton, dumbass."

Eric's lips twitched.

Chase snatched up the file. Flipped it open. Stared at the picture of the target.

Didn't say a word. Not one single word.

Cole took a peek at the file. Read the bio. *Vivian Wayne.* A scientist. One who appeared to be selling classified intel.

"She's...bad?" Chase's voice sounded funny? Rougher than normal.

Eric must have noticed the difference, too, because he frowned. "Appears that way."

"I'm...supposed to find evidence against her? Bring her down?"

"That's the job."

More silence. Chase was never silent.

He was also still staring at the woman's picture.

Cole nudged him. "You okay?"

Chase finally looked up. Blinked. Seemed to be a bit dazed. "Never better."

Now that was a lie. "You know her or something?"

"Never met her before in my life." His gaze went right back to the photo. "She's bad."

Eric and Cole exchanged a long look. "We covered that."

"Right." Chase pulled the photo from the file. Tucked it in his pocket. "I'm on her. I mean, I'm on the case." He spun on his heel. Marched out of the office.

Cole watched him go. Well, that had been weird as hell.

"Huh," Eric said.

Cole stiffened. *Don't start sounding like Chase.*

"What do you think was up with that?"

"I have no clue." Cole shrugged. "But I'm certain you'll be finding out. As for me, I have a honeymoon planned. Beautiful beach, incredible wife." He sauntered for the door. "Have fun working that shit out with Chase."

"Cole..."

He tossed a wave over his shoulder. "I'll send you a postcard. You'll love it."

"Cole..."

He spun at the door. "Thanks for taking Evie's case." Now, he was serious. "And thanks for always having my back." His back. The backs of all the agents at Wilde. "You gave me a second chance at Wilde. A chance to prove that I could be a good man."

Eric rose to his feet. "That's bullshit."

It was?

"You've always been a good man, Cole. You didn't need to prove anything to me or anyone else."

Aw. "Don't make me hug you."

Eric laughed. "Get your ass out of here. And *don't* forget my postcard. I'll be waiting on it."

The guy was a great boss. He was also a world class friend.

Cole headed out of the office. He passed Chase and caught his buddy peeking at the picture of Vivian again. Cole slapped a hand on the dude's shoulder. "Good luck."

Then Cole whistled as he headed for the elevator.

His whole life was waiting for him.

Evie was waiting.

And he was already eager for their next adventure to start.

The End

A NOTE FROM THE AUTHOR

Thank you for reading COUNTING ON COLE. I hope you enjoyed the story! Cole first appeared in BEFORE BEN, and, since then, he has popped up in quite a few of the Wilde books. His character has grown and changed, and I thought it was long past time that he had his own happy ending. I have always loved second chance romances, and since Cole was given a second chance by joining Wilde (so to speak!), it seemed fitting that a reunited love story be given to him.

If you'd like to stay updated on my releases and sales, please join my newsletter list.

https://cynthiaeden.com/newsletter/

Again, thank you for reading COUNTING ON COLE.

Best,
Cynthia Eden
cynthiaeden.com

ABOUT THE AUTHOR

Cynthia Eden is a *New York Times*, *USA Today*, *Digital Book World*, and *IndieReader* best-seller.

Cynthia writes sexy tales of contemporary romance, romantic suspense, and paranormal romance. Since she began writing full-time in 2005, Cynthia has written over one hundred novels and novellas.

Cynthia lives along the Alabama Gulf Coast. She loves romance novels, horror movies, and chocolate.

For More Information

- *https://cynthiaeden.com*
- *http://www.facebook.com/cynthiaedenf anpage*
- *http://www.twitter.com/cynthiaeden*

HER OTHER WORKS

Wilde Ways

- Protecting Piper (Wilde Ways, Book 1)
- Guarding Gwen (Wilde Ways, Book 2)
- Before Ben (Wilde Ways, Book 3)
- The Heart You Break (Wilde Ways, Book 4)
- Fighting For Her (Wilde Ways, Book 5)
- Ghost Of A Chance (Wilde Ways, Book 6)
- Crossing The Line (Wilde Ways, Book 7)

Dark Sins

- Don't Trust A Killer (Dark Sins, Book 1)
- Don't Love A Liar (Dark Sins, Book 2)

Lazarus Rising

- Never Let Go (Book One, Lazarus Rising)
- Keep Me Close (Book Two, Lazarus Rising)
- Stay With Me (Book Three, Lazarus Rising)
- Run To Me (Book Four, Lazarus Rising)
- Lie Close To Me (Book Five, Lazarus Rising)

- Hold On Tight (Book Six, Lazarus Rising)
- Lazarus Rising Volume One (Books 1 to 3)
- Lazarus Rising Volume Two (Books 4 to 6)

Dark Obsession Series

- Watch Me (Dark Obsession, Book 1)
- Want Me (Dark Obsession, Book 2)
- Need Me (Dark Obsession, Book 3)
- Beware Of Me (Dark Obsession, Book 4)
- Only For Me (Dark Obsession, Books 1 to 4)

Mine Series

- Mine To Take (Mine, Book 1)
- Mine To Keep (Mine, Book 2)
- Mine To Hold (Mine, Book 3)
- Mine To Crave (Mine, Book 4)
- Mine To Have (Mine, Book 5)
- Mine To Protect (Mine, Book 6)
- Mine Series Box Set Volume 1 (Mine, Books 1-3)
- Mine Series Box Set Volume 2 (Mine, Books 4-6)

Bad Things

- The Devil In Disguise (Bad Things, Book 1)
- On The Prowl (Bad Things, Book 2)
- Undead Or Alive (Bad Things, Book 3)
- Broken Angel (Bad Things, Book 4)

- Heart Of Stone (Bad Things, Book 5)
- Tempted By Fate (Bad Things, Book 6)
- Bad Things Volume One (Books 1 to 3)
- Bad Things Volume Two (Books 4 to 6)
- Bad Things Deluxe Box Set (Books 1 to 6)
- Wicked And Wild (Bad Things, Book 7)
- Saint Or Sinner (Bad Things, Book 8)

Bite Series

- Forbidden Bite (Bite Book 1)
- Mating Bite (Bite Book 2)

Blood and Moonlight Series

- Bite The Dust (Blood and Moonlight, Book 1)
- Better Off Undead (Blood and Moonlight, Book 2)
- Bitter Blood (Blood and Moonlight, Book 3)
- Blood and Moonlight (The Complete Series)

Purgatory Series

- The Wolf Within (Purgatory, Book 1)
- Marked By The Vampire (Purgatory, Book 2)
- Charming The Beast (Purgatory, Book 3)
- Deal with the Devil (Purgatory, Book 4)
- The Beasts Inside (Purgatory, Books 1 to 4)

Bound Series

- Bound By Blood (Bound Book 1)
- Bound In Darkness (Bound Book 2)
- Bound In Sin (Bound Book 3)
- Bound By The Night (Bound Book 4)
- Forever Bound (Bound, Books 1 to 4)
- Bound in Death (Bound Book 5)

Other Romantic Suspense

- One Hot Holiday
- Secret Admirer
- First Taste of Darkness
- Sinful Secrets
- Until Death
- Christmas With A Spy